DAUGHTER OF DESTINY

Kyra.

From earliest childhood she had known that she was set apart from ordinary mortals—that she possessed powers that both thrilled her with possibilities and shadowed her with peril.

In the center of the holy circle of tall stones she had been commanded to make her way through a land filled with violence to the legendary Temple of the Sun where she at last would learn her destiny.

Now Kyra stood upon a windswept height, looking down at the awesome Temple below . . . not knowing what would await her when she descended . . . knowing only that she had come too far to turn back from her fearful, fabulous fate. . . .

This is the second volume of the trilogy *The Sacred Stones* and tells of the further adventures of Karne, Kyra, and Fern and of their meeting once more with Wardyke the priest whom, with the help of the Lords of the Sun, they overcame in events chronicled in *The Tall Stones*, the first of the three novels describing the mystic civilization of pre-Roman Britain.

THE SACRED STONES Trilogy

The Tall Stones
04365-2 $1.95

Temple of the Sun
04393-8 $1.95

Soon to be available from Popular Library:

Shadow on the Stones

The Temple
of the Sun

by Moyra Caldecott

POPULAR LIBRARY • NEW YORK

THE TEMPLE OF THE SUN

Published by Popular Library, a unit of CBS Publications, the Consumer Publishing Division of CBS Inc., by arrangement with Hill and Wang, a division of Farrar, Straus and Giroux, Inc.

Copyright © Moyra Caldecott 1977

All Rights Reserved

ISBN: 0-445-04393-8

Printed in the United States of America

10   9   8   7   6   5   4   3   2   1

For Rachel,
Stratford, Julian and Oliver

with love

The Warning and the Journey

The High Priest, the Lord Guiron, was in the Great Circle of the Temple of the Sun by himself, the dawn rituals over, the other priests and initiates departed. He too should have left and be attending to the business of the Temple.

Something held him back.

Something made him break his routine and pace the Tall Stones around the circumference, not as a priest drawing energy from them, not as a suppliant speaking with spirits, not as Lord of the Sun in robes of splendour with the power to roam the world at will, but as an old man suddenly lonely and afraid.

It was as though the people leaving the Circle after the Ceremony this particular morning drained him of his significance. He had not felt this way before, or not for many years. He had been in the Circle alone many times, as High Priest it was his Right, but it had always sustained him in his confidence and strength.

Now he felt like a peasant who had wandered unwittingly into a Sacred Circle and was overwhelmed by his own smallness and in awe of the Giant Forces surrounding him.

He, Guiron, Lord High Priest, was afraid.

Afraid in his own Temple?

Afraid of what?

He did not know.

The shoulders he usually carried so straight and proud were bent.

"What is it?" he kept asking himself.

But for all his knowledge of the Mysteries, and for all the control of Mind and Body he had learned through the long years of priesthood, this time he was an ordinary man faced with an uneasiness to which he could not put a name, which he could not define.

He thought of entering one of the two Inner Circles within the Great Circle which were reserved for very special occasions. Perhaps their extra strength would give him back his stature as a Priest.

But as he approached the Northern one, it was as though he were held back.

"Not now," a voice that was not his own voice spoke within his head. "Not now."

Feeling himself an exile he stumbled slightly and returned to the Outer Circle. Beyond the immense Standing Stones that carried the flow of Spirit power from earth to sky, from sky to earth, the high ridge, walled with rough chalk blocks, rose above him, cutting him off from the rest of his fellow men. It was designed to isolate the Temple for its work, to concentrate its energies and keep intruders out, and he now felt as much a prisoner as a small beetle would that had fallen on its back within a steep-sided hole.

There were things in his past that he did not wish to think about. He pushed them back into the darkness. Long years of service as Priest of Light had surely undone whatever harm he might have done once long ago!

But from the crevices of darkness in his mind unease was stirring and this time he could not put it down.

With no one to observe him he allowed himself the luxury of tears and put his head against a Tall Stone to the

8

East of the Circle, a Stone for which he had always felt a particular affinity. He put his arms around it as though it were a man and could give him comfort.

"Lord," he whispered, "Lord of Light. Help me."

He tried to clear his head of the irrational and disorderly murmurings of his mind.

Where was his training now?

Slowly order came.

Slowly the clamour of his fear died down.

He tried to visualize, to call before him a picture of what it was that threatened him.

He could feel a low drumming or throbbing in his head. Whether it was from within himself or from within the rock he pressed himself so closely against, he could not tell.

He listened to it and it seemed to him at last that it was the sound of the ocean, beating relentlessly against the shore, the ocean rising and falling, swelling and subsiding, and upon its vastness there was a small seed, a fragile boat tossed among the waves, that bore within it something that threatened change to him and the Great Temple that lay around him.

The image was not clear.

The menace was not strong.

It was a hint, a stirring, a whisper . . . but it was there.

He strained for a clearer vision.

It would not come.

But pain entered his body from the North, so it was from the North that he expected the threat to come.

He pulled back from the Stone with a sudden movement and with a surge of great determination he pulled himself to his full height as a Priest, his eyes sparked with his old fire of office and, turning his face to the North, he spoke these words aloud and with great authority.

"You who come from the North to bring disruption and change to this man and this place, turn back. Turn back! There is no welcome for you here!"

He tried with all the force of will and thought at his command to reject the unknown intruders and turn them from their course.

9

His Will was strong, the beam of his Thought powerful, but the deep and featureless blue of the sky into which he thrust his desperate barb gave no sign that it had reached its mark.

"So be it," he thought, and turned to leave the Circle. "I have tried, and I will try again!"

In the North Kyra stood upon the cliff she had just climbed and stared at the sea that lay impassively silver, ominously vast.

They had sailed in their frail homemade boat since the first stirrings of Spring and the journey that lay behind them, which had seemed so long and painful, was nothing to the journey that lay ahead of them.

She could see her brother Karne, tall and fair and bronzed, out beyond the rock line of the shore fishing for their lunch. Fern, his wife, who was heavy with child, was gathering driftwood on the pebbled beach for their cooking fire. When Kyra was with them the community of their love gave them each strength and comfort, but from the height of the cliff top they seemed very small and vulnerable against the immense panorama that stretched as far as she could see and then . . . beyond . . .

The joy of purpose that had sustained her in their travels since they first set out suddenly deserted her, and she looked at the huge landscape of impenetrable forest behind her and the seascape that lay forever and forever below her and a sharp cold feeling of fear stabbed her heart.

"How is it possible," she thought in panic, "how *dare* we venture into this vastness and hope to find our way!"

Appalled at the foolhardiness of their journey, the immense scope of it, and the inadequacy of their preparation for it, she decided they must turn back at once to their comfortable little village where everything was known and loved, understanding and achievement easier.

"Karne!" She called. "Fern!"

She must tell them at once before it was too late and they were lost forever!

But no matter how loud she shouted the thin whistle of

her voice was blown backwards on to the land and dispersed among the tough coastal grasses and flowers that lived on the thin crust of earth above the unfathomable dark rock.

"Karne!" She called again. "Fern!"

But there was no way they could hear her.

She started to scramble down the cliff, loose pieces of rock and earth scattering under her feet and hands. Sea birds shrieking with indignation flew up from hidden ledges and her heart began pumping with an urgent and powerful fear.

She must be careful.

On the way up, so intent on the moment by moment examination of the beauty of the rocks and the lichens nearest to her, she had not noticed how sheer the cliff was. Now, looking down, she was shocked at the danger of the descent.

Karne and Fern looked up on hearing the pebbles rolling down the cliff and saw Kyra coming down too fast for safety.

They both gasped and called out.

Fern ran immediately over the sharp and uneven rocks, the child lying within her body making her progress clumsy and painful. Karne, thinking that Kyra was being pursued, ran back to the boat to fetch his sling catapult and stood high upon a rock where he could see further up the cliff, the stone in his sling held back, the leather thong taut, ready for action.

But it soon became clear Kyra was alone. Whatever was driving her to such careless speed was not visible to their eyes.

She slid the final slope in a flurry of stones and landed in a heap at Fern's feet, considerably bruised and shaken, her skin grazed in many places, but otherwise unharmed.

Karne was angry.

He raged for several moments at her recklessness.

"I am sorry," she brought out breathlessly, and repeated it when his words continued the bruising she had just suffered from the cliff, as Fern helped her dust herself off and wash the open places clean with sea water.

"What were you trying to do?" Karne demanded at last indignantly.

"I tried to call you from the cliff top," she said miserably, smarting as the salty water touched the open grazes.

"We did not hear you," Fern said gently.

"Of course we did not!" Karne exclaimed, looking at the height of the cliff. "How could we *possibly* have heard you?"

"I know. It was foolish. It just seemed so urgent . . ."

She hesitated. Things were not so clear at the bottom of the cliff as they had been at the top.

"What was so urgent?" Karne asked sternly.

"I thought . . . we ought . . . to turn back," Kyra said in a low voice, aware that this would not be received well by Karne.

They stared at her.

"Turn back! Why?" Karne demanded.

"It just seemed . . ." Kyra's voice was losing conviction every moment, "at the top of the cliff looking at how huge the ocean is and thinking about the journey . . . it just . . . all seemed . . . impossible!"

"But the Lords of the Sun *told* you to make the journey!" Fern cried.

She herself would not have been sorry to turn back, but she knew Kyra had been commanded to attend The Temple of the Sun to study for the priesthood. Without Karne's help and protection she could not make the journey, and without Karne, she, Fern, was not prepared to live. So their journey had become her journey.

Kyra was silent.

Karne was silent too. His anger was gone. He knew his sister well and the burdens she had to bear, the fears she faced from time to time.

"It will not be an easy journey," he said, quietly now, "but it *is* necessary."

"Karne . . ." Kyra said in a very small voice.

"Yes," he said gently.

"Sometimes I think I am not fit . . . It seems to me I

12

may have misunderstood. It is very *possible* that I misunderstood," she pleaded.

"I do not think so, my sister," Karne said soberly.

"Think back on all that has happened," Fern said. "You *know* you have been chosen! You *know* you have special powers not many people have! Powers that could and should be trained for use within the priesthood."

"But," Kyra said sadly, "there are so many ordinary things I want to do. Surely if I were fit to be a priest I would have my mind on higher matters all the time?"

"You are not a priest yet," Fern reminded her. "There will be years of training."

"But I do not *want* to reach the point where ordinary things do not matter to me any·more!"

"And I do not think you ever will reach that point," Karne said seriously. "You are training to be a priest, not a god. Maal still enjoyed ordinary things. Maal even made mistakes. Remember?"

Maal was their friend and teacher, the old priest of their community whom they had loved and trusted, and who had been cruelly ousted and then destroyed by the false but powerful priest-magician Wardyke.

"Maal always said the Universe is made up of ordinary things," Fern said. "It is in our Seeing of them, our appreciation of them, that they become extra-ordinary, that they take on splendour and magic. So you will not have to give up ordinary things. They will just become for you less 'ordinary'. You will have *more* Reality, not less!"

Kyra was somewhat comforted, but the sight of all that endless ocean, that endless land, that she had seen from the top of the cliff came back to her. She felt again that sudden cold twinge of fear.

"How will we ever find our way?" she said, tears coming to her eyes. "Oh, Karne, everything is so huge, and we are so small!"

He put his hands on her shoulders and the warmth of the contact made her feel less small, less alone.

"There is no point in thinking about it like that," he said briskly after a pause, "there is a fire to be made, fish to be roasted. I, for one, am starving!"

Kyra could not help smiling.

It was so like him to busy himself with practicalities and take one step at a time! And yet he had vision too and knew when two steps were necessary.

She looked at him with great love and trust, and then turned to help Fern with the fire.

After the meal, while the other two made the boat ready for sailing, Kyra clambered over the rocks to the furthest and largest one standing almost like an island in the sea.

She needed to think.

She remembered Maal with aching heart and all that he had taught her before his death.

She called on him for help. She called on The Lords of the Sun, on the spirits who lived in the realms that led to the one God who was Nameless but the Source of All.

"Tell me what I must do!" she cried aloud in pain, her voice becoming part of the water crashing onto the rock, part of the rock, part of the light splintering off its surface and the dark germinating in its depths.

Fern and Karne on the beach packing away the things in the boat simultaneously felt they heard a sound and looked up to see Kyra poised triumphantly on her rock, raised as tall as she could be, pointing with dramatic excitement to the swelling sea.

As the eyes followed her finger they saw, rising from the sea in dark and rhythmic folds, the bodies of innumerable dolphins, plunging, rising, plunging, rising, travelling the ocean with their slow and ancient dance, and all of them moving South. Moving South!

Kyra had her answer.

They launched their little boat of wood and hide and followed the course they had planned to the South, keeping land always in sight to the West of them.

It was during Fern's watch one night that, for the first time, they lost all contact with the land and with their course.

She sat huddled in her fur cape hour after hour while the other two uncomfortably and fitfully snatched some restless sleep. Karne had shown her the star she was to keep always behind them in the North and the others she was to watch progressing across the sky, the dim, dark hump of the land always to the West.

For the first hour of her watch her eyes grew weary with the number of times she checked their direction against those frail points of light.

But during the second hour the moon rose and she was overwhelmed by the splendour of its rising.

Without her realizing it and perhaps because the wind had subtly altered its direction, their little craft began to move along the spectacular silver path towards the moon. The dark and brooding ocean became transformed into a sparkling, shimmering mist of silver. "Moon Metal" her people often called what we now call silver, and the sea shone now with moon metal.

Darkly the deeps may have been waiting beneath the shining ripples of the surface, but Fern was no longer conscious of them. She no longer noticed the passage of the night, the progress of the stars, the disappearance of the land shadow to the West. She saw only the moon and felt the urge to reach towards it.

As the moon rose higher in the sky Fern urged the little craft faster along the metal path, taking out the paddle and scooping the silver water back to add speed to its progress.

Her first exultant urge to speed turned to despair as the great disk lifted higher and higher, further and further from her reach.

She stood at last, arms uplifted, calling to the moon with a strange and unnatural call.

Kyra jerked awake with the sound, seeing the girl transformed.

"Fern!" she cried in alarm.

Fern did not hear her, but stretched her arms to their limits . . .

The moonlight caught her eyes and to Kyra they seemed to be made of moon metal.

She seized her and shook her. The boat rocked dangerously and Fern's eyes became pools of dark.

15

"Come back!" Kyra cried. "Fern, you are possessed!"

Karne grumblingly awoke now and stared bewildered at the scene.

He saw his sister Kyra shaking Fern violently, felt the boat rocking.

In an instant he was up and in control. He pushed Fern and Kyra down with oaths of command, seized the paddle and righted the spinning and jerking of the boat.

Fern crouched with her head against Kyra's breast sobbing and shivering. Kyra enclosed her with her arms and comforted her with soft sounds.

"What is this?" Karne shouted. "What have you done?"

Kyra looked above Fern's head and could see no land to the West and the stars they had set their course by were not where they should have been.

They were caught in a sickly white light in the middle of darkness, far from home, far from anywhere they knew, and creeping over the face of the moon was the dark hand of a cloud.

Within a short while the stars had gone out one by one, the whole sky was overcast and they were in absolute darkness.

They sat huddled together, the cold they felt as much from within as from without.

Karne and Kyra had quietened Fern's sobs and had silently agreed to say no more about the incident. What was done was done, and now they must think what to do next.

"There is nothing we can do, but wait for morning and the light," Karne said.

He held Fern close to him, knowing that what she had done she had not done deliberately to bring them into danger, but that something from deep within those mysterious levels we all have within ourselves had stirred and an urge to reach and follow something she herself could not control or understand had taken over.

In the darkness, drifting with the deep sea currents, the three young people and the unborn child waited.

16

They saw no sun in the morning, but they knew it had risen because the black pit of darkness in which they had been marooned gave way to a dull and sombre grey, neither sky nor sea distinguished in any way.

Gloomily the three made breakfast of wheat biscuits and water from the goatskin bag. Up to now they had fed off the land each day and had not needed to draw on their emergency store of food.

Karne stared around him at their featureless world.

They had pulled down the rough sail in an attempt not to travel any further off their course, and lowered strings of fibrous rope over the side to watch which way they drifted, hoping their rudimentary knowledge of currents and tides, gleaned from fisherman friends, would help them decide which way land lay.

It was Fern who noticed the first sea bird and after that they concentrated on the sky and noted with desperate attention which way the birds flew. But this at first was not much help as the birds seemed to come and go from many directions.

Kyra buried her face in her hands and tried to "feel" the presence of the land. Karne kept quiet, knowing this was a power Kyra sometimes had which she was hoping would grow with training as a priest.

Fern joined her in her concentration, thinking of the forests and the growing plants with whom she had lived in close harmony all her life. She needed them now and called on them for help.

At first no help came.

The sound of the slap, slapping of the water against the side of the boat was all they were conscious of, that and the coldness of the air that enclosed them.

Karne watched the ropes, counted sea gulls and noted the direction of the drift of flotsam.

Gradually through the darkness in her head Fern began to feel little stirrings, hear little sounds like leaves rustling, small animals moving through undergrowth. . . .

She opened her eyes with excitement and found Karne

17

pointing in the same direction, and Kyra looking decisively along the line of both their pointing fingers.

Laughing, they all talked at once.

"I am sure it is that way—I heard forest sounds," Fern cried.

"And I saw a gull carrying nesting materials in its mouth travelling that way. It must have been returning to the cliffs!"

"And I," Kyra said dreamily, "felt the presence of a Sacred Circle and someone in it calling to us."

They looked at each other joyfully and set about turning the boat around to head in the direction they had all agreed was the right one.

While Fern was following the moon they must have drifted a long way off course and it took them the best part of a day to reach again the comfort of the land.

Great was their delight to see at last a darker smear of grey upon the Western horizon, and even greater was their pleasure to distinguish the tall stones of a Sacred Circle crowning the highest point above the sea as they drew nearer.

They were still a long way from their destination, the Great Temple of the Sun where the Lord Guiron waited so uneasily for them, but as they pulled into the rocky cove at the base of the cliff that housed the Stone Circle Fern was singing and Kyra's eyes were shining. People who used the Tall Stones of a Sacred Circle to communicate with the spirit realms must be of their own kind, and it would be good to be among such people again. Karne, who felt the responsibility of carrying Kyra and Fern safely over so great a distance and through so many dangers, was particularly relieved to break the journey for a while and seek the advice of people who would certainly know these waters and this coast better than he did.

He leapt into the shallow water and hauled the light craft as high out of the sea as he could, the girls joining him with enthusiasm.

It was almost dark but they could still see fairly well, and when they finally drew breath from all the effort of

18

attending to their boat they found that they were not alone.

Standing on some rocks a short way from them and holding in their hands what looked like clubs stood several men, rough and uncouth, clad in furs and not in woven cloth.

Kyra, Karne and Fern froze, unsure of their next move.

The men stared at them and they stared at the men.

The first movement came from Kyra who took a step or two towards them in spite of Karne's warning touch upon her arm. She stood vulnerable, her hands empty and open in front of her, as though showing them that they had nothing to fear from the people from the sea.

At the same time she tried to project friendly thoughts towards them, knowing that all people respond, whether they know it or not, to the thought flow from others.

Her overtures must have succeeded because they approached and there was no menace in the way they came. Their faces were smiling and friendly, though dirty, and as they drew nearer Karne could see that the sticks they carried were not clubs, but bundles of rushes, probably dipped in fat, to use as torches against the dark of the night that was fast closing in around them.

The men spoke their language but with a more guttural sound. From what they said it became clear that the travellers were expected. Their priest had sensed their presence at sea during the dawn watch in the Sacred Circle and sent greetings and offers of hospitality to the strangers.

Karne accepted with gratitude on their behalf.

While the leader of the group and Karne exchanged these words, two of the men busied themselves making fire with a bow-like tool. It spun fast on a piece of kindling wood until it smouldered and set light to the rushes which became their torches for the climb up the rocky cliff path.

At the top of the cliff the whole village seemed to have gathered to greet the strangers, but the one who stood out among the others was the priest, the only one clad in woven cloth and wearing leather on his feet. He was shorter than his charges but of enormous bulk, the folds of his garments falling over a great belly. He raised his two plump hands to them in salute while the villagers crowding behind him waited eagerly but silently to join their greeting to his.

"Welcome, my friends. It is not often I have the pleasure of sharing my hearth with one of the brotherhood," and he looked straight at Karne who stood tall above the girls and slightly ahead of them.

Karne was puzzled by this, but said nothing more than polite greetings in reply.

"Come!" the priest said imperiously but kindly, indicating that Karne should follow him.

Instantly the rest of the villagers closed in on Kyra and Fern and, chattering excitedly, led them off away from Karne, to the group of wooden huts surrounding a small circle of open fires.

"You will eat with us," some said.

"Our house is your house," others cried, and Kyra and Fern could see that they were to be quite smothered with hospitality.

Although the people were very different from their own the whole atmosphere was so friendly and festive they did not think to feel alarm.

Both girls were glad they would have the comfort of sleeping in a warm house for a change, but both wondered somewhat anxiously what had become of Karne. There was no sign of him or the priest.

When Kyra could at last make herself heard above the hubbub of questions and friendly offers of food she ventured to ask where her brother might be.

"He is with the Lord Yealdon, of course," she was told as though her question had been a foolish one. "He will eat well and sleep soft. You have no cause to be concerned. It is a great day for the Lord when he has someone of equal stature to talk the Mysteries with!"

Again Kyra felt a small twinge of puzzlement, but she was hungry and tired and cramped from the long hours on the boat and soon dismissed thoughts about her brother and the priest to enjoy the good roast deer and pungent root ale. The firelight flickered from every side, dim figures wove in and out through it and when the light caught their faces she saw nothing but friendliness and pleasure.

After the eating and the drinking, when Fern and Kyra were feeling decidedly dizzy from the ale, the villagers performed a dance for them, singing a strange song very different from any the girls had ever heard before. It seemed to be a hunting song accompanied by a ritual dance. Half the dancers had antlers fixed to their heads on strange masks and tails of fur hanging between their legs, while the other half had spears which they pretended to throw from time to time.

The dance started slow, the hunters close to the ground stalking their prey, the "animals" feeding peacefully and unaware of danger. Almost without Kyra and Fern noticing it the tempo of the slow drumming music and muted song changed, becoming faster and faster, louder and louder. The chase was on! The "animals" leapt and twisted trying to escape. The "hunters" circled and pursued, drawing their trap tighter and closer.

Kyra and Fern found themselves caught by the savage rhythm of the beat, so unlike the music of their own peaceful farming community, and began stamping their feet in time to the dance. The impact of so many stamping feet raised the dust and the air seemed to vibrate with frenzy. Dust and sparks and smoke mingled with the dancers, the heady smell of ale and of roasting meat, the loud and louder chanting of so many throats, began to work on Fern and Kyra so that they found themselves leaping up and joining in, a surge of primitive ecstasy burning them up like the stubble in a field of straw on fire on a windy day.

Kyra could feel the sweat pouring from her, but she could not stop dancing. It was as though she was *being* danced, rather than herself dancing. The drumming of her feet had become her own heartbeat.

On and on the sound went, the movement went faster

and faster until at last a composite scream broke from the throats of all the dancers . . .

"Kill!"

Ice cold the word like a flung dagger stopped all movement, all frenzy, instantly. Kyra was dimly aware in the immediate and deathly silence of the humming whine of dozens of spears travelling through the air.

"Oh you gods," she cried within herself, "they have not killed them!"

She tried to pull herself together enough to see what had happened, but the dancing and the ale and the unaccustomed emotions of the whole evening had told on her and she could feel herself slipping into unconsciousness. Her last thought as the weirdly falling dust disappeared from her sight was for Fern. Fern who carried a child within her body and must surely be feeling even worse than herself.

Karne seated on a thick rich bearskin rug within the priest's comfortable house, which was some way from the feasting and the fires, could hear the sound of singing and the loud thud of stamping feet, but it was very much a background noise and he did not take much notice of it.

He was amazed at what he saw. The dwellings of the villagers he had noticed in the firelight seemed no more than temporary shelters against the weather. In his own village the houses were built with pride and care, circular and of wood and rushes, bound over with hides to keep the weather out. They were built to last a man's lifetime. He wondered if these people were nomadic. He had heard of such people, wanderers who had not learned the way to use the land skilfully so that it yielded year after year the crops needed for sustenance. People who used the land once and then moved on. Hunting people. Restless people.

But the priest's house was sumptuous with the most magnificent furs Karne had ever seen hung from every beam and spread across the floor. He was given a sweet wine made of honey to drink, and bowls of rich and tender meat, spiced with nuts and herbs he had not tasted before, to eat. Several young girls slipped in from time to time silently and discreetly to replenish their goblets and their bowls.

At first he was delighted with it all, but gradually as more and more wine was pressed upon him and his refusals were ignored, he began to have misgivings. The friendly face of the priest seemed to him too friendly. He smiled too much and his plump hands that had been raised in greeting with such dignity began to look greasy and unclean as he fingered the food.

Karne wondered at the great disparity between the style of living of the priest and his people. He seemed an alien among them. In Karne's own community the priest Maal, who had been with them for many years, had held a position of great respect and, although master of Mysteries that the ordinary people never questioned, had a relationship with them that was friendly and loving.

Karne noticed that the fat priest had many large rings upon each finger, some in silver and some in gold, but one in particular he noticed and disliked. It was of a greyish metal that he had not seen before and was shaped like an eye. As the priest's hands moved the eye seemed to glint and gleam and never take its attention off Karne. He tried to shake himself free of the feeling, telling himself that it could not possibly be an eye that could see, but was a blind piece of metal fashioned by a man, but, whether it was the wine or whether it was the monotonous and softly droning voice of the priest, Karne felt himself slipping further and further away from the reality he knew how to control.

"It is not often we welcome such a distinguished traveller as yourself," the man said at last, smiling.

Karne through his confusion knew enough to try to protest that some mistake was being made, but his voice seemed to come out thin and dim and carry no conviction. The priest ignored it.

"You are too modest," he said, still smiling, indicating to the girl with his much beringed hand that Karne's cup needed refilling.

"No . . ." said Karne feebly.

"I insist," the priest said, smiling.

He paused a while, and Karne struggled to work out what was happening, but his mind was too confused by the influence of the wine.

"I must hold on," he told himself desperately, "something is not right!"

But the man's charming voice was speaking again, soothingly, softly.

"I have been cut off here among these barbarians for longer than I care to remember!"

He said the word "barbarian" with great venom and bitterness. Karne wondered what the girl who stood behind him to serve the wine was thinking. These were her people and although she was poorly clad and possibly not as advanced in knowledge and skill as the girls in his own village were, she was by no means deserving of such scorn.

He had thought it was a priest's duty to educate and guide his people, not to keep them in a state of savagery and then despise them for it.

"We could exchange knowledge and ideas," the fat priest continued smoothly. "It is many years since I learnt the Mysteries, and you are young. There must be many new things taught in the Temple Schools these days that would add to an old man's strength. You could teach me these things, while I," and here he leaned very close to Karne and his rheumy eyes seemed to leer into the boy's, "could teach you things I have learnt over the years of practice as a magician-priest that no school ever taught or ever would. I have powers that would startle *you*, young priest!"

"I assure you . . ." Karne began feebly, really worried now, realizing the misunderstanding had been allowed to go too far.

"No, do not protest," the old man's voice was suddenly sharp. "I assure *you* I need to know what they are teaching these days and if . . ." and here he paused and his face was harsh and cold, "if you refuse my offer of a peaceful trade . . . I have ways of taking what I want . . ."

There was a cruel and relentless edge beneath the

24

smoothness of his voice now and he raised his right hand slightly, turning the deadly eye of his ring towards Karne so that just briefly, as though it was a taste of things to come, the firelight in the brazier glinted off its metallic surface and pierced his eyes with light so icily inhuman, that for a moment he was blinded.

Karne was afraid now, deadly afraid. He had tried to tell the man he was not a priest, but to no avail.

He struggled to gather together his bemused wits and think of ways to outwit his formidable foe. Before he had noticed the extent of the man's unpleasantness he had thought to tell him that he himself was not a priest, but that his sister Kyra, although not yet a priest, was at least a candidate on her way to training.

Now he realized he must protect Kyra and somehow deal with this man himself. His heart felt heavy. Not only was his own mind befogged by the wine, but his adversary was obviously a trained and unscrupulous magician.

Karne tried to remind himself that it was he, Karne, who had finally outfaced Wardyke, the false priest who had destroyed their friend Maal and taken over their village, but it had not been an easy victory and he had had the help of Kyra, Fern and the Lords of the Sun behind him.

As his thoughts raced to find a way out, his senses brought him something else to worry about. Kyra and Fern were with the villagers and the dance and music he had been vaguely conscious of as part of a festival occasion, he noticed now had the same cruel undertones as the voice of the priest before him. It would not take much for Kyra and Fern to become prisoners of these people.

"Speak," the fat priest said now, smiling again, knowing that he had made his point and could afford to hide the barb of his threat once more under his ingratiating manner.

Karne could see a bowl of water to the left of the tent.

He rose and boldly took it in his hands.

The man watched warily, the hand with the ring tensed for action.

But Karne showed no sign of threatening him. Standing

25

as tall and commandingly as he could, he lifted the bowl of water high over his own head and then tipped its icy contents over himself.

The man was puzzled, but said nothing. He continued to watch him like an animal watching its prey.

The shock of the cold water had done what Karne hoped it would do, clear his mind, freshen his body and sharpen his wits.

"You know as well as I," the young man said now as sternly as he could, "our brotherhood is sworn to secrecy."

"But not among ourselves," the man was quick to reply, leaning forward eagerly, knowing that the vows had been instituted to prevent the quite considerable power of the Mysteries from falling into the hands of those not ready to see their full implications and use them wisely.

Karne looked at him coldly, standing tall above the bulky but seated figure.

"What is it you wish to know?" he said at last.

The man leant forward, his eyes for the moment failing to hide his real feelings. It was clear to Karne his host needed some specific piece of knowledge very badly, and would kill to get it. His face was twisted with a mixture of greed and anxiety.

"Of late it has become difficult for me to . . . contact . . . certain . . . people . . ."

He was trying to choose his words carefully, but every moment Karne was more certain that the man was now the suppliant and he the one in the position of power.

As Karne grew bolder, the fat priest Yealdon grew less sure of himself. Karne remembered what he had learnt —the crux of all power is belief and confidence.

"What people?" he said sternly.

"The Lords of the Sun," Yealdon muttered the words so low it was as though he hoped Karne would not hear them.

Karne's heart leapt. This was good news.

One of the skills a priest was trained to have, vital to his work, was the ability either himself to "spirit-travel" across the world to seek the help and communion of other

26

priests, or in times of stress to call upon the Great Lords of the Sun, who were the highest in the hierachy of priests and who moved most freely about the world in spirit form, most knowledgeable in the Secret Mysteries.

Karne felt almost sorry for the man. A priest who could not communicate with other priests and The Lords of the Sun was cut off in his own isolated village, among people with whom he could not exchange thoughts and ideas, particularly as in this case he had taken no trouble in the past to educate them to any kind of companionable level.

Karne's own people were simple enough farmers but they were not ignorant savages. The rapport between the old priest Maal and his people had been good, and he had kept the vital elements of priestly wisdom continually renewed and refreshed by contact with his peers across the world. When they were in difficulties and Wardyke had usurped his place and ruined their ancient ways of life, Kyra, a mere child, but with training from Maal and a natural aptitude for priestly powers, had called upon The Lords of the Sun for help, and they had generously given it.

"And what . . ." Karne said boldly, "will you trade for my help in contacting the Lords of the Sun?"

Yealdon almost crawled forward. He began to look more and more like a toad. The boy could feel the balance of power in his own favour. The man was crawling to *him*. He needed to know what he thought the boy knew, more than anything else in the world.

"I can make an enemy die," Yealdon said eagerly, "by nothing more than the use of this ring!" And he took the one that had so disturbed Karne off his finger and held it triumphantly aloft.

It glittered balefully in the firelight.

Karne swallowed imperceptibly. He had not conquered his fear of this man completely, though so far he had it well hidden.

"You mean you will trade your ring for the knowledge I can give you?"

Yealdon smiled and his eyes were evil. He cradled the

27

ring within his hands, holding it close to himself as though it were the most precious thing in the world.

"I will trade anything you ask," he purred, still cradling the ring.

"I ask the ring!" Karne spoke loud and clear.

There was a deathly silence between them for what seemed to Karne like a very long time.

"Certainly," Yealdon said at last, but Karne knew it was a lie. "First the knowledge, and then the ring."

"No," Karne said, his heart beating loud against his ribs. "First the ring, and *then* the knowledge!"

"But how do I know that you will not cheat me?" Yealdon almost spat out the words.

"How do I know that you will not cheat *me*?" Karne replied.

Deadlock.

The two eyed each other warily.

"You may take my knowledge and then kill me with the ring, thus keeping both!" Karne said.

"You may take my ring and kill me, and so save yourself the trouble of giving me the knowledge," Yealdon countered.

"Why should I do that? Would a priest of the Brotherhood do that?" Karne asked.

"Would a priest of the Brotherhood do what you suggested I would do?" Yealdon snarled.

Again the two watched each other silently.

Apart from the heaviness of the old man's breathing it was uncannily quiet. The serving girls had left them alone.

Karne became aware that even the sound of stamping and singing had ceased from the direction of the huts.

How he longed for Kyra's strength to help him at this moment.

He had no plan. He knew only he must keep the balance of power as it was now, and stall for time until he could think of a way of dealing with the situation. He had no secret knowledge to give the man, nor if he had would he have given it.

Karne realized that his own belief that the ring could

28

kill was adding to its power. If only he could doubt enough that it could harm him, he would be safe from it. But the glint of the dull and unusual metal, the acrid smell of some strangely potent herb that was burning in the brazier, the heavy, staring eyes of the man before him, all helped to dull his mind, and primitive fear was gradually undermining his control.

To break the influence of the priest, surrounded by his tricks of power, Karne forced himself to move with a last and desperate effort of will.

"I will give you the knowledge you ask for, and I take your word as sworn upon the Tall Stones of The Temple of the Sun that you will use no treachery." Karne spoke at last. "Now, follow me."

"Where are you going?" Yealdon spoke sharply and uneasily.

"To the Sacred Circle," Karne said as calmly as he could. "You must know that knowledge of this kind can only be passed within the Sacred Circle!"

Yealdon was not pleased. He had hoped to find out what he needed without leaving the protective ambience of his house. But he took a rush light from its holder and by its low and flickering flame the two found their way to the top of the cliff where the Tall Stones rose darkly against the grey surge of the sea. The sky was still overcast but the clouds had thinned considerably in places and a faint and eerie light emanated from the moon behind them, not enough to make the silver path upon the water that had so bemused Fern, but enough to make the land and the Stones of the Circle darker than the sky or sea.

The village lay silently behind them, the fires reduced to embers and no sound coming from the dark huts. Karne wondered if Fern and Kyra were safely asleep. He knew they were extremely tired.

How he longed to be far away and safely sleeping too!

As they approached the Circle Karne was faced with another problem.

In his community it was an ancient law that no one but the priest or at special times designated by the same law, village Elders, could enter the Circle. It was full of power that ordinary men were not trained to handle or withstand. Kyra had been afraid but she had so far progressed in her apprenticeship that she could enter safely and use its ancient forces.

Karne had no right to tamper with the mysterious forces in the Circle.

He was afraid.

But what was he to do?

In despair he called to Kyra for her help, and in that moment of desperation believed implicitly that she would come.

"Why do you wait?" Yealdon cried impatiently. "The night will not last forever!"

Of that at least Karne was glad.

"I must first consult with The Lords of the Sun," Karne said, trying to hide the tremor in his voice. "They may not wish you to have this Secret Knowledge. There may be a reason they have withdrawn themselves from you."

Karne caught the glint of the deadly ring as Yealdon raised it warningly.

"And if I die," Karne said loudly and clearly, though in his heart he was feeling very far from bold, "my Knowledge dies with me!"

He called again for Kyra deep inside himself. Why did she not hear? She had the power to enter men's minds and see their thoughts. Why did she not now see his?

"Push me no further, boy!" Yealdon said with anger in his voice. "I have waited a long time for this Knowledge, and I can wait a while longer."

He too was trying to control his face and voice. He did not wish Karne to sense his eagerness and impatience. He did not want to wait longer! How many winters and summers must pass before the sea threw up another priest upon his shore. Maybe never, and he had grown too fat and lazy, used to comfort and routine, to endanger his life by travelling on the sea or through the dark and savage forests that ringed his hunting village to a depth no man had ever measured. For some while now he had not been able either to leave the place in the flesh or in the mind, nor could he reach out to other priests in the world on any spiritual level. He had absolute power in his own small community, but in a sense he was a prisoner there. This was the first contact he had had for a long, long time with anyone outside his village. It was a kind of miracle. He might never get another chance.

Kyra came out of her faint (or was it sleep?) in the dark interior of a foul smelling hut. She could see nothing, but heard snoring and heavy breathing all around her. Her first thought was for Fern and she whispered her name, but received nothing back but further grunts and snores. She tried to still her fears and concentrate as Maal had taught her to, to sense with her inner senses where Fern might be.

She sensed nothing from Fern, but kept half seeing at the corner of her eye in the dark an image of Karne. When she turned to look directly at him he was gone and it was only the dark blankness of the hut she could see.

It seemed as though he were trying to tell her something.

But what?

Fern?

She must find Fern.

She sensed danger but whether it was to Karne or to Fern she could not make out.

She was sure neither of them were in the same hut as herself.

She must crawl out of it somehow.

She must have air.

She almost choked on the staleness of the smell.

It seemed to her as her senses gradually became used to her surroundings and the dark that the hut contained far more people in a more confined space than ever would have been allowed in her home village. The roof was low and as far as she could make out the only opening was a small hole to one side, through which she would have to crawl. No one could go in or out of this noisome hut except on hands and knees.

31

The task of reaching the hole (she refused to call it "doorway") was not an easy one. She was surrounded by gross and noisy sleepers and she dared not to wake them.

Tiny movement by tiny movement she prepared to make the journey, pausing every moment to check that the general level of the sleeping noises had not dropped in any way. Luckily for her the excitement of the night and the potency of the root ale had made the rude sleepers sleep heavily and deep.

Her head was aching and her thinking was not as clear as she would have liked, but at least she was conscious and was making progress to the hole.

At one point while she was climbing over a man's body, his arm came up to hold her down to him, his lips muttering something to her. Her heart almost stopped beating and she lay against him as still as stone, feeling the dead weight of his muscular arm upon her. But after a while by the limpness of his limbs she realized he was still asleep and she carefully released herself from his embrace and continued creeping to the hole.

At last outside!

She took great gulps of air.

And as her head cleared she heard within it quite distinctly Karne's cry for help.

At the same time she saw Fern sitting on her haunches before the last remnants of a fire, rocking backwards and forwards on her heels, rubbing her arms and trying to warm and comfort herself.

"Oh, Kyra," she sobbed when her friend put her arm around her shoulders. "I have been so frightened and alone. I thought you were dead when they carried you off, and I cannot find Karne anywhere."

"Did they kill anyone?" Kyra asked anxiously.

"I do not think so. It was a mock hunt. The ones with antler-masks fell flat when the spears flew, but I saw them get up afterwards. I have been so frightened! These people are not like our people. I insisted on staying out here by the fire. They wanted me to sleep with them in those horrible huts, but I would not. They could not understand it and were really rough with me."

"Are you hurt?" Kyra asked quickly.

"Only a bit bruised, I think. I finally made them understand and they left me alone. I think they were too tired to keep it up for too long. Oh, Kyra, I am so thankful you are all right! But Karne! Where is Karne?" Her voice was desperate.

"He is in danger, I fear. I can sense a call from him. Come, we must go to him."

"Where?"

"Be quiet a moment. I must 'feel' the direction of the call."

She stood still, concentrating, and felt the flow of Karne's anxiety coming to her from the Sacred Circle on the cliff top.

Compared to the inside of the hut, the night was relatively light. She and Fern stumbled many times, but nevertheless made their way swiftly to the source of his danger.

Within the Circle they could make out the figures of two men. One slender and tall, one bulky and gross. Her brother and the priest.

Kyra sensed great evil and danger surrounding her brother and stood in the shadows unseen by the man trying to locate the centre of the menace. She held Fern, who wanted immediately to run to Karne, and indicated to her to keep silence and be still. Fern obeyed, though it was painful for her to do so.

Kyra felt the priest was greedy and unclean, but somehow weak. She did not sense the strength in him that Karne had had.

No, the menace was not coming entirely from the priest.

What then?

Something the priest wielded?

A dagger perhaps.

She had seen cruel daggers forged of bronze and sharpened to a deadly cutting edge.

No.

Something else.

She heard Karne's voice raised unnaturally high and saw his hands rise up above his head.

"Lords of the Sun!" he was declaiming.

What was he doing, she thought with horror! He knew he had no right to be within the Circle and certainly no power to raise the Lords of the Sun.

Had her brother gone mad, and was this the menace that she sensed? Karne had always longed to have the powers she had!

She drew nearer, trembling with anxiety.

"Continue!" she heard the fat priest's voice commanding Karne.

"You, Lords of the Sun," Karne repeated and hesitated again.

Yealdon moved closer to him and lifted his right hand with something that glinted in it, but which Kyra could not make out from this distance.

"You, Lords of the Sun and Spirits of the many worlds that lie within our world! . . . Come to the aid of one who wishes to preserve your ancient laws against the one who would betray them!"

His voice was loud and ringing.

Kyra caught the message, and in that instant saw with great clarity what the priest held over Karne to make him do what he was doing.

She shut her eyes and formed a mental picture of the ring he held towards her brother. She felt the malevolence of its power and she visualized it shattering in a thousand pieces. At the same time she joined her voice to Karne's, leaping into the Circle and repeating loud and clear the prayer he had just prayed.

Yealdon screamed as the ring he held above his head seemed to burn his fingers. He dropped it, shrieking with the pain, and as it hit the stony ground it shattered and splintered into a thousand fragments, some of them striking his cheeks and causing them to bleed. Tearing at his own face as though it were on fire Yealdon further ripped his own flesh, convinced the ring had turned against its Master.

Quickly Karne seized the hands of Kyra and Fern and they ran fast and low for the path that led down to the bay where their boat was moored. The first glimmerings of the dawn light helped them and they were away, bruised and shaken from the scramble down the cliff path, before the villagers awoke amazed to find their priest crawling on his hands and knees within their Sacred Circle, muttering and sobbing and sifting through the earth to find thin splinters of metal, his face a mess of tears and blood.

He looked up to find them staring at him and for an instant fear of *them* showed in his eyes.

In that instant he was finished as the tyrant he had been.

Where the splinters of the ring had struck his face, sores festered and never healed.

Illusions

When the time came to leave the ocean and turn their little craft into the wide and muddy estuary of the river that cut deep into the land, the three tired and discouraged travellers felt a surge of new hope and energy.

It marked the end of the first phase of their journey.

Fern was particularly glad. She sat in the front of the boat as they rode in with the tide, her long red-gold hair blowing back with the wind and her voice raised in song. Although they would still travel for many days on water, the land with all its rich profusion of growing things would be near. She could talk with the trees, "feel" the surge of living sap in growing plants, take guidance and comfort from her familiar green world. The ocean was so cold, so unfamiliar and so vast. She knew the same force that gave life to the land was no less present in the ocean, but somehow she could never feel it there. She who had never been lonely in her life although she had lived most of it alone, tasted loneliness for the first time on the great and surging deeps. She would have clung to Karne but he was always busy keeping them afloat and moving in the

37

right direction. Lines of concentration from staring into distances were becoming a common feature between his eyes. She turned to Kyra, but Kyra too seemed occupied in ways within herself that Fern could not share.

The land was Fern's medium, the forests and the thickets her domain. She would be happy there.

The meeting of the river waters and the sea was not easy to navigate. Several times their little boat nearly capsized in the turbulence and Karne and Kyra were kept very busy and nearly lost their nerve and balance. But once through this obstacle, the tide and a following breeze carried them easily to where the estuary narrowed and became a river.

Ayrlon, the new priest of their home community, had said that for many days they could travel inland on this waterway. It led West and gently South. But when they found the course turning sharply North as it did at one point, they must leave it and travel overland for a while until they found another South-flowing river. There were many such and he gave them advice on how to choose the best. Luckily their boat was very light and could be carried between them when they had to cross the land, and it would always be useful as shelter in the night.

"Always keep a fire going," Ayrlon had advised. "The forests are full of animals, some of whom may not be friendly. Fire frightens them and keeps them at a safe distance. Where there are caves use them, but look first that they are not inhabited by man or beast. Make your fire in the mouth of the cave. Many bears, wild cats and wolves seek shelter there from time to time.

"Where you find villages rest with them awhile. Do not push yourselves too far too fast. You will find many dangers and difficulties on the way and if you are tired you are that much less able to deal with them.

"Give my greetings wherever you find people of our faith. I made many friends on my journey North and it is possible you will meet with them and they will give you kinder hospitality for my sake."

38

Kyra, Karne and Fern had listened to everything he had said.

It had been a good day for their village when he arrived. The snow was still on the ground but the earliest shoots of Spring were beginning to show through it. He came quietly, with none of the dramatic showmanship Wardyke had used that fatal Midsummer's Day the year before.

The people took Ayrlon to their hearts within a few hours of his arrival. He was a quiet man, small in build. He listened more than he spoke, but those who told him of their troubles knew he understood and walked away comforted, though more often than not he had said nothing.

Kyra tested her feeling for him by a long night vigil of prayer and meditation near Maal's grave, and in the morning knew for sure her first feelings had been true. He was to be trusted with her village, and their customary ways of peace would be safe in his hands.

When she left she looked back with pain to leave her much loved home, but with calm in her heart knowing that everything was now as it should be.

The first night up the river they camped on high ground on the Southern bank in a dull and drizzling rain.

Fern rushed about, ignoring the wet, joyfully gathering special roots and shoots to eat. Karne and Kyra could hear her talking excitedly wherever she went as though she were greeting long lost friends.

They busied themselves by setting up the boat as tent and trying, at first unsuccessfully, to find a place where it was possible to make a fire. They had just succeeded in encouraging a rather damp and smoking version to ignite when Fern returned, still happy, but dripping wet, her hair clinging in long wet strands to her shoulders and back, water trickling off the end of her nose.

The next day they paddled upriver still in rain and camped damply upon the bank again.

The third day was better. The sun came out and their spirits were so uplifted that they made much greater

39

progress and found, when it was time to camp, a small community of people living on rising land a short way from the water's edge.

After the initial suspicions were allayed the villagers made them welcome and they enjoyed a real feast of river trout and heard many tall stories of river demons and monstrous forest ogres.

Karne went fishing with the men the following morning and learnt to glide so silently in the water that the fish were not alarmed at his presence and he was able, after many attempts, to dart his hand out and seize a fat fish before the creature knew that it was in danger.

He shouted and danced with joy at his first success so much they all had to move to another reach of water to continue their fishing, every fish within a great range having been frightened away by his exuberance.

Kyra and Fern took some of the women into the forest and spoke to them of the gentle tree spirits and the living force that flowed through everything and had its source in that which was limited by no Name, but had power and energy to drive life's multifarious forms within a great and ever harmonious pattern.

The river women listened attentively, but the girls could see they could not understand what was being said.

"No matter," Kyra said to Fern, "it is like planting a seed. The ideas we give them now may lie dormant in their minds for many years, but one day the warmth of some experience will stimulate them into growth."

"But what about the ogres?" a woman asked fearfully, looking around.

"*You* give them their ugly shapes, their terrifying attributes and then cower in the night from them."

"But we *feel* them around us in the dark!" the woman said.

"What you feel are the urges in your own minds to evil, and you give them shape and form with your imagination. You put them outside yourself so that you need not feel guilty about them, so that you need not fear *yourselves*!"

The woman looked at her with eyes that comprehended nothing of what she was saying.

"Have you not felt hate for someone and wished him harm?"

"Yes," the woman admitted reluctantly.

"Then you have felt guilty to feel such hate, to wish such harm, so you have pretended to yourself that it is not *you* hating, not *you* wishing harm, but some other creature, some monster, some ogre. And you vividly imagine it destroying what you want destroyed. But gradually this image becomes so real to you you begin to believe it exists apart from you. You tell others and they join their fears, their hates, their guilts to it as well. And so it grows and grows in your minds until you have all forgotten how it first began!"

"But children have gone into the forest and been eaten by the ogres!" Some of the other women joined in now.

"The children may have been killed by wild boars or wandered so far they have not been able to find their way back," Fern said. "There may be a thousand natural dangers in the forest which could be overcome if you could control your fear of them."

"Fear can kill," Kyra warned. "It is very powerful. If a child is fed on stories of monsters and ogres and it goes into the darkness of the forest, the cracking of a twig trampled by a small deer, the whirring of a bird's wings, could so destroy the balance of its mind that it might run and stumble deeper into the forest, terrified, no longer taking care, a prey to any natural danger."

The women looked doubtful, but as though they wanted to believe.

"If you like," Kyra said after a pause to think, noticing that they were not ready to understand such teaching yet, "Fern and I will go into the forest and pray to the Spirits of Light we know and they will drive whatever it is you fear away from this place forever!"

"The forest is not safe!" the women cried.

"Kyra has magic powers," Fern said, realizing what Kyra was trying to do. "She has started training as a priest."

The women were still puzzled. They lived cut off from

41

the rest of the world and had no Sacred Circle and no priest.

"I have magic powers greater than the ogres that you fear," Kyra said with confidence, "and I will destroy these monstrous ogres once and for all if you will do exactly what I say."

They did not fully understand even yet, but knew enough to realize that these strangers were very different from themselves. The one called Kyra spoke with such authority and conviction they were prepared to believe she was some kind of magician.

The women began to draw back from them a little after this and their friendliness was now tempered with caution.

"While we are in the forest asking the help of our Spirit Gods make me a model of the ogre that you think lives in the forest. Fashion it of river clay and bring it to me at the river bank when it is ready," Kyra commanded.

"There are several types of ogre," someone said.

"Then make them all for me . . . in clay . . . as nearly as you can to how they look."

Fern looked at Kyra, but said nothing.

For the rest of the day the women worked busily at the models.

The men returned from fishing and were told the story. Some argued. Some helped. But by mid-afternoon they were all taking part in the activity even if it was only to offer advice about the look of some particular eye or nose.

Karne took Kyra aside.

"What on earth . . . ?" he said.

She put her finger to her lips.

"It may help to dispel their fears. Why not this way, if they are not ready for the truth as we know it?"

He shrugged and smiled and left her to it, setting about the task himself of gutting the fish they had caught and roasting them on the fire.

Kyra chose sunset for the staging of her exorcism.

She, Fern and Karne built a small circle of river boulders on the narrow sandy beach just below the bank, scooped out the sand from within it, allowing the water to seep up from below.

When the models were prepared, the sun a red and gigantic sphere sinking into the tree tops to the West, the villagers gathered to watch with some apprehension as Kyra lowered the hideous clay figures into the little pool of water she had prepared.

She walked round and round the circle many times chanting improvised prayers of exorcism, Karne and Fern meanwhile scooping more and more river water over the models.

Gradually the clay softened, the hideous features disintegrated and, as the sun finally set with a shaft of brilliant light catching the ripples in the river close beside them, the last ogre dissolved and was no more than muddy water.

As this happened Karne, Kyra and Fern raised their arms and sang a song from their own village, a moving, rising hymn of praise to Light and Life and the Spirit Guardians of the World.

So sweetly did the sound of their voices mingle with the birds homing to their nests, so uncannily did the last shaft of light from the sun fall now upon the little circle of stones and dye the muddy pool of water the colour of blood that the villagers gave a great gasp of relief and *believed* their ogres were finally dead.

That night the villagers sang and danced to the strangers, and this time there was no menace or cruelty in the dance as there had been in the hunting dance of their last host village, where, although no one was actually killed, the lust for killing was in the air.

This dance was only of joy, and the air was filled with feelings of release.

A day or two later the three were sorry to move on. They had made friends. The villagers believed that their monsters had been destroyed and they had been taught to pray to the friendly spirits of the River and the Forest and the Sun for help and comfort in everything they did.

43

Karne had learnt to fish in a new and exciting way.

Fern had found plants she had not encountered before.

And Kyra had been taught to weave baskets of river reeds far superior to any she had ever seen before.

They parted with warm feelings, villagers and travellers each having benefitted in some way from their time together.

Overland travel was not easy. The boat became ever more cumbersome and heavy to carry and, after several rivers had degenerated into rocky rapids before they had a chance to make for shore, it became virtually useless as a boat. They decided at last to abandon it and make their way as far as possible by land, crossing rivers when they found them by inflating their water carrying skins to use as floats and then refilling them with fresh water on the far side.

Kyra was particularly sorry to see the boat go.

The last day before it finally sprang a leak too serious for them to mend had been in many ways idyllic.

For most of the day they had drifted and paddled gently down a very quiet and narrow river, the mossy banks close beside them, honeycombed with the holes of little furry river creatures who came frequently out to swim or bask on floating logs, totally unafraid of the unfamiliar creatures drifting past them.

Karne hummed quietly as he occasionally pulled the paddle through the water to keep it on course and Kyra lay back upon their sleeping rugs and other travelling things, gazing at the sliding slopes of interlocking branches and light new leaves above them.

They were in a kind of green tunnel. The reflections of the trees below them and the trees above, leaning sometimes down to water level, caused reflection and reality to join on an interface that was neither reflection nor reality, but a kind of otherness into which Kyra's thoughts slipped and received a new and deeply stirring peace.

Light played its part, sparkling between the leaves and flickering in the green world reflected in the water and in Kyra's eyes. She hardly dared breathe for fear of dispelling the delicacy of the beauty that moved her spirit through so many levels of awareness.

Karne and Fern were forced to bend their heads to avoid the branches of white hawthorn blossom and their hidden protective thorns.

They were happy too, but in a different way from Kyra.

Fern leant her body against Karne and they felt totally together, absorbed within each other, the green sunlight clothing them in one garment.

Kyra did not notice when the boat stopped and Karne tied it to the brown and knobbled root of a tree. She lay still, gazing upwards in her own secret world, while he and Fern left to find a private place of their own among the tendrils, flowers and grasses.

The day had to end.

But not one of them would ever let it fade in the slightest detail from their memories.

It was one of those precious days, seemingly out of time.

The next day was rougher. Rapids battered at their boat, and muscles grew tired with hauling it in and out of the river, climbing banks, cutting through undergrowth. The whole character of the land had changed remarkably with the change in the rock formations.

From the slow and gentle progress through a wide and meandering valley, hills began to close in upon the river and chasms of rock, with small trees and bushes clutching a precarious living in shallow crevices in their sides, took the place of the mossy peaceful banks they had loved so much.

By midday they agreed the boat's usefulness was finished. From Ayrlon's description they had about exhausted the navigable rivers leading South. They decided to leave the boat, strapping everything they could carry about themselves, and set off to climb the steep side of the chasm wall, hoping to have a better view of the land still to travel from the top.

Fern found the climb with the added weight of her unborn child more than she could bear at times, and Karne, noticing this, suggested they make camp for the night on a broad shelf of rocks and grass, little more than half way up. There was a good overhang of rock to shelter them and plenty of dry wood for a fire, their goatskins were full of fresh water, and they had a plentiful supply of fresh hare meat caught by Karne earlier in the day with his catapult.

While Fern rested and Karne attended the cooking fire, Kyra wandered off to explore. She felt restless and did not want to settle yet to the chores of making camp.

The rocks of these mountains were different from the ones she knew nearer home. She fingered them and brooded, wondering what it was she felt in them that seemed to lead her on and stir some feeling in her that she could not explain.

She kept moving further and further from the camp site, led on by a kind of urge, almost a kind of hunger. Tender and beautiful ferns grew from the cracks in the rocks, lichens of greater variety than she had ever seen clung to the long exposed surfaces of stone and the older branches of the trees. Hanging festoons of filigree lichen, reminding her of pale silver-green hair, hung from the twigs high above her.

But it was the rock cliff that was speaking to her.

It was something inside the rock cliff that was calling her name.

Puzzled, she wandered on and on, looking without realizing it for an entrance into the cliff. The sun had disappeared behind the hill on the opposite side of the chasm before she found it. The shadow was cold, but it was still light. No doubt on plains beyond the hill the sun was still shining. She knew it was not yet time for night and looking upwards she could still see the sun shining on the topmost branches of the trees at the top of the cliff face under which she was standing.

The entrance was half closed over with tangled briars, but she felt the darkness and the emptiness behind them and knew that there was a deep cave there.

She thought about it for a while. Should she return to

46

the others and tell them? Perhaps they were meant to use it for their camp.

She felt strongly, but in an undefined way, that she was *meant* to find this cave.

But it would take her a long time to return to the others and by the time they had carried all their belongings back to the cave night would be upon them.

She decided to have a quick look inside the mountain herself, and then return to the others.

She peered inside and was surprised to see how deeply the cave had eaten into the rock. It was larger and darker than any cave she had ever encountered before, but still she felt the need to explore it.

She ignored the little chill of fear that rippled under her skin and looked around for a suitable branch to serve as a torch. Having found one she worked to set it alight and finally she was ready to bend the briar bushes back and enter, in some trepidation, but nevertheless impelled by a force she could not control.

The flame of her torch took her through the fairly capacious entrance hall of the cave, the only thing here to startle her being a sudden flight of bats that fell from the roof and swirled like dark and solid smoke about her head. She could not prevent herself screaming and throwing herself at once upon the dry and sandy floor. Luckily, although she dropped her torch in her panic, it did not go out and after the bats had swarmed once or twice in wide arcs and had settled back to their places, and she had given herself a stern reprimand for having given way to such a foolish fear, she was ready to continue.

After a while the cave wall showed two separate crevices, wide enough for a human to pass through. She hesitated, knowing that it was foolish to go further but still unable to resist the urge to do so.

She chose the right hand crack and proceeded down a fairly adequate passage way. She became more and more convinced it was leading her to some special place, and so eager was she to find out if she were right and so easy was the passage to follow that she did not notice that it branched frequently in many directions and she had long since turned off from the main one leading back to the entrance cave. The passage she was following was becoming narrower and narrower, lower and lower, sloping always downwards deeper into the mountain.

The torch light flickered on the walls beside her and suddenly she became aware that it was not bare, smooth rock she was seeing, but that the light and shadow of the guttering flame was throwing up in relief what seemed at first to her to be the most amazing man-made carvings. The walls were full of the shapes of creatures, many of which she recognized from the sea, but some she had never seen or dreamt of before.

She stopped and touched them, staring with astonishment. One came away in her hand and she stood transfixed with the perfection of a sea urchin, each detail of tiny radiating spots where the living spines had been joined to the shell perfectly preserved. But in stone! Cold hard stone.

What skill the carver must have had to bring such detail to his carving!

She gasped again.

The wall was full of them, not only upon the surface, but where she broke them off there were others in the rock behind. Shells she remembered from the beaches.

But all in stone.

Icily the realization came to her that these were no man-made carvings.

Living things had turned to stone.

She shuddered and touched her own cold flesh.

Would she too turn to stone in this weird place?

Was it some baleful influence, some dark force, that had led her there, not the Spirits of Light she was wont to follow?

Fear gripped her now and she began to shiver uncontrollably. As she did so the torch in her hand shook and the creatures in the walls seemed to mock her with a strange dead dance.

She turned and ran, horribly aware that she had come a long way and her torch would not last much longer.

The sea urchin was still clutched in her hand. She moved to throw it away, but something made her keep it and she put in in the carrying pouch at her waist. If she ever saw them again she would show it to Karne and Fern.

She ran and ran, grazing her arms against the narrow jagged walls, scarcely thinking which way to turn as each new gallery of darkness opened its entrance to her blind and hurrying form.

At the peak of her panic she turned the corner in a passage that she now realized she had never been down before and stood staggered and breathless at what she saw.

Before her, illuminated fitfully by the still burning stump of the torch in her hand, was a gigantic cavern, the far recesses of which disappeared into darkness, but where the light touched Kyra could see that from the magnificently high ceiling to the floor it was hung with spectacular columns of crystal.

Forgetting her fear Kyra stood stunned. Tumbling in folds like a water fall turned to ice, great curtains of dazzling white fell around her, gigantic statues of translucent stone arose on every side, icicles of stone hung from the domed roof to join flowers of stone upon the floor.

This was what she had come for!

Her heart rose and it seemed to her a crescendo of splendour, almost like a song of triumph but using no earthly means of sound, soared around her, through her and above her.

She was in ecstasy with the beauty and the greatness of it.

She moved forward, walking in wonder, through the exquisite filaments of crystal.

She could hear water dripping and in the centre the cavern floor was lower than the rest and filled with a milky liquid.

Staring into it, her light picking out the reflections in it, she was suddenly jerked into fear again as her torch, burnt now to its very end, scorched her hand and dropped into the water.

As suddenly as the darkness had revealed this splendid,

dazzling sight to her, as suddenly it snuffed it out and she was in utter blackness.

Fear welled back and she turned her head every way trying to see something, anything, any variation in the dead blackness of the hole in which she was trapped, that would give her some idea of what direction she should take to find her way out.

But there was no variation.

She stood very still, listening to her heart beating fast and the drip, drip of the water from the roof. She wondered if there was any way she could make fire, but she had no wood with her and everything in the cavern was wet, the walls, the floor, the rocks, the hanging veils of crystal.

Her own skin felt damp and clammy.

"I must think," she told herself.

But all she could think about was that she was deep inside the earth, deeper than in any tomb.

"I must move about. I must feel for the entrance," she told herself, knowing that if she stood still and thought about her situation any longer the fear that was already clouding her mind would take possession of her completely.

Cautiously she moved.

She established the pool of water was ahead of her by finding her feet and ankles suddenly immersed in icy liquid.

"Good," she said to herself, "that means the entrance is behind me."

She turned carefully around. She had never noticed before how difficult it is to be sure how far you have turned, when there is absolutely nothing to which you can relate.

But she had to make a decision.

Carefully she eased herself forward, hands held out in front of her, knowing there were many hanging columns in the way. Where was their brilliant, luminous, crystalline splendour now, she thought bitterly. All their magnificence came from the little flame she had carried in her hand. Darkly they waited now as no doubt they had waited in the same darkness while the sun a million times a million times shone upon the fortunate creatures of the earth's surface.

How she longed for light!

Gradually she progressed across the cave, bumping herself against rock, feeling her way, slipping and sliding, but at last coming into contact with what she was sure was the wall of the cavern.

She sat awhile to rest, her heart thumping and her breath coming fast. She told herself there was nothing to worry about, she had found the wall and it was just a matter of time as she worked her way round it until she found the entrance. She refused to think about the confusion of passages beyond.

After a while, too cold to be still for long, she started to feel for the entrance. The cold, damp hardness scraped her fingers, but she found no hole. She moved and moved, always in the same direction, always her hand upon the wall. Time passed that there was no measure for. Only her weariness and despair told her that she had been going a long, long time.

At last she paused. She *must* have been around the full extent of the cavern. She must have been!

She tried again.

Again.

The fear was becoming uncontrollable. She could feel cold sweat upon her forehead.

If only she could see!

She stared and stared into the dark and for a moment fancied that she saw a lighter dimness to one side.

Her heart leaping she moved towards it, but she missed her footing, slipped and twisted her ankle. Now tears of pain were in her eyes and she was trembling and shivering with cold, pain and fear.

The lighter patch she had thought she had seen was now upon the other side of her. She turned her head and felt there was another lighter patch where she had looked before. It seemed to her the cavern was no longer so dark.

It also seemed to her that she was no longer alone.

"Who is there?" she called, her voice rasping with fear.

51

The sound echoed eerily around the cavern and came back to her as a hiss.

Trembling, still she tried to see, to listen for someone other than herself, and then she felt presences and could see dim figures.

She called to them and raised herself in spite of the pain of her ankle, and they drew nearer.

But as she saw them more clearly she screamed aloud. Sickly vapours they were, in monstrous shapes.

"No!" she screamed. "No! No! Not you!"

She pressed her hands to her eyes to shut them out. She tried to run and fell again.

Weeping and bleeding and frantic with pain and fear she felt it was the end of everything for her!

And then . . .

And then somewhere in her mind a thin thread of memory came to her.

"These are not *real*," she told herself. "It is my fear that calls them into being!"

She remembered the clay ogres and the water, and felt ashamed that she could presume to teach others about the images of Fear and yet fall prey to them herself so easily.

She forced herself to open her eyes.

But they were still there.

The Fear was still in her.

No matter how she reasoned with herself she could not drive them from her presence.

She remembered Maal and prayed for his help. He had told her many times of all the Spirit helpers in the endless realms of different Realities. They too had no form but that which thought gave them. Humans invented forms for them, just as she had invented forms for her fears and for the evil influences she could feel around her.

She shut her eyes again and forced herself with all the inner strength she had to visualize forms of Light and Love and Kindness, Spirits that would help and protect her.

When she opened her eyes again the crystal rocks seemed to glow with inner light.

She forced her mind to obey her will.

She drew herself up to stand as straight as she could.

Her ankle hurt but she ignored it.

She told herself again and again she was not afraid.

She was protected by hierarchies of helpers who came when they were needed.

Her fears had created the others. Her confidence would destroy them.

"I will think only of love and those I love," she told herself, and thought of Maal, of Karne and Fern, but mostly of . . . someone else.

Another figure appeared to her now and the shadowy ones she had hated seemed to draw back and begin to fade.

Standing before her was the one she had called most urgently, one of the powerful Lords of the Sun, the young priest from the desert Temple of the South, from across the sea. The young priest she had met in "spirit-travel" when she was seeking help against Wardyke.

He held out his hands to her but did not approach, and although she gazed at him with such joy she thought her heart would burst, she did not dare make a move towards him.

"You have passed the first test," he said quietly.

She looked her question.

"The illusions of Fear are powerful, but you have recognized them for what they are."

She noticed there was no sign of the demons now, only the beautiful young man shining with the same strange light as the crystal columns.

"Can you do the same for the illusions of love?"

She stared at him.

She longed for him.

She began to reach out her hands, to move forward.

He stood still, appearing very real, watching her with great kindness, but with a question in his eyes.

She paused.

"The illusions of love?" she asked herself, and then, "What am I doing!" she thought. "As a priest people will come to *me* for help and I must not fail them.

"You are here and not here," she said aloud, steadily,

looking directly at him, "as I am. What we appear to be and what we are, are very different."

"This shell I use, called 'Kyra', I can throw away this moment and will suffer no loss. I am more than Kyra. I am God's creation, and God 'creates' by 'becoming'. Nothing can be separate from Him. All of Him, all the time, is in everything He has 'become', is in me now, and I would feel the joy and power of it if my mind would only stop holding back the realization that it is so.

"The Real Me is Forever and Everywhere. I am One with All that Is."

She was in the dark.

She was not afraid.

When Karne and Fern found her the next afternoon she was sitting cross legged on the floor of the cavern, her face composed and calm, and she looked up at them as they stood, their faces grey with anxiety lit by the torches they carried, as though it had only been a few moments that she had been waiting for them, instead of a whole night and the best part of a day.

The Birth of Isar

About the time the moon reached full for the third time since they left their home village, Fern began to feel the child in her body was ready to be born. She who had always been so lithe and agile was beginning of late to be clumsy, to feel her body cumbersome and heavy, and many times she accepted the helping hand of Karne over rocks and ridges where before she would have scorned to be so dependent.

At night she could feel it moving inside her restlessly and she lay under the stars staring all night into the immensity of the sky and wondering about the child that was to be born.

It was not Karne's child, but Wardyke's, the result of rape and fear. Karne and she had discussed it many times since he had recovered from the initial pain and shock of the knowledge and they were agreed that the child who would be born was an individual in its own right and must not suffer in any way for something which was not its fault, the manner of its conception. Fern had carried it and nourished it. Karne would father it and protect it. Wardyke was long gone, punished and banished for all the things that he had done, and he had no more part in this new life.

Fern believed passionately that everything that lived was its own Self and belonged to no one but to the Great Source of Life Itself, and that was not "belonging" in "the slave to Master" sense, but in "the lover to lover" sense. The loving and the wanting to belong and to be part of the whole harmony of Existence was the only binding force. It was your choice if you chose to be part of it and to flow peacefully with it. Just as it was your choice if you chose to reject it and to drift into disharmony and chaos, suffering pain as you beat your head against the constricting walls which were of your own construction.

Fern, who had once said so ringingly, "No man can own a tree!" knew more than anyone that no one could own a child. Children were born through the medium of male and female flesh, but this was just a kind of door through which they stepped into the world from regions where they had lived millennia before.

The role of parents was to cherish and nourish the infant in its bodily form, teach it how to use the new and unfamiliar tool of flesh it had been given, until they sensed that it was ready to recognize the obligations and powers of its nature and walk freely as it was meant to do.

One morning after such a night of staring at the stars Fern told her husband and Kyra her friend, calmly, that the baby's birth was very near.

They had made camp in what had once been a clearing in the woods. From the charred marks on boulders and the remnants of animal bones upon the ground, it would seem it had once been inhabited and then deserted. Nature had started to reclaim it and young slender saplings of birch, hazel and alder were growing from the undergrowth of bracken, bramble and flowering plants. It was a beautiful place, full of bird song and early sunshine.

Kyra and Karne looked at each other. They had planned to rest at the next community they found while

Fern had her baby among friendly and helpful people, a priest at hand knowledgeable in the ways of healing in case anything should go wrong.

But Fern insisted that she could go no further and that indeed she could wish for no better place for the birth of her child.

She looked up at the shimmering leaves and the slender silvered trunks of the young trees.

"These are my friends," she said. "I would rather be among them than among strange people."

"We need water," Karne said, beginning to feel anxious and bustle about, putting more wood on the fire.

Kyra stood still and seemed to be listening, though not necessarily with her ears.

"There *is* water," she said. "I will fetch it for you."

She took all the skin bags they had and set off to the East.

"Watch where you go!" called Karne sharply, remembering the terrible long night and day Fern and he had spent worrying about her the last time she had wandered off to explore. They had only realized she was not coming back when it was too dark to risk looking for her. They had passed a sleepless night and a worrying morning before they located the entrance to the cave. The bending back of the bushes and the remnants of the fire she had kindled to light her torch had shown them where she was. When Karne had seen the ramifications of the passages within the cave he had insisted on returning to camp to bring all the ropes and fibres he could find so that they could tie some to the entrance and always have a thread to follow back.

It was in this way that they had tracked her through the labyrinth and found her at last.

This time Kyra was not away long and returned with plenty of fresh water to warm at the fire to wash the little creature when it finally emerged.

They made Fern as comfortable as possible and sat close to her while she worked to bring her baby into the light. Karne cradled her head and shoulders in his arms when the effort seemed too great, and Kyra waited to receive the child into the world, her heart beating with a strange excitement.

What an awesome mystery this was, the clothing of the immortal in the mortal, the Spirit from regions far beyond our knowledge, opening its physical eyes in our world, our reality.

She was always amazed how suddenly the last phases of the immensely long process passed. One moment Fern was lying in Karne's arms as she had always known her. The next moment her face distorted with effort into a stranger's face, and then there was the slithering arrival of a whole new Being upon the soft grass.

Swiftly Kyra did her part as she had seen others do in her home village when children were born, and soon the strange new person who was to be from then on an integral part of their lives was washed and wrapped in soft woollen cloths and held close to the breast of a mother whose face was transformed with joy and love.

Karne leant close, thinking more of Fern than the child, but happy too.

There was no look of Wardyke in the tiny creature, but much of Fern. Upon his head, standing up on end like fur upon a squirrel's tail, was a shock of Fern's red-gold hair.

Kyra found herself crying with delight, and kept touching the tiny, perfect hands.

"Look at the nails!" she said. "How can *anything* be so small and yet so beautifully just as it should be!"

This set them all to laughing and the rest of the morning passed joyfully in tending their new charge and wondering at the magnificence of its construction.

When Fern and the baby at last were sleeping in the warm sunlight, Karne and Kyra sat a little apart talking softly.

They both felt tired, but unable to relax. They talked of many things but mostly of the thought that had struck both of them as they watched the little creature feeling blindly for the source of milk and nourishment in its mother's breast, wonder at the sheer miracle of consciousness, the primitive form the baby now showed which in a

58

few short summers would become as complex and as sophisticated as their own.

"This experience more than anything I have ever had," Karne said, "has convinced me that we do not just begin in flesh and end in dust. Nothing could learn as much on so many levels as this child will need to learn to reach the kind of consciousness that we now have, unless it brought with it some skills and aptitudes, some form of memory or consciousness, which would give it readiness to accept all that this world can teach, interpreting it upon its ancient knowledge."

Kyra smiled.

She knew that many times in the past Karne had doubted much of what she and Fern and Maal believed. It was good to see that he had now found a way of understanding and accepting.

Later they talked of Wardyke and wondered if he had left his trace upon the child as Fern had left the colour of her hair.

Karne's face grew grave when they were discussing this. He would say nothing to Fern and he wished it had not even arisen in his mind, but he could not stop a faint trace of misgiving.

"I would feel happier, Kyra," he said at last in a low voice, "if you would try to reach within the child and set my mind at ease upon this point. Pray for it, weave protection about it. Give it strength to withstand any influences that would be harmful to it or to Fern."

He did not mention himself. She knew his concern was only for his wife.

"I will try," she said, "but you know my powers are very uncertain, they sometimes work and they sometimes do not. I can promise nothing."

"Try," Karne said firmly.

Kyra carefully took the baby from its mother. Fern stirred slightly and murmured Karne's name, but did not wake. Karne sat beside her while Kyra took the baby to the other side of the clearing, sat upon a boulder and rocked it gently in her arms. When she was sure the disturbance of the move had not woken it she kept it still, cradled in her arms, and lowered her own head to rest her forehead on its forehead. Karne could see her going very still, as she had many times before when she was sensing things beyond the capacity of his own senses.

He watched with great attention but could not see her face nor anything that would indicate to him what she was thinking as she held the child.

At first she was distracted by the sweet snuffling noises. the baby made as it slept, the way its mouth and cheek muscles moved as though it were dreaming of sucking, and she had to fight her loving sentimentality and force herself to ignore the baby shell and look for the real self within.

The immediacy of the soft, warm forehead upon hers began to fade and gradually images began to come to her, images of distance and feelings of wandering in strange places. Nothing definite at first. Nothing that she could recognize.

The feeling that she had most persistently was of another world, of skies that were not blue but like burnished copper, of people who protected themselves from light instead of seeking it. Of strange plant forms that grew in darkness and withered with the touch of the fiery light that radiated from more than one giant sun.

She felt a fear of light. She found herself longing for the cold dark cave she had been trapped in recently. Strangely she could see in the dark. Or could she? Was she looking at objects outside herself or were they all projections from her own mind, as in dreams upon this earth?

"Strange to be afraid of light," she muttered to herself. "Light goes always with the highest forms of Understanding and Awareness . . . the light of the Spirit Realms . . . the light of God.

"Are these people evil then, that they seek the Dark?"

She searched herself, the child, for more information, but felt no trace of evil.

"Light is a construct too, a Symbol," she thought she heard the words within her head. "Light and Dark have no relevance to what Eternally Is. You have made an idol of Light, as others have made idols of wood and stone. You can see in darkness *and* in light.

"You do not See.

"The Seeing is You."

She was puzzled by this, but stored it in her memory to ponder upon at another time.

"Is this child in my arms from this strange world of burning suns?" Kyra asked the voice that seemed to be speaking these words within her head.

"The child is called Isar and lives now upon your earth. Ask no more of him than that."

"I must ask one more question," Kyra cried. "Please, I need to know. Will he have Wardyke's lust for power and cruel needs?"

"The child is called Isar and lives now upon your earth. Ask no more of him that that."

"But . . ."

But she knew there would be no more answers.

She opened her eyes and looked at the child within her arms. His eyes were open now, but instead of the wandering bluish blindness so familiar in newborn babies' eyes, she knew he was looking directly at her, and *seeing* her.

She stood up and held him out to Karne.

"His name is Isar," she said quietly, humbly. "I know no more than that."

And Isar he was called.

When Fern felt rested and strong enough to continue on the journey Kyra wove a little carrying basket for Isar and Karne strapped it on to Fern's back.

When they had left the waterways they had thought that they would have great trouble making progress towards the South across the land, most of which was deeply forested. But they soon found the network of trackways that Ayrlon had described to them. The whole country seemed to be criss-crossed with narrow tracks that led straight from Sacred Circle to Sacred Circle. Where the tracks had become overgrown and difficult to follow there was always something they could use to sight their course upon, a Tall Stone standing singly, directing the eye to a notch on a far hill and indicating the direction of the track, or through a burial mound raised above the landscape, or even through a series of shining ponds leading the traveller onwards with little flashes of light. Sometimes there were marking stones or, on hill tops, cairns built up high that could be seen for great distances.

Strangely when they were on the track, however indistinct it might be, Kyra could "feel" a kind of power flowing through it that led her on. On several occasions when markers had disappeared and Karne had insisted the right direction lay one way Kyra would argue and claim that she could "feel" it was in another direction altogether.

After the second time Kyra had been proved correct Karne gave up and left the orientation entirely to her, no matter how illogical it seemed at times. It was as though she were following definite but invisible lines of energy that ran through the earth, which at some points had been marked visibly by the inhabitants of the area, but which at other points had not.

Where they came upon well-worn, well-marked tracks they knew they could not be far from human habitation and they rarely failed to find welcome waiting for them in villages. Many times they were sorry to move on and leave new found friends behind.

Where they found a Sacred Circle Kyra would question the priests about The Temple of the Sun, and the picture she built up of it intrigued her more and more. There seemed to be a great deal of inconsistency in the descriptions and she formed the impression that it was something different for each priest who had studied there.

She wondered what it would be for her.

Not all the Stone Circles they encountered gave rest and peace to their weary limbs and spirits.

One day in a mounting storm they hurried to follow Kyra's instincts that told them a Stone Circle was not far away. The branches of the trees above them were groaning and creaking ominously in the rising wind and they

62

hoped to reach its shelter before the storm broke. Clouds like the black wings of night were closing in on them.

Isar upon his mother's back howled and sobbed. Fern took her husband's hand and they walked faster than they had ever walked, in silence and growing fear. The storm had some strange quality about it, some malevolence that seemed supernatural.

Kyra was troubled. She "felt" the Stone Circle not far away and yet she also "felt" a kind of warning.

"Perhaps we should stay here," she said, "and see the storm out before we go any further."

"No," Karne said, "at the Circle there will be houses. We must be under cover when this breaks."

It seemed sensible and in the wild cry of the wind there was such menace they could think of nothing else but getting to the village as quickly as possible.

They hurried on.

As the rain broke from a black sky ripped asunder by a tremendous dagger of lightning they saw the Stone Circle before them, livid in the eerie light of the storm.

But nowhere in sight were the houses that they had expected and longed for.

Karne ran forward, the rain already soaking him through and tearing at his flesh.

Nowhere were there houses.

The Circle was deserted, overgrown with brambles and stinging nettles.

It seemed a long time since anyone had used this desolate place for worship.

Fern crouched against the dead trunk of the only tree in the area and tried to protect her baby from the icy stinging rain and the constant frightening flashes of lightning.

Kyra stood in the middle of the Circle soaking with the water that poured over her and tried to "sense" where the nearest shelter would be.

Nothing came to her but a feeling of great evil. This was a cursed place.

"We must leave at once!" she tried to cry out, but for some reason she seemed trapped where she was and her voice would not carry through the storm to the others who were crouched together, outside the Circle.

Her limbs were becoming cold as stone and impossible to move. Terror was in her heart. She remembered the feelings she had first experienced when she had tried to "spirit travel" for the first time and had thought she was dying, but this was somehow different. Different and more horrible.

Meanwhile Karne and Fern had been startled by the visitation of an old and hideous crone who appeared apparently from nowhere and suddenly beside them.

When Karne had pulled himself together from the shock he spoke to her as boldly and as calmly as he could.

"We are travellers, weary and far from home. Is there a village or shelter nearby we may use while the storm lasts?"

The woman laughed harshly.

"There is no shelter here," she said.

"Nearby perhaps?"

"Nowhere! No shelter anywhere!" she almost screamed.

Fern was trembling uncontrollably with fear and cold, but Karne managed to keep himself enough under control to say sternly,

"Old woman, you must live somewhere! Will you not give hospitality to strangers?"

The old creature shrieked with laughter and as suddenly as she had appeared she vanished.

Karne put his arms round his terrified wife and child and tried to think what to do next. He looked for Kyra and saw her in the Circle, crouching in an unnatural position as though she were being twisted and knotted by an invisible force.

Not pausing to think but that he loved her and she was in trouble he rushed into the Circle and seized her stiff and icy form and dragged it back to where Fern and Isar were weeping against the dead wood of the old tree trunk.

He rubbed his sister's icy arms and slapped her stony face.

64

"Help me!" he cried to Fern, and they rummaged in their bags and found what furs they had and wrapped Kyra in them, all the while calling her name and beating and rubbing her, trying to get the blood flowing again.

"She is dead!" sobbed Fern.

"No, she is not, but she will be if we do not get her warm!"

They clung together, their own bodies trying to warm each other and her.

Mercifully the rain and storm began to pass and when Kyra finally opened her eyes there were already breaks appearing in the windy clouds.

But Kyra's eyes were bloodshot and feverish. Her lips, blue with cold, uttered strange sounds as though she were talking another language.

They had brought her back to consciousness, but she was in some kind of dreadful fever and incapable of speaking to them in any way they could understand.

Fern and Karne looked at each other in despair.

"It is this place," Fern said, shuddering. "It is full of evil. See, no trees grow, no birds fly about or sing! We must get her away from here."

Exhausted as they were, Fern gathered up all she could carry and Karne lifted his sister in his arms. They had no idea in which direction to walk, but they knew they had to walk.

Stumbling with pain and weariness, at last, at nightfall, they saw the fires of habitations, and the people of the village took them in.

Karne told them their story, while Fern and Isar and Kyra were put to bed in a warm house and covered with dry fur rugs.

Once rested and refreshed Karne and Fern were told the story of the derelict Circle they had so unluckily stumbled across in the storm.

"It is said that in the ancient days a witch lived in that place, an old crone, hideous and disgusting, who had the power to make herself into a beautiful young girl for brief spells of time.

"All the communities had refused to take her in and

she lived alone, riding the wind it is said and causing storms to devastate the crops of all the villages that had refused her hospitality.

"One day a handsome young man and his friends were walking in that place and found her in her temporary guise as a beautiful young girl, and the young man fell in love with her. He spoke of taking her to live with him and told her how much he loved her and how he would never leave her.

" 'Not even when I am old?' she asked.

" 'Never!' he said, gazing at her beauty.

"At that moment the spell she had put upon herself wore off and she returned to her hideous, ancient self.

"He drew back in horror, and he and all his friends turned to run.

"But she stood upon a boulder and screamed at him,

" 'You promised never to leave me, and you never will!'

"And with that she cast a spell that to this day no one knows how to break.

"The young man and his friends were turned to stone and anyone who crosses her path within that circle turns to stone as well!"

Karne and Fern were horrified.

They remembered the unnatural, twisted stiffness of Kyra, the terrible coldness of her flesh . . .

Had they saved her just in time from that dreadful curse?

Kyra was very ill for a long time, and even the priest who had some knowledge of healing was doubtful of her chances of survival, but she did not die, nor did she turn to stone.

One day her fever seemed to have gone and they told her the story.

She lay for a long time with her face turned to the wall, tears dripping down her cheeks, too weak to say anything.

But that night her fever rose again and in her delirium they heard her call again and again for Maal, complaining that he had promised to return to her and be with her.

In the early hours of the morning, Fern, keeping vigil by her side, thought she heard Maal's voice speaking from Kyra's mouth, saying quite distinctly that he *would* return, but that he had not promised it would be in *this* lifetime.

When Kyra recovered enough to be aware of what was being said to her Fern told her of this.

Kyra could remember nothing, but tears gathered in her eyes as she listened to Fern's words.

"I want him in this lifetime! I need him *now!*" she said, her face pale and desperate.

Fern stroked her head.

"You think you need him. But no one knows what he truly needs. Maal will come to you when you really need him."

Kyra wept.

She felt so weak, so tired. It was all too much to bear.

After a while she drifted off to sleep and in her sleep she dreamed fitfully about the cave she had been trapped in and the strange stone shells and sea creatures she had found so deeply in the earth.

When she awoke she felt in her carrying pouch for the perfect stone sea urchin she had brought from the cave.

She turned it over and over in her hand. She knew there was something she was ready to learn and it was somehow connected with this stone shell.

Was it that the Universe was full of forces that we did not understand and that they were available to us if we made ourselves available to them?

Words that Maal had said about Good and Evil came to her now. To him Good and Evil lay in the motive, the will, behind an action, not in the action itself. A force that could be used for Evil, could just as easily be used for Good.

The stone shell lay in the palm of her hand. Why or how it had been turned to stone she did not know, but she felt no trace of evil in it, no menace, only significantly that it was part of the natural processes of the Universe.

"I will keep this with me always," she said to herself. "It will be to me like Maal's stone sphere with the spiral markings. It will be my talisman, my centre of strength. I survived the test within the cave," and she knew this had been a severe and important test, "and I survived the cursed circle. I will take it as a sign. A power has been brought to my notice and I will use its positive energy and not its negative. For me it will bring life, not death; spirit, not stone."

Having decided this she held it in both hands and tried to *will* herself to feel better.

"My talisman will cure me," she said firmly. "The mysterious force or energy that transformed it from living shell to stone, I now reverse!"

She concentrated her whole being on what she was trying to do.

She felt the cold stone warming in her hands and began to tremble, wondering briefly if she was mistaken in trying to use it in this way.

The trembling grew more violent.

Karne and Fern returned from being with the villagers to find her seated on her rug clutching her hands together, and shuddering from head to foot as though she were in the grip of some supernatural force.

"Kyra!" they cried, "Kyra!"

But she could not stop shaking.

Thinking that it was coldness that made her shiver so they pulled all the rugs that they could find over her.

"No," she said at last, pushing them aside. "No, I am not cold."

Gradually the shaking stopped.

She sat quite still and carefully released her hands. The knuckles had gone quite white with the tension of her fingers gripping the stone talisman.

She looked at it for a few moments and then looked up at them with a beautiful smile.

"It worked!" she said.

"What do you mean?"

"This is my token of power. It will work for me whenever I truly need it. I was meant to find it and I was meant to suffer in the finding."

"Are you sure it is not an evil power like the witch who

68

turned those men to stone?" Fern asked anxiously. She was ill at ease that something that had once lived and moved in the ocean should now be stone and buried deep in the earth.

"It will be what I make of it," Kyra said. "Its powers can be used for good or evil."

"Do you mean you will be able to turn living things to stone!" Fern cried in horror.

Kyra looked at her.

"Did you learn nothing from Maal?" she asked. "If he would not call Spirit power to do evil work for him, I would not call this strange power to do evil work for me."

The answer did not really satisfy Fern, and she was never really at ease with Kyra's talisman at any time, but she dropped the subject now and turned to tend to Isar who was ready for his milk.

Kyra insisted on standing up in spite of their protests and claimed that she was completely cured and felt strong enough to walk.

Karne tried to persuade her to spend at least a few more days at the village, but when he saw that she looked perfectly healthy, he decided to delay their journey no longer and they set off the following morning.

The last stages were relatively easy. It was late summer and the weather was warm and pleasant, fruits, nuts and berries were ripe for picking, and a track along a ridge was so well trodden and wide that it seemed designed for pilgrims to The Temple of the Sun.

They found themselves singing as they walked and were often joined by other travellers for days at a time. The ridge way was mostly clear above the forest level and the view on either side of mildly rolling countryside, frequently cleared for terracing and planting, comforting. Unfortunately it was also above the spring line and Karne had to make frequent descents to find water when they made camp for the night.

Villages were more frequent than they had been and seemed to grow larger and larger. When they remarked on this to the people in one of the villages, they laughed and suggested they should wait until they saw the size of the community that served The Temple of the Sun before they were impressed.

"In these parts we call it Haylken, the valley of priests and kings."

"Kings?" Kyra asked.

"It used to be a place of kings in the ancient days," they were told, "but now there are only Spear-lords who walk in procession with the priests with gold upon their heads, their women decked in amber and in jet."

"They might as well be kings compared to us," the wife of their informant said. "We farming people all bow to them, and what they demand of us we give them. When they ask our labour no one dares deny it."

"In the valley nearer the Temple each village is ruled by a Spear-lord. But here we are still free."

"One came to our village once," a boy said eagerly, "and carried on his wrist a hawk with yellow eyes who did his bidding and tore at flesh whenever he commanded it!"

"Birds are sacred and should not be used thus," Kyra said.

"If you had been here I wonder if you would have spoken so boldly on the subject then," the boy's mother said.

Kyra was silent.

She remembered the time when she had "travelled in the mind" to The Temple of the Sun to meet the great Lords who gave help in the matter of Wardyke. She had seen many such tall, grand people as the villagers described, but no hawks to tear at flesh.

"Haylken," Karne said musingly, " 'the valley of priests and kings'. It has an exciting ring to it!"

His eyes shone.

For a long time he had chaffed at the constrictions of his own village and longed to travel to the centre of the world. The Temple of the Sun was this for all their countrymen and now that they were nearing it he found that it was not only a place of priests and learning that Kyra would enjoy, but of splendour and adventure that would have challenges for him.

Fern was not so pleased. She loved the country life and would have preferred to settle in a forest glade somewhere nearby and leave Kyra to her studies in this strange, alarming place. But she knew Karne would not be content with this, so she and Isar must follow and see what comfort they could find in this valley of priests and kings.

"There must be trees there and growing things," she thought. "We will make a garden and draw it about us like a veil, and live our lives as quietly there as though we were in the heart of a wood."

Karne was as anxious now as Kyra to finish their journey. Even he, with all his restless energy, had had enough of travelling and of discomfort and danger.

"First you will see the Field of the Grey Gods," an old man told them. "Then on every side the smooth round humps of the burial mounds."

"The Grey Gods?" Kyra enquired.

"Yes. The Grey Gods in anger among themselves shattered the mountains in the ancient days and scattered their debris over all the area. It is said the stones have magic properties and none but priests dare approach them. The gods in olden times helped the priests to take some of the tallest stones to build their Sacred Circles, but no man alive today can tell when that occurred."

Kyra was intrigued. She longed to learn about the powers of stone. Would she be allowed to approach the Field of the Grey Gods when she was a priest and learn from their secret energies?

"Come," she said to Karne and Fern, "let us be on our way."

They left with many offerings of food from their friends and many warnings not to be tempted to enter the Field of the Grey Gods no matter what happened.

"Not even animals go in there," called one voice after them.

"And do not forget to bow the knee to the burial mounds," another called. "Much evil comes from lack of respect to the dead."

Fern shivered slightly and wished she were back in her own village, her own wood.

Karne gazed about him impatiently as though he half hoped something would pounce and need to be fought off.

Kyra fingered the stone sea urchin in her hip pouch and said a little prayer for help and protection from the Spirit Realms.

"We will be all right," she said at last. "We have come so far and through so many dangers, and it *is* the wish of The Lords of the Sun that we should come to this place. We will have protection."

"And anyway," Fern said hastily, "there is no reason for us to go anywhere near the Field of the Grey Gods *or* the burial mounds. We will stay on the track and make our way straight to The Temple."

"I wonder if they know you are coming," Karne said to Kyra. "I mean . . . did The Lords of the Sun . . . ?"

"Of course. Remember the vision I had the night Maal's white stone turned to the green jade of the High Priest?" And she fingered the jade pendant that hung about her neck on a leather thong.

She heard the High Priest's voice as she had heard it in her vision. "You who now have my mark upon you will follow me and learn what I have to teach."

She had no real doubt that she was expected, but what exactly would happen when she arrived and how she would know where to go worried her somewhat.

They stopped talking and proceeded in silence, each with their separate and different thoughts.

By evening they had seen nothing of the Field and the mounds and settled with some disappointment to another night of camping.

Isar was restless in the night and cried a great deal. Whether he sensed his mother's anxiety or whether there was something else that bothered him in the night so close to the Field of the Grey Gods they could not tell, but when the morning finally came none of them had had much sleep.

They broke camp earlier than usual and when the sun had barely started its journey across the sky they suddenly came upon the field of grey rock they had been told about.

They stood amazed.

It did indeed look as though an angry god had scattered broken rock in every direction, and it was almost as though plant life as well as animal life did not dare venture among the magic stones. The grass was poor and a few brambles and briars grew, but the trees stopped neatly at the edge of the Field as though a giant knife had cut a swathe and forbidden them to advance further.

For a great distance the rock seemed to have been dropped in chunks from above, instead of pushing up from within the earth as it normally does.

They stopped and stared for a long time, and then continued on their way, looking always over their shoulders to see if the rocks were still there.

Isar wept inconsolably.

Kyra would dearly have loved to venture off the path and try her secret senses against them. Surely at last she would be able to tell what it was that made priests choose one stone rather than another for their Sacred Circles.

"I will just . . ." she began, unable to restrain herself any longer.

"Oh, no, you will not!" Karne said sharply, seizing her arm just in time.

"I would not go far . . . just let me test that stone there . . . it is hardly in the field at all!"

"Do not let her, Karne," Fern said anxiously. "We have been warned and Isar can 'feel' something here. I know he can. Listen how he cries!"

"We have only been warned by simple superstitious people who understand nothing, and Isar is just hungry and tired of travelling. If I can stand within a Sacred Circle and not be harmed, surely one stone . . . ?"

"No!" Karne snapped.

"Why not?" Kyra challenged. "Surely you do not believe the story that they told!"

"What I believe or do not believe has nothing to do with it! We are near the end of our journey and I do not want any more delays!"

Karne could be very authoritative when he chose. "There will be time enough for you to test yourself against those rocks . . ."

"With priests to guide and help you," Fern added.

Kyra sighed deeply.

It would be good to reach their destination at last.

She allowed herself to be persuaded and they continued on their way.

They saw many burial mounds as they had been told and bent the knee to every one of them.

And then they gasped, for what they saw they were not prepared for, in spite of all that they had been told.

Below them on a plain and on gently rolling hills that stretched as far as they could see, there was a sight that took their breath away.

A giant circle of raised earth, overgrown with grass, and within it the hugest Standing Stones they had ever imagined, and running towards it and then out on the other side, like the curving body of a snake, an avenue of Standing Stones that seemed to run forever.

The Temple itself stood in some isolation, but beyond it in every direction stretched clusters of habitations to the horizon.

How many people lived around and served this Temple? The number was unbelievable! Kyra began to feel very insignificant and very much afraid. Fern sensed it and held her hand. She was horrified herself to think of so many people living so close together. The forests and wild places seemed mostly to have been pushed aside, and little plumes of smoke from cooking fires seemed more common than the trees.

They stood upon the ridge way looking down upon the scene for a long time, trying to make some sense of it.

They noticed that the houses nearest the Temple were the largest. Some were circular as those in their own home village were, but many were long and straight as though they housed a great many people under one roof.

Fern looked beyond at the spreading landscape wondering where her own small hearth would be. She noticed that what had at first appeared to her to be an unruly mass of houses formed a kind of pattern. The habitations were in groups with fields and trees dividing them from their neighbouring group and each one seemed to be centred on a home much larger than the others. The plain was dotted with small villages, not one vast shapeless mass of people as it had at first appeared. The travellers were not used to seeing two villages nearer than a few days' travelling and this is what had confused them at first.

Fern was a little less upset.

"What is that strange hill?" Kyra pointed beyond the Temple, to the South West, where a tall unnatural-looking hill rose suddenly from a flat field.

"It looks manmade, but there are no Sacred Stones upon it!"

"It must be some kind of burial mound," Karne said.

"But who would be so great as to command such burial splendour?" Kyra asked, awed.

Indeed it was a gigantic mound, steep sided and different in character from all the other mounds they had seen. It had a kind of sombre majesty, a brooding watchfulness.

"We will find out nothing by standing here," Karne said decisively. "Before the night we must find a place to settle."

They started moving again, Kyra and Fern growing more and more ill at ease as they approached the Temple. It was so huge!

"We will leave the ridge path here," Karne said. "This track leads down towards the Temple."

"I do not think we should go directly to the Temple!" Kyra said nervously.

"Why not? It is to reach The Temple we have travelled all this way!" Karne said impatiently.

"Perhaps . . . we should make some enquiries first among the villagers."

"You have not come as a villager. You have come to be trained as a priest!" Kyra could sense a note of determined pride in Karne's voice. She remembered those early days when there was no doubt he felt possessive of her powers. He had encouraged her to use them and driven her well beyond her own wishes in the matter.

Her nervousness was making her fall back into her old submissiveness to him, but she was older now and grown greatly in inner strength, and managed with an effort to assert herself at last.

"We will wait here," she said suddenly, with great determination, "at the crossing of the paths, and I will go into the Silence and look for guidance."

Karne looked as though he were going to protest.

"Sit!" she said with a sternness that surprised even herself.

Karne sat.

Fern sat close beside him and was glad of the time to rest and suckle Isar. She was not looking forward to meeting so many strangers.

The Arrival

Kyra sat apart from her companions and composed herself. She knew that the most crucial part of the process that Maal had taught her was to forget herself as "Kyra" completely, and "open" herself to the influences from deep within herself and from the Universe, the influences that were always present but not always noticed. As the trick to use upon her unruly "surface" mind, she chose this time the flight of a black bird she had noticed in the sky, circling round and round, round and round, in a perfect and harmonious arc. She followed it with her eyes for some time, and then closed them, following it still, but now as a projection of her mind. Round and round the black bird went until she was aware of nothing else. Faint sounds that had been rising from the valley, the rustle of grass as Karne moved about impatiently, the chattering of nearby sparrows faded. She heard nothing, felt nothing, thought nothing, saw nothing but in the inner recesses of her mind the circling of the black bird. For all she knew it might have long since ceased to circle in the sky that Karne and Fern could see.

It existed now only within herself.

Gradually she let the image go, the black bird fade, until nothing was in her mind but a kind of readiness, an emptiness that was waiting to be filled.

Maal had warned her that at this time she must be particularly careful not to have any preconceptions. She must wait in readiness, expecting Nothing. She was not waiting for something she already knew, but for something . . . she knew not what.

So she sat. Very still.

And after a while it seemed to her she was not sitting on the grass any more, but was drifting upwards, as gently as a gliding bird on a current of air. She could see everything below her in perfect clarity and detail. She seemed to imprint the pattern of it on her consciousness and knew she would never forget a single detail of it.

Then she felt herself turning as the black bird had turned, arcing slowly and with dignity at first and then gradually going faster and faster until the whole scene was spinning and blurring. She could see the landscape now as nothing but a series of whirling circles.

The air above them seemed to whirl and spin in the same way and she found herself caught in a downward whirlwind spiral to land in the greatest circle of them all.

As she touched earth all movement ceased and she was alone in stillness surrounded by giant Standing Stones and giant ramparts of earth.

She thought she had her eyes open and was truly standing there, but to Fern and Karne upon the ridge way she was still sitting cross legged at the crossing of the two paths, in silence, with her eyes closed.

She looked around her and could see no one. The black bird she had watched was perched on one of the tallest Stones nearest her, watching *her*.

She felt strangely ill at ease under its scrutiny.

Was it a spirit?

Would it understand if she were to speak with it?

She bowed to it at last.

The bird stared at her unblinking.

"My Lord," she said politely to it, "if you have been sent to guide me . . . please guide me!"

She heard a chuckle from behind her and blushed to find she was no longer alone.

A girl a bit younger than herself and slightly deformed was watching her with great amusement.

"Do you always talk to rooks?" she asked, smiling broadly.

Kyra was embarrassed.

"No . . ." she stammered, "but I thought . . ."

The girl laughed out loud.

"We have all kinds of people here, but none who talk to rooks! Is he your god?"

"No, of course not . . ." Kyra said indignantly.

"Then why . . .?"

I thought he might be a messenger," she muttered defensively, still feeling foolish. The girl seemed more than ordinarily mocking and unsympathetic.

"Oh, well," the girl said shrugging, "anything is possible! But to me he is just an old rook looking for a worm."

And as she said it he dived and seized something in the grass, tugged fiercely for a few moments and then flew off with his long and wriggling victim in his beak.

"You see!" the girl said triumphantly.

"I know it must have looked foolish . . ." Kyra said, trying to be friendly, though she felt irritated by the child. "But I *am* looking for someone to show me the way. Perhaps you . . ."

"Where to?" the girl asked sharply.

Kyra hesitated.

Where to begin?

"I am a new student," she said at last, "and I do not know where I have to go to be accepted."

The girl stared.

"I mean . . . I have just arrived from the far North. My brother, his wife and baby and myself have been travelling since early Spring to reach this place. And now I do not know exactly where to go or what to do."

"What are you doing in the middle of The Temple?"

"I . . . am not sure . . . I suppose I was lost . . ."

"No one is allowed in here except the priests and those that they have chosen."

"What are *you* doing here?" Kyra asked quickly.

The child certainly looked neither like a priest nor a student.

"Oh, I am useful about the place," she said airily. "I go where I please."

Kyra decided not to follow this up until she had settled some more important questions for herself.

"Could you tell me where to go?" she asked as politely as she could.

"I suppose to the house of the High Priest would be the best place," she said, looking at Kyra's jade pendant. "It seems you are one of his."

This at least was something!

"Where will I find this house?"

"I will take you there." She turned jauntily and immediately began to hop and skip away from Kyra. Kyra had to run to keep up with her, but strangely felt no breathlessness or strain no matter how fast she ran.

They passed through the Circle of Tall Stones and found a narrow entrance gap in the high earthen bank. Kyra noticed that the bank looked higher than it had appeared from a distance as there was a deep ditch around the inside. Where it was broken for exit and entrance, a wooden bridge was across the hollow. It seemed of flimsy build and possibly would be taken away on certain occasions.

Kyra stared around her at the magnificence of the carved and decorated wooden houses the girl led her among. She saw many of the spiral and concentric circle motifs she had noticed on the wooden columns of Maal's house and on many rock faces during the journey. She began to feel more at home and less afraid as she remembered that Maal had been here and learned his skills in this place. She would learn the Mysteries too and be a priest among priests, not a frightened girl among strangers.

The girl led her to the largest circular house of all and stopped.

Kyra stared at the tall columns flanking the entrance, the beautifully high, thatched roof, the strangely shaped river worn boulders arranged in a double row leading to the entrance. She noticed that they were of different stone to the Tall Stones of the Temple, and fancied she saw in them the tracing of shells and sea creatures similar to the ones she had found in the passages leading to the giant cavern.

"Is this the house of the High Priest?" she asked, her voice low with awe and respect.

When the girl did not answer, Kyra turned around and found that she was no longer there. As silently as she had appeared, so silently had she vanished. Kyra heard a sound above her and looked up, On the highest point of the High Priest's house the rook she had seen earlier was sitting, and he was watching her.

"Oh no!" she thought, and in that instant found herself back upon the path beside Karne and Fern and baby Isar, their dusty travelling packs beside them and her own worn sandals upon her feet.

"At last!" Karne cried in relief. "I thought you were going to sit there forever."

"Have I been here all the time?" Kyra asked, amazed.

"Of course. Where did you think you had been?" Karne answered irritably; and then, remembering Kyra's peculiarities which in his impatience he had overlooked, he added more kindly, "Have you been 'spirit-travelling'?"

"I suppose," she said, still confused.

"Where did you go?" Fern asked eagerly.

"I think I know where we must go now," Kyra said standing up and stretching her stiff limbs. She looked around to see if she could locate the rook, and was half relieved to find that she could not.

She did not know what to make of him. Bird or spirit? Which?

"That is a relief," Karne said, at once picking up their packs.

81

"The path you suggested *is* the right one," Kyra said to her brother. "I know now where the High Priest's house is, and we must go there . . . I think! . . ." she added under her breath. Once her visionary experiences were over she was never sure she had actually had them. At the time they always seemed so real. But as soon as they were over, she wondered . . .

But Karne had no doubts.

They made their way quite quickly down the hill and towards the grand houses nearest to The Temple.

"Which one?" Karne asked as they drew nearer.

"It was one of the round ones . . ." Kyra's voice sounded a trifle uncertain.

"Which round one?" Karne persisted.

"Do not push her so hard, Karne," Fern suggested gently. "She will find it if she is left in peace."

Fern had always noticed her own and Kyra's instincts worked better in quietness and without harassment.

Kyra eventually found the house and stood hesitating on the path between the river-worn rocks. She looked up at the topmost point of the thatch and again was relieved to find there was no sign of the rook. She glanced around her, half expecting to see the strange girl who had brought her here the first time, but she too was nowhere in sight.

When her eyes returned to the entrance of the house she was startled to find the High Priest standing quietly observing her.

She had seen him before in "spirit-travelling", but to Karne and Fern he was a stranger, and they held back in some confusion.

He was immensely impressive, tall and regal, clad in long and flowing robes with a huge and elaborately carved jade circle upon his breast.

His eyes in his bearded face looked deeply into their own, one by one.

It was as though they were frozen to the spot unable to move until he had explored their minds more thoroughly than they themselves had ever done.

They had the uneasy feeling that there was *nothing* they could keep hidden from him.

After what seemed a long and gruelling experience, he moved forward a step and smiled. They were instantly released from whatever it was that had kept them so rigidly in his power.

He held out his hands to Kyra in greeting and smiled at her.

"I believe you have something for me," he said.

She was horrified. Of course, she should have brought a gift!

He was holding out his hands still as though he was sure she had one.

But what did she have that she could possibly give him?

And then, as though in a dream, she found her hand going to her hip pouch and drawing out her stone of power, her precious sea urchin.

She found herself holding it out to him, offering it to him.

He smiled and accepted it with a slight bow of the head.

"I have been waiting for this," he said in his deep, gentle voice.

Kyra tried to suppress the signs of her disappointment. She did not want to part with it. It was her own, and within it she felt were concentrated great energies and powers that only she could use. Through suffering she had learned the secret and earned the right.

As though she had said these things aloud the High Priest smiled at her and said quietly,

"You are not ready for such a thing, my child. When you have learned how to use it properly and control it, you will receive it back."

She felt ashamed of her ungenerous thoughts, but she was not sure she liked the ease with which the tall priest seemed to see into her head.

Karne and Fern were looking quite terrified.

The High Priest now took another step forward and held out his hands for Isar.

Fern drew back instantly, her eyes suddenly sparkling like an animal protecting its young.

No one was going to take her baby from her!

Karne too suddenly recovered his courage and took a defensive step forward to protect the child.

"Nay," the priest said kindly, "I will not take the child from you or harm a hair upon his head. I wish only to give him my blessing. He is a stranger in this world and needs more protection than you can give him."

Karne and Fern looked less worried, but still did not offer the child.

Kyra felt only goodness and kindliness emanating from the man.

"It will be all right," she said reassuringly. "I am sure he will not harm the baby."

Karne stepped aside, but still kept a wary eye upon the priest.

Fern found herself holding her baby out to him as Kyra had found herself offering him her most precious possession.

The priest took the babe in his enormous hands and held him aloft.

Isar stared unafraid into his eyes.

Something passed between them, but not even Kyra could interpret what it was.

At last the old man handed the child back to its mother, and there was a strange look upon his face.

"What is it?" cried Fern. "What did you see?"

The priest said nothing.

"Tell me!" shrieked Fern with unaccustomed passion.

Again the priest was silent.

"Please!" Kyra pleaded with every level of her being.

The man spoke at last, but slowly, as though he were choosing his words very carefully.

"This child and I have been destined for a long time to meet."

"Is it good . . . the destiny I mean . . . or is it bad?"

Fern's face was anxious and strained.

The priest's face was thoughtful, removed.

"Please!" pleaded Kyra yet again.

"It is good for one of us, and bad for one . . . but I cannot yet see . . . for which one good or which one bad."

Fern was crying and holding Isar close.

Karne put his arm around her.

"We will keep him away from you," he said. "You need not see each other ever again. It is Kyra who has come to work with you, not us."

The priest smiled a shade mockingly.

"You underestimate the powers of destiny," he said. "There is no way you can prevent the crossing of our paths. They have already crossed."

"But," Kyra said, "have we no control over what happens to us? Is everything laid down?"

"Our meeting was laid down as the result of our own actions. That is why I can see it in his eyes. But what we will make of the meeting, that is up to us."

"And that is why you cannot see which one will suffer, which one benefit?"

The High Priest looked at Kyra with approval.

"I see you will fit well in to our ways of thought."

And then he looked at the tired and dusty travellers on his path with the kindliness of a host, all shadows gone.

"You need somewhere to rest and refresh yourselves. I will call someone to take care of you.

"In the morning, at sunrise," and here he looked at Kyra only, "you will come to this house again. And you," he said to the others, "will be shown where you may build your house and live in peace within the community."

"Will Kyra not live with us?" Fern asked anxiously.

"No, she must live in the College with the other students. From tomorrow her way and yours must part."

"Will we not see her again?" cried Karne now in dismay.

"You will see her, of course, but not all the time."

The three were silent. Sad. Astonished at how fast their lives were changing. The journey had seemed so long it had lulled them into thinking that things would always be the same.

They had never really thought about how it would be at the end of the journey.

As they stood, the long shadows brought by the setting sun creeping around them, a black bird swooped past them and landed with a whir of wings upon one of the river sculpted stones just behind them.

Kyra spun around and standing on the path beaming at her was the peculiar little girl she had met before.

There was no sign of the black bird after all. It must have flown away.

"This is Panora," the priest said calmly. "She will show you to the guest house for the night."

Isar who had been so calm when the stranger priest had taken him from his mother seemed very restless in the night again. The guest house was comfortable and warm and Panora appeared from time to time with bowls of delicious food and helped them light the little lamps of earthenware filled with oil that they had never seen before. She even helped set up a little hammock for Isar which could be rocked to comfort him to sleep.

"He does not like it here," Fern said. "I can feel it."

"As soon as it is morning we will look for a place for our home as far from the Temple as it is possible to be without being too far from Kyra," Karne promised.

"Will you help us, Panora?" Fern asked the spritely girl. She liked her and allowed her to jog Isar up and down upon her knee.

Kyra still felt ill at ease with her. She could not decide what it was, but she thought it must have had something to do with the way she disappeared and reappeared so suddenly.

"I am here to help," Panora said cheerfully, "and I will sing Isar to sleep if you like."

"If only you could!" Fern cried. "But it seems to me we are in for a bad night."

"Not necessarily," Panora said cheerfully, and started to sing. It was a weird little song like nothing any of them had ever heard before.

"It is not even our language," thought Kyra, but that

86

was her last thought until the morning. The song did its work not only on the restless baby but on the others too, and within moments they were all fast asleep.

Panora stood a moment looking at them all with amused eyes, and then flicked her fingers. Instantly the little lamps went out and the travellers were alone in the guest house in the dark, peacefully and dreamlessly asleep.

Kyra woke as a beam of sunlight shafted through the door.

She was alert at once, remembering that she should have been at the High Priest's house at sunrise.

Shouting, she poked and nudged Karne awake.

"I am late!" she cried "I must go!"

She left him waking slowly as though from a deep and drunken stupor.

She ran as hard as she could in the direction she remembered. There was pale sunlight everwhere and people were going about their early morning business as though everything were in order.

Breathlessly she arrived at the High Priest's house to find no one there but Panora sitting on a rock and drawing pictures in the dust with a long stick.

"Hello," she said cheekily.

"I am late," almost sobbed Kyra. "What can I do now?"

Panora's eyes twinkled as she squinted into the sunlight above Kyra's head.

"Follow that rook!" she suggested, and laughed hilariously.

Kyra was on her way before she realized how ridiculous it was, but she was so confused by the strange girl, who by now she was quite convinced was no ordinary girl, that she followed the bird who she was also convinced was no ordinary bird.

She found herself, hot and breathless, in time to join a procession led by the High Priest over the little bridge into the Temple.

She was not dressed as the others were dressed and felt conspicuous and awkward.

The High Priest walked first, clad in very regal robes, and behind him many people of different ages, the younger ones at the back of the line, but all clad in neat tunics, well-tied sandals, with different coloured cords about their waists.

"The cords must be some kind of indication of the progress of their studies," she decided, and looked around anxiously to see if there were any there like her without cords at all.

No. It seemed she was the only complete beginner.

She saw many of the others looking at her curiously, but no one spoke. She was ashamed that she had left in such haste she had not been able to comb or plait her hair and it stood around her shoulders now in a blonde and tangled mass.

Once within the Circle the little procession made a slow progress around the circumference of the outer ring of Stones.

This was followed by a hymn to the Sun not unlike the one Maal had often spoken at the dawn. She began to feel less lost and strange. Ritual words were comforting, specially ones that linked people from so many different places.

She began to join in the responses to the hymn and found herself chanting quite a few that she did not know she knew. The voices of the others seemed to draw the right words from her until she was not sure if the sound she thought she heard from the voices outside herself was not actually her own voice from within. In some way she had become part of a composite Being and the strength of all the people in the group was in that Being.

At the end of the hymn the High Priest raised his arms and they were all silent. She knew she had to bend her head and shut her eyes. She did this and remained a long time in darkness and in silence.

In this state she knew that her first studies would be of dreams. How she knew this she could not say. But the knowledge came to her with the force of a command.

Simultaneously they all opened their eyes though no spoken word of command was given. She found herself following a particular group of students, knowing that they were the ones to be studying dreams.

She sat with them, crosslegged on the grass, at the feet of a teacher who asked each one in turn to relate the dream of the night before. Afraid that she would be asked to describe hers she racked her brain to remember what it had been. But her memory was blank. Since the beginning of that eerie song from P---- as she woke in the morning, everything in her mind had totally disappeared.

She gave up and listened attentively to the other students.

Each told what he had dreamed, the teacher interrupting occasionally to question and draw something out that the narrator had apparently been trying to hide. He seemed greatly skilled at knowing when the truth was being spoken and when it was not.

When the dream was exposed enough to satisfy the teacher, he began to ask questions of the class and draw out of them what they had understood by it.

Kyra was amazed by some of the suggestions and felt unwilling to expose some of her most secret fantasies to the scrutiny of these apparently ruthless critics.

After a dream had been analysed by the class and Kyra was sure there could not be a single thing left in it unaccounted for, the teacher would step in and reveal yet layer upon layer of significance hitherto hidden in the symbolism.

She was staggered at how complex a reflection of every level of consciousness in a person a dream reveals.

She was glad that for this day at least there was no time left when it came to her turn, and the class was dismissed before she had to speak.

The teacher indicated that Kyra and a boy called Vann were to remain behind. He smiled kindly at the two of them, more kindly than he had during the lesson. Kyra had begun to think she was afraid of him, his tongue had been so sharp, so ruthless in its quest for honesty.

"The two of you are new," he said now, and Kyra looked with relief at the boy and he at her.

"What is your name, girl?"

"Kyra," Kyra said, relieved to find that not everyone in this formidable place could see directly into her head.

"And where do you come from?"

"From the far North," Kyra said.

"Vann is from the West country. From the mountains."

She smiled at him. He was not good looking, but had a pleasant face. Although he looked older than her, he was smaller in build.

"He has been here a day longer than you and will show you where you will live and where you will find food. You will both wear an orange cord until you have passed the tests I set for you. Meanwhile you will work hard and obey me in everything."

"Yes, my lord," she said humbly.

"Now go. You must be hungry."

She was.

The First Training and the Test of Dreams

While Kyra was settling in to her new life in the College of Mysteries, Panora was helping Karne and Fern find a suitable place for their new home.

Isar and Panora seemed to have a bond between them from the first and the girl became more and more a part of their lives, carrying the baby upon her hip while they walked from village to village looking for the one where Fern felt most at home. Karne agreed for Isar's sake that they should go as far from The Temple as they could and at last settled for a village that lay beside the banks of a stream, particularly rich in leafy shade and moss. The people seemed friendly and pleasant and not unlike the country people they were accustomed to in the North.

"The first thing to be done," Panora said, "is to visit with the Spear-lord and ask his permission to join his community."

They had heard of the Spear-lords before they had reached the Temple, and Fern looked alarmed.

"In our village we have the priest and seven chosen

Elders to look after us," she said. "We know nothing of Spear-lords!"

"Here it is different. The Inner Council of The Temple is the ultimate authority in the land, but in each village a Spear-lord rules his own people. They serve him and do his bidding in all things and in return he gives them protection and tenure of some of his land."

"How did this come about?" Karne asked with interest.

"In a time the oldest people now living heard their grandparents talk about, a tall warrior people came to this land from over the sea. They were so strange and grand, carried such weapons and wore such clothes, the local people offered no resistance but welcomed them as lords. Many of them became priests in The Temple and took powerful positions on the Council. In time the custom we now have came about. It seemed to happen, naturally, without violence. No one even questions it these days."

"Are they still warriors?" Karne asked.

"We have had no wars here for many generations. But I have seen them fight amongst themselves with long daggers and axes, sometimes in anger, but more often for the sport of it. Some of their weapons are very beautiful. I have seen a dagger held to its haft with pins of gold intricately worked in a magnificent design."

Karne's eyes shone. How dearly he would love to have such a dagger.

"Is this way of the Spear-lords a good way?" Fern asked.

"If the Spear-lord is a good man, it *is* a good way. If he is not . . ." Panora shrugged and did not finish her sentence.

"And what of the Spear-lord who rules this village?" Fern asked anxiously.

"Look around," Panora said, " 'feel'."

Fern looked around.

"I feel peace here."

"And in the eyes of the people who live here?"

"I see peace."

"Then he is good," she said shortly. "You would feel it if he were not."

She led them through the village to the Great House standing clear of the other houses, half way up a gradually sloping hill. Fern was happy when she noticed there were healthy looking plants and trees clustered about it.

The Spear-lord, Olan, was not at home, but his wife and daughter gave the strangers a warm welcome, a drink of milk and a sweet-tasting honey cake to eat.

It was clear they knew Panora well and Fern noticed with surprise with what respect these grand and elegant people treated the ugly, unkempt little girl. They listened to her request with favourable smiles and for a moment Fern fancied she had seen them bend the knee in a slight bow to her when she first entered their house. But she dismissed the idea from her head as soon as it entered. It could not be! To her Panora was just a friendly village girl who had adopted them because she was lonely and because she enjoyed organizing things and showing people round.

Olan's wife and daughter were very beautiful and calm people, dressed in fine woven garments, both with earrings and bracelets of gold. The inside of their house had low couches spread with rugs of fur from animals they had never seen.

Fingering an unusual spotted fur Karne asked if the animal had been hunted locally.

The woman smiled.

"No," she said, "these have come from over the sea. My husband has visitors from many lands. We often exchange gifts of local artifacts for things we do not find here."

She held up a cup to the light that came streaming through a slit in the wooden wall, and it glowed translucently with a kind of amber light.

In answer to Fern's unspoken enquiry she said, "Yes, it is amber."

Fern was overwhelmed by the beauty and the richness of everything she could see, and by the grace and warmth of the two women.

It was arranged that Panora and Olan's daughter should go with them to choose land for their home. It was made clear that Olan's permission had still to be granted but, as Olan's wife said, looking significantly at Panora, "if it is the wish of the High Priest, the Lord Guiron, there should be no difficulty in obtaining it."

Again Fern felt there was something being communicated between Panora and the woman that they could not intercept.

And so it was that before the autumn turned all the leaves to the colour of fire Karne, Fern and Isar had set up house. Fern had even succeeded in starting the rudiments of a garden by taking plants already rooted and growing from the woods and fields and, with great tenderness and care, transplanting them to enclose her little home.

"It will be better in the Spring," she told Isar. "The seeds I have planted will grow then. You will see. You will live in a garden full of love and loveliness and no harmful thing will come near you!"

She held him very close and kissed the top of his head. He was most precious to her. Most precious! She could not bear to think of the strange shadows that hovered over him.

Panora came on most days to help them or to play with Isar. She brought them many tales of what was happening in the other villages or at The Temple and so, although they hardly left their own small place, they were not out of touch with the rest of the area.

Karne grew to like and admire his Spear-lord Olan very much. He worked on Olan's land for part of each day, but most of his time was spent on the strips of land he had been given for his own. The community cattle, sheep and goats were kept together and the villagers took it in turn to tend them, to lead them to pasture in the morning and back to the communal compound at night. Each villager had his mark upon some of the beasts. Not all belonged to the Spear-lord.

Karne made sure both his land and the land of Olan under his charge was well dug and turned over before the frosts came to harden it. That first autumn Karne and

Fern had never worked so hard in their lives, but they were together, and they were happy.

The Southern soil showed white when it was turned over and the strip fields waiting through the long winter for the early Spring sowing made the landscape seem unusual to Karne. From the rugged North with its hard rock and dark earth, the soft, pale shading of the fields made them look ghostly and unreal.

Olan laughed when Karne told him this.

"It is real enough in the Spring when the wheat is growing boldly. You will see how real it is!"

Fern delighted in the colours of the autumn trees, the gold and bronze of leaves and black of branch against the chalky earth.

She began to feel less homesick for the North.

Meanwhile in The Temple College Kyra's life was very different.

Although her main work at first was concerned with the significance of dreams she soon found that all the branches of learning in the Great College were interrelated and from dawn to dusk under the guidance of different priests, they studied not only dreams, but group and private meditation, healing, divination, prophecy, and, together with these more spiritual disciplines, disciplines of the body, control of muscles, of breathing, of every part of the body including its use together with creative imagination to design and make physical objects of satisfaction and beauty.

Under the guidance of Maal she thought she had learned a great deal about "going into the Silence" within herself. In that Silence she could be away from the distractions of the outer world and aware of the subtle and numerous realms of consciousness within her which linked her with the Whole of which she was an organic part. In The Temple College she found what she had learned from Maal was only the beginning. She learned greater control of herself, so that when she chose to "go into the Silence" she went smoothly and efficiently instead of plunging in clumsily and almost accidentally.

She learned that what she did in the "Silence" was not only of benefit to herself, but like a stone in a pool of water, the influence of it spread out in ever widening circles around her.

Not only in the "Silence", but all the time, whether she knew it or not, she was influencing with the flow of her thought people outside herself and they were influencing her.

Thought became more than just the rambling monologue she was accustomed to hearing within her head.

It became a Force that she respected, a force that perhaps had shaped the Universe in the first place, but certainly shaped the day-to-day existence of all around her.

Each person creates his own world by his own thinking. It is given shape by how he sees it, and how he sees it depends on how he is, inside, from the first moment when he begins to notice the Universe around him, through his struggles to understand it, using all the tools at his disposal, his body, mind and spirit, until at last he stands fully Aware and Conscious of All the implications and subtleties of the Whole.

"In the study of this force we call 'Thought'," the teacher said, "we use many methods. Before we can use its power to influence the world around us we must learn its power to influence us. We will not have the final mark of the priest upon us until we have learned not only what 'Thought' is and how to use it, but Who We truly Are and how we stand in relationship to the Universe as a Whole. Once we understand this we will use 'Thought' as a tool and not as a weapon, and it will be safe for us to be released upon the outside world as priests."

They were taught that the Thought that came from their "surface" minds was the least significant, least reliable of all the forms of "Thought" available to them.

In the silence of meditation, consciously and with strong self control, they explored the realms of understanding most close to the all enveloping Being of the Universe, but in their study of dreams they became familiar, through painstaking interpretation of image and symbol, with the deeper layers of their own personal being.

96

With the dusk their studies were not done. Sleeping became a kind of work as well. For it was sleep that gave them the material for their explorations of the inner levels of their consciousness.

When the priest-teacher thought it advisable they worked within the Sacred Circle, using its ancient forces to strengthen their own powers of understanding, but all the preliminary discussions were held outside the Circle.

In the Winter hide tents were erected for their shelter in the worst of the weather, but Kyra noticed one particular group never used the tents and in the fiercest, coldest conditions sat cross legged and flimsily dressed at the feet of their Master.

"Why is that?" she asked, and was told that this was yet another branch of training that must eventually be undergone, training to control one's body in such a way that heat or cold, pain or pleasure, could have no effect upon it.

Kyra remembered how Maal had controlled his own dying, lying buried in the earth for a long while apparently dead, and yet not dead.

"They can even walk through fire and are not burned," Kyra's informant told her.

"You mean they just do not *feel* the burning?"

"No, their flesh does not even *show* the burning!"

She was amazed once more at the incredible power of "Thought."

Each day was so full of interest she scarcely felt the passing of time and woke one morning after a dream of Karne and Fern to realize that she had not seen them for a long time.

She determined to ask for time off from her studies to visit them.

That morning she told her teacher of her dream and how it showed quite clearly that she was missing them.

He smiled.

"I see you are an expert already," he said, and his voice was slightly mocking.

She decided not to rise to this and asked instead, politely, if she might have the day off work to visit them.

He did not give her a straight answer to this, but turned to the whole class and said,

"This day here is a special ceremony, the inauguration of a new priest. We are expected to attend. We will take positions on the West of the avenue half way between the Sanctuary and the Sacred Circle. When the procession has passed us we will enter the avenue and follow it as far as the earth ring. It is our privilege to stand upon the ridge and watch the ceremony from there."

"Do the ordinary villagers see the ceremony too?" Kyra asked a neighbouring student in a whisper.

"No. It is a great honour to be allowed to witness an inauguration. It is because it is part of our training in the Mysteries that we are permitted."

Kyra was sorry about the villagers, but excited that she at least would have a view of it. All thoughts of visiting her brother and Fern went from her mind.

In making her way with her new friends to their position beside the avenue she was amazed to see the crowd that had already gathered. The land on either side of the Processional Way was filled to bursting point with men, women and children, many of whom looked as though they had been there since the night before. Families had brought food to eat and she saw many a water skin and ale jar handed around.

She had to cling to the arms of her friends, Vann and Lea, so as not to be separated as they pushed and jostled towards the position their teacher had told them to take up. But for all the unruliness of the throng she noticed the Processional Way itself, between its tall and sombre Standing Stones, was kept completely empty. The earth between the Stones was as hallowed as that within the Circle. She herself dared not put a foot upon it, although she was sorely tempted to, to escape the pressing of the crowd upon her back.

The procession was to be at noon and she was just feeling tired and bad tempered at the length of the wait, when she heard her name called and she saw her brother

Karne pushing through the crowd, carrying Isar upon his shoulders and dragging Fern by her arm behind him.

"Karne!" she shouted excitedly and flung herself at him.

In spite of the lack of space they managed to kiss and hug each other satisfactorily. She was amazed how Isar had grown and developed in the short while she had not seen him. He seemed very cheerful to be upon his father's shoulders above the crowds and banged his little fists upon Karne's head from time to time as though it were a drum.

"Oh, he is lovely!" Kyra cried, her eyes quite misty to see them all again.

Fern hugged her.

"We have missed you so much. Our home is lovely and we long to show it to you. We were talking about you last night and planning how we could possibly see you. Karne hoped we might meet you today, but when I saw the crowds . . ." She threw up her hands and laughed.

It was indeed amazing that they should find each other in such a crowd.

Kyra remembered her dream and the way her teacher had mocked her for settling so quickly for one simple interpretation. It might simply have been her yearning to see her family again that had made her dream as she did, but in the light of what Fern had just said, it could have just as easily been the flow of thought from them that she had intercepted in her relaxed dream state. On the other hand, *they* could have been influenced to think and talk about *her* at that very time because she was dreaming so vividly about them.

And there was yet another factor to consider in her dream, the interpretation of which seemed to be growing in complexity at every moment: the incredible chance of their meeting in this milling crowd this very day.

Was this a prophetic dream?

Or did their mutual longing for each other "pull" them together through the crowds? Did they unknowingly follow a beam of thought as though it were a path?

Suddenly a hush fell upon the crowd and above it Kyra could hear the clear and haunting notes of many horns blown together in a rising cadence. The sound made a little shiver pass through her body. Even Isar looked in the direction of the horns and stopped his happy gabbling. A little frown gathered on his forehead which gave him a very wise, old look.

The procession had begun.

The High Priest, the Lord Guiron, in regalia of great magnificence, walked first. He was almost unrecognizable in his long purple robes, the great collar and crown of gold and jade heavy upon him. His face was like a mask, it was so still and cold. His eyes were gazing straight ahead like stone until he was almost level with them and then Kyra was startled to see his eyes swing to the side and meet instantly and directly those of Isar raised above the crowd on Karne's shoulders.

Kyra suddenly felt an icy wind blow from one to the other, and her own flesh caught between them raised goose-pimples with the chill of it.

But as suddenly as it had happened it was over, and Kyra, looking around, could see no evidence that anyone else had noticed, until she saw Fern weeping and pulling Isar off her husband's shoulders, pressing his face into her breast and murmuring over him sounds of great comfort but of no meaning.

Kyra noticed that Fern was shivering too.

But Karne had not noticed what had happened and was puzzled at his wife's reaction. When they spoke about it later he said he had been so busy watching the clothes of the priests he had not noticed their eyes and tried to tell the girls that they had imagined it. But his voice did not carry much conviction.

When Kyra became aware of the Procession again she saw priests of every rank in robes of crimson and in gentian, their faces framed in the unfamiliar stiffness of helmet or crown.

Behind them followed the tall figures of the Spear-lords and their wives, clad in even greater splendour than the priests.

Then came the horn players and behind them the drummers.

Further back still a small group of very old priests walked, dressed in simple white robes with no jewellery or finery of any kind, and in their midst walked the young man who was to be inaugurated as priest this day.

He too was dressed with the greatest simplicity and carried himself with great dignity.

But Kyra noticed as he passed close to them a little muscle in his cheek was twitching.

She knew how he must be feeling, and thought to the future when the procession would be for her.

When he had passed and after allowing a discreet gap to form, the students were led into the Avenue to take their part in the procession.

Just before she was pulled forward by her fellow students Kyra looked back and saw Fern still in tears cradling Isar and now Karne, aware at last that something was wrong, had his arms about them both and was trying to lead them out of the crowd.

She longed to stay with them but was pushed forward by the current of her new position in life, and had to leave them behind. As she walked the Processional Way her feelings were torn between her old loyalties and her new.

"Karne will look after them," she comforted herself at last. He had inner strength as well as muscle, and she knew he loved both Fern and Isar most tenderly.

The ceremony in the Circle took a long time and the students who stood upon the earth bank well away from the action grew restless and began to talk among themselves.

On seeing Panora moving about quite freely among the honoured members of the ceremony, Kyra turned to Lea and asked why such a little girl of no particular significance was allowed to be among that most exclusive group.

Lea did not know, but someone who overheard the question leaned forward and joined in the conversation.

"She is no ordinary child," he said darkly.

"How do you mean?"

"Did you not know that she is the daughter of the Lord Guiron?"

The man could not help but be pleased with the effect his words had upon his listeners. Several other students crowded around to hear more. Kyra was stunned.

"But the High Priest lives alone!" one student said.

"I have never heard of a wife!" another added.

"And Panora certainly looks more like a ragged waif than the daughter of a wealthy priest!"

"He has no wife, nor ever had one," the informant told them.

"Only a child?" one student said with a laugh.

"Yes ... and no ..."

The man was obviously enjoying spinning out the mystery.

"How do you mean?" Kyra demanded.

"Well, she is not a child in the ordinary sense of the word. In fact, she does not really exist in the ordinary sense of the word!"

Now he had his listeners spellbound.

"Tell us!" they demanded.

He told them.

"When Guiron was still a young man, before he became High Priest, he fell in love most deeply, but with no hope of taking her to wife."

"Priests are allowed to marry," someone said, "although it is not usual."

"Aye," the man said mysteriously, "but only with real women!"

They gasped.

"He had the misfortune to fall in love with a spirit woman who lived on a lake and was only seen when the mists came down thick upon it."

"A spirit woman?"

"Aye. As part of his training as priest he had to spend a night alone on the lake, experiencing the dark and the stars. But during the night the mist grew thick and he could not find the shore. He found instead this beautiful spirit woman. She told him she was not of flesh when she could see the way he was gazing at her, but he would not listen and *would* have her. She tried many ways to fend him off but he used his priestly powers to overwhelm her, it is said, and she bore this child we call Panora."

"When he was young, you said," Kyra mused, "yet Panora is still a young child, certainly not more than fourteen summers, and the Lord Guiron is an old man now."

"Panora never ages and comes and goes as she pleases. She is more spirit than girl."

Kyra could believe it!

"Where is the lake? Where is her mother?"

"No one knows. When he became more powerful as a priest the lake was drained on his order, and the woman has never been seen since."

"But how is the story known?" Vann asked. "Surely no priest would have been made High Priest if he had such a shameful incident in his past?"

"All I know," the man said defensively, "is what I have been told by the old villagers who were present when the Lord Guiron became High Priest."

"So it could be no more than an idle tale?" Lea said.

"Explain Panora then!" the man challenged.

"She could be just an ordinary waif."

"No, she could not. She was found sitting waiting for him at his door, mocking him, when he returned from his inauguration as High Priest, and he looked as though he had seen a ghost. People tried to send the child away, but he said she was to be admitted to his house and no one was to disturb them. Before she went inside she called out loud and clear to all who were gathered there, that she was the daughter of the spirit woman of the lake and the Lord High Priest.

"When she was seen again she avoided answering questions and no more was said about it as the Lord Guiron was held in great respect. But there are some who remembered the night and the day he had been missing on the lake and how wild he had looked on his return. The legend of the spirit woman was well known and there

103

were some who had wondered if he had encountered her even then, long before Panora's appearance. When they remembered how he had wandered about distracted and alone on the shores of the lake for a long time and then had insisted the lake was evil and must be drained, Panora's claim began to seem more real."

"But Panora is quite plain and the spirit lady was supposed to be so beautiful?"

"She must have been like her mother in some way or he would not have recognized her and looked so horrified!"

Kyra remembered how strangely Panora seemed to appear and disappear, and the very definite position of privilege she held with The Temple. She could see her now within the Circle watching everything that went on.

"She *is* a waif . . . between two worlds . . ." Kyra thought, and a twinge of sympathy for the child disturbed her.

And then she thought of Isar.

Panora was always with him and she was the daughter of the man whose destiny it was to cross with Isar.

Fern thought he was safe and far away from Guiron in her new home, but Panora was a constant link with the very danger she was trying to avoid.

At first she thought to rush to Fern and advise the little family to return North, as far from Guiron as they could. And then she remembered what the High Priest had said: "You underestimate the power of destiny."

Something had to be worked out between them, either now or later, and there was no escape.

She would warn Karne to be on guard with Panora, but she would not encourage them to believe that it is possible to escape one's destiny by moving one's position on the face of the earth. Something more was required. Something from deep within the two protagonists.

As the winter progressed Kyra's interest in her studies continued to grow.

During dream study they learnt how to project images into each others' sleeping minds as she and The Lords of the Sun had already done to Wardyke in the past. But at that time she had scarcely known what she was doing or how she did it. She learned now how to control her visualizations and their projection, either as direct images or in a kind of symbolic code.

"As you learn to master the art, my children," the teacher said to them one day, "some of you may reach the point where you can project 'cold', but most of you will never reach beyond the point where it is strength of feeling, passion, that sends the message across and manifests it in another's mind."

Kyra was not sure of the extent of her own powers in the matter but decided one night to put to use what she had learned for her own ends.

When she had first come to The Temple of the Sun she had expected to see the young priest from the desert temple in the South as one of the teachers. In the vision she had received of her own arrival and acceptance at The Temple, she had seen him quite clearly with a group of students from his own country surrounding him.

She had seen his image in the cavern when she had called so desperately for help, but since her arrival at The Temple she had seen no sign of him, nor found anyone among all those she had questioned who had heard of him.

She knew he was one of the great Lords of the Sun, but she was not sufficiently advanced in her studies to be allowed to attend the lessons on "spirit-travelling" in spite of her early experiences.

All the students had experienced in one form or another some unusual power before they were called for training, but once they were at The Temple these "experiences" were ignored, and they all started from the beginning, the priesthood claiming, with some justification, that the "experiences" had been uncontrolled and accidental.

The young priest she longed to see appeared not to be at The Temple at all. Lying in her sleeping rug that night she decided to try and find out where he was. She persuaded herself that this would be a good test of her capacities and that she was doing it as part of her training in dream travel.

She composed herself for sleep, emptying her mind of everything but the young priest, projecting her longing to see him with great passion into the dark and lonely night.

At first she wondered why the moon and stars were bobbing about in the sky and then she realized that she was on a boat and the boat was in rough seas.

A boat?

She was surprised.

She had expected the desert temple with the tall red sandstone columns fluted at the top like palm trees.

For a moment she thought she must have failed, and then she wondered if perhaps she had not.

There must be some reason for the dream of the boat.

Perhaps it was a symbol.

Sometimes when one tried to project fear into the dream of one's partner in an experiment and used the most frightening image of a demon one could think of, the partner saw a perfectly ordinary dog. At first it seemed as though one had failed but then it emerged in discussion that a dog had savaged him as a small child and ever since "fear" was associated with "dog" for him. The experiment had not failed after all.

She decided to explore the boat.

She passed the steersman but he did not notice her and this gave her boldness. It was a strange ship. Larger than she had ever seen. Grander. Yet made almost entirely of reeds.

She found where the crew lay and stood beside them one by one, willing them to stir in their sleep and turn their faces so that she could study them.

But he was not there.

Sad at heart she willed herself to leave the ship and try to reach the temple in the desert.

But she woke instead, restless and tossing, in her own sleeping place in the long house of the College.

She lay awake most of the night thinking about the dream, but in the morning did not mention it to her friends nor to the teacher.

The full turn of the moon later it was Kyra's time to be tested.

She was to compose herself for sleep, asking deeply within herself for some kind of guidance or lesson from the spirit realms.

No student was allowed to think of her this night and she herself was to try totally to empty her mind of all its usual images and thoughts.

A year ago she would not have been able to do this, but now as a result of the training she had received, she found it quite easy to do.

She lay totally relaxed, alone and empty of all thought. So empty indeed that she was not aware of the crossing over from wakefulness to sleep.

Next day she had to tell the class her dream and give her interpretation. On this she would be judged fit or not to move on a stage further in her studies.

In her dream she had been present in a huge temple building such as she had never seen. A building built on many levels of different kinds of wood and stone, flags and fluttering streamers blowing in the wind from every jutting peak and rib of the many timbered roof.

The Temple was built against the side of a mountain, each floor higher up the mountain, and surrounding the whole thing were other mountains of great height and beauty, white with snow and dazzling in the sun.

Within the Temple were great works of art. Wise men were studying scrolls with little markings on them which Kyra knew in her dream were symbols which they could understand within their heads.

Her own people had no such thing as writing, but in the dream Kyra understood what writing was and how it was being used to store the knowledge of a great civilization.

She walked about looking at exquisite paintings hanging on scrolls from the walls, at Statues carved with perfect precision from the hardest rock. She heard great men discussing learned ideas.

So great and splendid was this storehouse of knowledge, and so magnificent and advanced upon her own civilization, that she concluded she was seeing a vision of the future.

This was the first part of the dream.

The second part was horrible.

Suddenly from the sky came monsters in vast hordes. They dropped black rocks upon the beautiful shining building, and as the rocks touched they roared and flashed and whole sections of the walls disappeared in smoke and flame. Pieces of roof and wall and statue were flying everywhere, and everyone was running about and screaming.

Only one group of men seemed to stay calm. There were seven of them and they walked calmly to the courtyard that was in the heart of the Temple, and went to a tree that grew in the centre of the courtyard. The leader lifted up his hand and picked a single seed pod from the tree and then the seven turned and walked away.

Through all the corridors they walked quite calmly among the screaming, running people, the falling timbers and the splinters of rock. The scrolls of paintings were in flames, the scrolls of writing utterly destroyed.

The seven men picked their way past the debris and the flames and went out of the temple by a small side door, low on the mountain and not far from a forest.

They looked back as they entered the forest and saw the last of the Temple laid flat.

The monsters in the sky were not content with that but continued their work of destruction on every living thing they could see or on any fragment, man-made or natural, that belonged to the civilization they were determined to destroy.

The seven men hurried through the forest as the demons turned their attention to the living trees and began to blast them with their fiery rocks.

As the last cover was destroyed the seven men entered a dangerous rocky chasm.

One by one they were killed.

But before each died he passed on the green seed pod they had been so carefully carrying to the next man who was still untouched.

Kyra, watching it all, was in despair.

The flying monsters were determined to destroy the men as they had destroyed everything else.

As the last man saw that there was no way out for him he flung the seed pod into the river far below him and Kyra saw it swirling off in the white and boiling waters of the rapids.

The last man stood with quiet dignity watching it go until he too was blown to pieces as his companions had been.

Kyra woke remembering the utter desolation that had once been the most magnificent civilization she could ever have imagined.

The class listened spell-bound to her story. It was a message from the spirit realm. Of that there was no doubt in their minds. None of these things had ever happened to Kyra in this life, and there were things in the dream that she could not have known about or seen.

After a long silence the teacher said to Kyra,

"What have you learned from this?"

They all knew that with spirit messages you always took the meaning that came to you at the moment of waking. This was part of the message.

They never discussed, or analysed, these kind of dreams even if the interpretation that came with them seemed at first illogical.

"I learned that nothing is ever completely destroyed, but lives on in another form. What is past nourishes what is present, and what is present nourishes what is future, and there is no changing this.

"And I learned that the Temple I saw was not only in the future, but was also in the past. This had all happened before and would happen again. The Circle and the Spiral are the most potent symbols of Being known to man.

"The Seven Men of Wisdom, the Guardians of the Mysteries, rescued the seed pod rather than any of the fabulous paintings or scrolls of writing, because it contained the tiny germ of Life that would grow again wherever it landed into another civilization. This one was finished, but a new one could grow as long as this mysterious seed containing spirit-force was preserved.

"I realized this world, or any other world, could have had many such civilizations which had disappeared and grown again, as it were, from seed.

"And we who grow do not remember the others, no more than the seed remembers the tree from which it was taken, or the tree remembers the seed from which it grew. But the tree would not be what it is if it had not come from such a seed. And the seed would not be what *it* is had it not come from such a tree."

The High Priest Guiron who was present at the examination of Kyra stood up and raised his hand above her head.

"You have done well.

"But remember always, graduating from a class means only that you are now fit to *begin* to learn what there is to learn, and that you have some idea in which direction to look for knowledge."

The rest of the students drummed their feet on the ground and looked at her with smiling faces as she passed along in front of them.

She felt very happy.

Divination

The first thing Kyra learned in the class for divination was that the power of divining was not in the object itself, but in the mind of the "Seer", so that it was perfectly in order for them to use anything they liked as aids to divination.

"Our 'surface' mind," the teacher said one day, "is not only crude and noisy, the most inadequate form of consciousness we have, but also arrogant and shrewd. It has been used for so long it is loth to give up its domination. For this reason, before we have the skill to change easily and accurately from it to the subtler regions below, where we are sensitive to influences travelling invisibly from person to person, Spirit to Spirit, we have to use little subterfuges, little tricks, to 'outwit' our 'surface' minds.

"For this reason some people throw pebbles or sticks, and make their decisions on the way they fall. Others burn bone and examine the pattern of cracks. Others kill animals and peer into their entrails, and yet others consult Oracles and are given words which can be interpreted in many different ways.

"Where you have been hindered by lack of confidence,

or by trying too fast to master a skill you are not ready for, where you have been staring so hard that you can no longer see, or so long that you no longer notice, a return to the quiet within yourself, a rest from the constant harassment of the 'surface' mind telling you what to do, filling your attention with irrelevant details, will be invaluable.

"Sit in front of a flower. Watch it grow.

"Relax.

"Being is easy if you do not work at it too hard.

"Understanding flows up from under the surface like a spring and brings you refreshment from times and places long forgotten by your 'surface' mind. Everything you have ever learned in this life and in the ones you have lived before, is preserved, available, if only you know how to reach it."

The students sat spellbound. Their new teacher was a vigorous and lively man who paced up and down in front of them as he spoke, using gestures energetically to emphasize each point.

Kyra knew much of what he was saying already, but if she had learned anything in the past year, she had learned how necessary it was continually to renew and reinforce one's knowledge of truth. But she wondered if the "surface" mind the teacher spoke about with such disdain was not a protector as well as an enemy; we need to draw on inner levels of consciousness from time to time, but to live so intensely aware of so much all the time would be exhausting. We need rest, not only from our "surface" mind, but from our "inner" mind as well. We *need* the kind of sleep that most people call their waking life, as much as we need the kind of waking that most people would call sleep.

The students practised at first by throwing little clusters of pebbles and trying to see what they could make of them.

Kyra was amazed how often her set of pebbles took on the shape of a boat. At last, worried about this, she turned to her student neighbour and asked what he saw in her pebbles.

"A tree," he said without hesitation and returned to his own.

"A tree? Surely not . . ."

She remembered the dream she had of the boat.

She trusted this teacher enough to talk to him about it. He quietly cross questioned her until without meaning it to happen the whole story of the young priest she was longing to see came out.

The teacher smiled.

"There are two possibilities here. Either you are longing for him to be on a boat coming towards you so that you force this image into existence. It is a wish-image. Or perhaps you have penetrated to a deeper level where you are in thought contact with him and he *is* actually on a boat coming towards you. Both explanations may be valid simultaneously. There is no limit to the number of levels that can be operating at once."

After they had spent a great deal of time using different methods to explore their own most secret knowledge, the students were told to each choose a partner and start to work with him. One would ask the question and the other would be the "Seer" and try to answer it.

Each student found some things worked better for him than others and the teacher encouraged them to choose the method they felt most at home with. Belief in its efficacy and a relaxed attitude was very important.

Kyra had a set of small, carved, walrus ivory pieces, beautiful to feel and touch, that her father had given her as a farewell present.

She had always found the quickest path for her to the inner realms was the path of visual beauty. The curve of something, light touching something with unusual delicacy, the sudden harmony of two reeds moving in a breeze . . . these things were enough for her to slip from mundane consciousness to a level where depth of awareness of anything was possible.

In throwing her ivory pieces, in calmly and deeply contemplating them, Kyra drifted into a state of receptive meditation, where the bond of inner communication between herself and Vann, who had asked the question, was so close that she could "feel" what he deeply wanted the answer to be, in fact knew himself what the answer was to be. He wanted to specialize as a Healer, but his "surface" mind told him he should leave the College as soon as he could qualify as an ordinary village priest because his family wanted him back with them.

Kyra looked at him, her eyes misty from staring at the exquisite ivory pieces.

"You have great potential as a Healer. It would be wrong to throw it away. Your family will understand eventually and be glad."

He knew this. He just needed to be told it.

He felt at peace at last.

One day their teacher strode briskly into their midst and asked them one question and then sent them away for a few days to think about it.

The question was: "Does a prophet really see the Future?"

The students argued amongst themselves and went for long walks alone to think about it and when he called them back again there were almost as many different suggestions as there were students.

When the teacher had heard them all he told them to sit down and he would give them a demonstration.

He sent Panora who was hovering around as usual to fetch a man who was famous as a Seer and Prophet.

Panora vanished instantly, overjoyed to have such a mission, and returned not long afterwards with a very old, very bent man Kyra had seen from time to time about the Temple environs.

He was led by Panora to stand before them and Kyra saw that he was blind.

The teacher asked for a volunteer to question the Prophet. Several students volunteered but Kyra was chosen.

She left her place and stood before the man.

"Do not ask your question aloud," the teacher said. "The Prophet is not only blind, but deaf. *Think* it! The rest of you must keep your minds as still as possible so that there is no interference in the flow of thought between the two."

Kyra was a little nervous now that she was so exposed, but seeing Panora's mocking face, she felt she had to continue. Somehow she disliked the girl. Perhaps she had never forgiven her for laughing at her that first day when she addressed that perfectly ordinary rook as "My Lord!" But surely she would not be so petty!

She took a few moments to compose herself. She had intended to ask if she would ever meet her young desert priest in the flesh, but somehow, perhaps because Panora was staring at her so fixedly, she found herself thinking about the High Priest Guiron, and what lay between him and Isar.

The old man took a long time to speak and some of the students began to be a bit restive. The teacher stilled them with a fierce look and there was unmoving silence again.

At last he spoke and his voice seemed to come from a long, long way away.

"A woman began the trouble and a woman will end it."

Kyra waited, hoping he would say more, her heart beating fast.

Nothing more seemed to be forthcoming.

"Will it be the same woman?" she found herself thinking.

"A woman that was loved was there at the beginning, and a woman that is loved will be there at the end."

And that was all he would say.

The teacher broke the tension with a sharp clap of his hands.

"That is all," he said to Kyra. "You will get no more."

And then he turned to the class.

"I am afraid Kyra chose a question that will not be of much use to you as a demonstration. Whether the answer has relevance or not will not appear for many years. I

115

should have put a limit on the kind of question to be asked."

He looked around at the disappointed faces of the students.

"I will choose another one of you, and this time the question must have an answer that can be easily checked. Ask it aloud first, that the class may know what you ask, and then in your mind that the Prophet may know it."

Kyra felt she had failed them in some way, and returned to her place disconsolate. It had been an "unsuitable" question, but she *did* want to know the answer.

The student who had now been chosen cleared his throat and said aloud to the class:

"Can you tell us the exact day and time of day we will see the very next complete Stranger from over the sea in our Temple?"

This time the whole class concentrated on the question and whether it was the force of all their minds working together, or whether it was because the question was simpler to answer, the answer was given almost immediately and without any of that eerie sound of distance he had had in his voice before.

"On the third day from this, precisely at noon, a young priest, his skin much burned by the sun, dressed in white and blue, with gold around his waist, will stand with the Lord Guiron in yonder Circle," and he pointed exactly as though he could see, directly at the Southern Circle contained as a sanctum within the Great Circle.

Kyra gasped. It was the very question she had wanted to ask, but had been prevented from doing so by Panora's disconcerting eyes. Had her mind influenced that of the student who had asked the question?

It *must* be her priest! The description fitted exactly.

She was so excited that her mind wandered far from the class she was attending and was only brought back to some kind of sense by the sharp and sarcastic voice of the teacher who could see that she was not listening and had trapped her with a question.

She blushed and stammered, but her mind was hopelessly out of tune with the class.

She caught Panora's eye and felt that she would like to shake her for the look of amused triumph on the girl's face. The thought of doing violence to her had no sooner left her mind, than the child laughed and snapped her fingers. Kyra momentarily turned her eyes away and when she looked back, in Panora's place, tugging at something in the grass for its midday meal, was a black and evil looking rook.

"Oh!" she snapped irritably, and stamped her foot.

"Perhaps it would be better if you left the class for a while, Kyra," the teacher said to her. "I can see you are not going to listen to a word I say."

"Oh . . . I am sorry . . ." mumbled Kyra, contrite. "I really will concentrate!"

"No," the man said, "you will waste the time. Climb upon the earth ridge, and walk the whole circumference slowly. When you have done that, return to me and tell me what you have learned."

In shame Kyra did what she was told.

"That Panora!" she caught herself thinking resentfully. And then, "No, not Panora. Kyra! My mind should be under *my* control, not at the mercy of every disturbing whim and influence."

She climbed the ridge and started walking, taking deep breaths of the wonderful early summer air, feeling the warm energy of the sun stirring her spirit, its light beautiful on everything it touched.

Some people thought of the Sun as a god, but to her it was enough that it was a channel of Power for the Limitless One, as she was herself.

When she returned to the class she was peaceful and refreshed, and the words of the teacher made sense to her.

"All I ask of you is that you learn as much as you can about everything you can," he was saying, "keeping a mind always open and ready to receive, and yet careful and guarded enough to weigh the new against the old, the unlikely against the likely. The more background understanding you can accumulate from the past the easier you will see into the future, for the one grows out of the other.

"No knowledge, no understanding, is ever wasted. If it is not immediately needed, store it, you will need it one day."

He gave as many examples of predictions that had failed as had succeeded, and pointed out that where the prophet had gone wrong it had usually been because he had not been patient enough to sift through all the knowledge he needed for the task.

"It is not only the present life of the man who asks for help that you must consider, not only what he *thinks* he knows about himself. You must search the inner levels of his mind and reach the real Self he might not even recognise. The time scale you must use must be as long as Time itself. He does not come into existence with his birth, nor leave it at his death. Remember this at all times."

After the class she asked Lea about the discussion that she had missed.

Lea told her that the prophet had probably scanned far and wide among the beams of thought that he was aware of in his dark and silent world and so came upon the young stranger who was thinking hard about their Temple as he approached it. The prophet visualized him from the man's own image of himself and gave the time of arrival the young man himself estimated.

This explanation pleased Kyra.

She thought about the more difficult matter of Guiron and Isar. But the prophet again could have scanned their minds for memories of ancient experiences and guessed the natural outcome of those events.

She was content that they should all be part of a great moving, expanding harmony and play their destined part in it, but she did not want to believe that every detail of their play was pre-ordained. That she was destined by some past act of her own to be upon a ship storm-tossed at sea she could accept, but in that situation she wanted to believe and did believe that there were still many different choices she could make to affect the outcome. And if her choice should result in pain or death, it was still her choice whether she let herself suffer it in anger and

118

despair, or whether she accepted it calmly as having some purpose in the Universe.

"We were warned about causing things to happen by predicting them," Lea said, interrupting her line of thought.

Kyra looked at her.

"He gave us an example of a man being given the exact time of his death. It seems it is quite possible the man died at that moment not because he was destined to, but because he *expected* to. Either he gave up taking precautions because he had no hope, or he might have even done things that would lead to his death, without realizing it, convinced that it was inevitable and the sooner it was over the better."

"So the prophet was a kind of murderer?"

"Yes. We have to be very careful what we say when people ask us to prophesy. Sometimes a whole community has been destroyed by a prophecy of doom. No doubt the prophet had good reasons for sensing its possibility, and he was right to warn them of it, but he should also have pointed out that it might very well be possible to avert by, say, a change of their way of life. Because they believed it was inevitable they gave up trying. Fear, despair and self-indulgence, the predators of the mind, moved in, and the community collapsed as the prophet foretold."

"It is a great responsibility," Kyra said.

"Yes," Lea agreed.

The Arrival of Khu-ren

On the third day from the day the Prophet had been brought before them Kyra took great trouble with her appearance and was late for class.

The morning seemed endless and she looked frequently at the position of the sun to establish when it would be noon.

"Kyra, the sun will not move faster no matter how much you wish it to!" Her teacher was regarding her with kindly amusement. She hung her head.

"I know you are all anxious to see if the prophecy will come true. At noon I will remind you of it and we will discuss it then, but meanwhile there is other work to be done."

Noon came and went.

The young stranger did not appear.

Kyra could feel tears burning behind her eyes.

The teacher himself was visibly disappointed, the prophet had never been known to be wrong before.

But as it turned out, although the timing was inaccurate, the young stranger *did* appear later in the afternoon, clad as the prophet had said, standing with Lord Guiron in the Southern of the two inner Circles.

The young man *was* the priest Kyra had been waiting for. She learnt from her enquiries later that he had brought a party of his own countrymen as students for the Temple College, and was the Lord Khu-ren, one of the distinguished Lords of the Sun, who would be staying for some time to instruct those who were priests already in the highest grade known to their culture, the grade in "spirit-travelling".

Kyra was full of joy and tried every trick she could think of to delay leaving the Great Circle after her class was over, but she was forced to move before the young lord finished speaking with the High Priest. Unless they were engaged in a specific training matter or part of a rit-ual ceremony the students were not allowed within the Circle. By using the Circle only for intense psychic in-struction or for religious and mystical purposes over long periods of time an atmosphere had been built up which gave the Temple the concentration of psychic power that was necessary for the immense tasks it had to perform.

The students were only allowed in at all because their bodies had gradually to grow used to the feel of such power, for the time when it was their turn to use it. The more elementary the classes they attended the shorter the time they spent within the Circle. Those who were nearly approaching the state of the adept and had passed initi-ation into the Higher Mysteries spent a great deal of time in the Circle.

But none but the very high stood within the Inner Circles "in the flesh".

Kyra remembered when she had stood in the most holy place of all, the Northern Inner Circle, but at that time she was not "in" her physical body, and neither was the young priest.

She had waited to meet him so long, and these few mo-ments that were left seemed longer than all the time be-fore!

She could not stay in the Circle, but she waited just out-side determined to see him as he left.

"What is the matter?" Vann asked her.

"Nothing," she replied, rather sharply.

"Are you not coming?"

"No. Go on without me. I will join you later."

She thought they would never leave, but at last she was alone.

She had a long wait and had almost despaired when she heard voices and the small group from the Inner Circle appeared. The Lord Khu-ren was speaking, and his voice, which she suddenly realised she had never heard before as all their communication had been through the medium of thought, was deep and melodious. He spoke their language, but a little haltingly, with strange intonations and every now and again he hesitated for a word which the Lord Guiron supplied.

She was startled at the strength of feeling that surged through her as he approached, and a little ashamed. She was even trembling.

As they came nearer and nearer she found herself stepping backwards, afraid now of the meeting, her feelings were so out of control.

It seemed to her he deliberately kept his head turned away from her and kept talking and looking at the High Priest.

Within moments they were past and it was all over.

He had not seen her.

Tears came to her eyes. She had wanted him to see her so desperately, and yet had feared it. The anti-climax of it not happening at all was too much. She turned and ran and did not stop until she reached the home of Karne and Fern.

That night she spent with them.

They could feel she was troubled and unhappy but she refused to tell them why.

She rocked Isar to sleep in her arms and there were wet patches on his soft head when she laid him down at last.

Karne and Fern were very happy to have her with them, but did not question her further when they could see she did not want to tell them what was troubling her.

She preferred to talk about their affairs, to hear all their stories of village life, of the friends they had made, and of the admiration they had for their Spear-lord, Olan.

"We have been very fortunate. I believe not all the Tall Strangers are as noble as Olan," Fern said.

"He is teaching me to fight with the long dagger of his people," Karne said excitedly.

"Whom do you want to kill?" Kyra asked, raising an eyebrow.

"No, not to kill. It is a sport and requires great skill. And there are horses here . . ."

"We have them at home too," Kyra said quickly.

"Yes, but here Olan has tamed them and some of the Tall Strangers have learned to ride upon their backs. He teaches me to look after them and soon he will teach me to ride as well."

"This is a great honour," Fern said, "because normally it is only the Spear-lord who may ride. Olan thinks very highly of Karne and treats him with respect."

Karne laughed.

"Other Spear-lords are not so pleased! Old Hawk-Eagle who lives over the hill to the South hates Olan and resents the fact that he treats a local peasant almost as an equal. He says it will make the other peasants restless and they will all be demanding equality soon!"

Kyra smiled.

Equality to her was something impossible on earth.

Every single person was at a different stage of spiritual evolution. There must be inequalities in this sense. There must be a kind of hierarchy of wisdom and responsibility. But from what she could gather Hawk-Eagle himself would be very low down in the hierarchy she had in mind, and this would not please him.

The trouble with people like him was that they thought they could impose an unnatural hierarchy on the world, making sure that they (however unworthy they might be) were at the top and everyone else (however worthy) would be below.

In the morning she was up at first light and out in the
124

cool and fragrant garden. Spider webs caught the dew and new flowers that had pushed out of their enclosing sheaths at night were turning their faces to the sun. She longed to stay in this peaceful and pleasant place with the ones she loved. For the first time she felt that she did not feel totally happy at the College. But she knew she would already be in some disgrace for not having told anyone where she had gone and for being away all night.

She ate a quick breakfast of fruit and milk and then ran as swiftly as she could back to the Temple.

She was late for class and in trouble as she expected. The teacher gave her a hard and searching look when she arrived flushed and out of breath, but said nothing. Her friends looked at her too, but there was no opportunity to question her then.

It was not until the rigours of their studies were over that they had a chance to speak to her.

"Will I be punished?" she asked anxiously.

"No, of course not. But you do owe him an apology and an explanation."

She set off at once to find her teacher and stood before him, with contrition on her face.

"I am sorry, my lord, that I was not present last night and was late for class this morning. I went to see my brother and his family and slept the night with them."

"You did not ask permission?"

"No, my lord."

"Did you think it would be refused?"

"I did not think, my lord. I just ran off."

He stared at her steadily. She dropped her eyes.

"You must learn more self control if you are to be a priest," he said at last, quietly.

"I know my lord," she said in a very low voice.

"Next time," he said " 'think'."

"Yes, my lord."

You may go now," he said gently.

How much of what was really in her mind he had seen she did not know, but she was grateful to him for not mentioning it.

On returning to her fellow students she was given a

125

small parcel wrapped carefully in a very fine piece of white cloth. She fingered it enquiringly and realised that it was not wool. It was a fabric she later learned was linen, unknown to her at that time.

"Where did it come from?" she asked, bewildered.

"One of the students who arrived yesterday brought it."

Kyra looked up immediately.

"A student?" her voice shook a little.

"He asked if there was a girl called Kyra from the North with us. We said you were in our class, but were not here at the moment. We did not know where you had disappeared to!" complained her friend Lea.

"But was it one of the students from over the sea, from the desert land?" Kyra demanded.

"Yes. He said . . ."

She was pulling it open now with trembling hands and heard no more. The others crowded round to see what it was. As the thin wrappings of linen were removed Kyra found lying curled up inside a necklace of blue faience beads of great delicacy and beauty.

She gasped, and her friends were amazed as she held it up to the light to see how exquisite it was and how subtly the colour and the light interplayed.

"What did he say?" she asked now, her voice strange and tense.

"I cannot remember exactly . . . just that it was for Kyra of the North . . . and I was to be sure you were given it."

"What name did he give?"

"No name. Only yours."

"I did not know you knew any of the new students?" someone said.

"How did you meet him? He has only been here a day!"

"Is that where you disappeared to last night?"

They were teasing her now and harassing her, but she was scarcely aware of it.

It would not have been from the student. She knew no students from that country. But she did know their Lord Priest.

She buried her face in her hands and started to sob.

126

This gave her friends pause and most of them left her alone after this, but her best friends Vann and Lea stayed behind.

"Tell us," they said gently, but she shook her head.

At last they too left her alone and when they were gone she took the necklace out of its wrappings and gazed at it reverently. She held it against her cheek and her eyes shone. She kissed it and put it carefully over her head and stared at it lying against her breast.

She moved the pendant of jade which she had worn for so long into her carrying pouch, so that the new necklace could lie in its place.

When she joined her friends again they could see that she was blissfully happy, but they could see also she was not prepared to speak about it.

The evening prayers came and went, and at last it was time for sleep.

She slept quietly and easily and her dream was as beautiful as the necklace.

Over the next few days she tried to see the Lord Khu-ren to thank him for his gift but there seemed no way of approaching him.

At first there was no sign of him and she was deadly afraid he had left the Temple area altogether, but then she heard he had been taken to see the College of Star Studies, the other Great Circle which was part of the complex Temple of the Sun, but built further South, away from the populous villages and the bustle of the main Temple business.

The priests who manned the College were particularly skilled in astronomical calculations and she knew there would be a time when she would study briefly with them. But now she was anxious in case the Lord Khu-ren would settle there and it would make it almost impossible for her to see him, but she was assured by Panora, who knew everything about everybody's business, that his visit was only temporary and his main work would be done at their own College and Temple Circle.

Relieved, Kyra waited impatiently for the days to pass

and at last was rewarded by the sight of him walking in procession with the Lord Guiron for the Harvest Ceremony. She could not approach him, of course, but she hoped at least to catch his eye.

As he came level with her on the processional route she would not have been surprised if the whole concourse of people had not heard the loudness of the thoughts of her mind *willing* him to look at her.

Whether the others noticed anything or not she did not know, but he did.

His eyes met hers very briefly and then dropped to the chain of beads around her neck. If she had had any doubts before that he had sent them to her they were dispelled now. There was a warm shine of recognition in his dark eyes and pleasure at seeing his gift upon her breast.

But the look, though intense, was very fleeting.

The priest that walked beside him came between them and he was carried past. He did not turn his head to look at her again, but then she knew that no priest upon the Processional Way was supposed to look anywhere but strictly ahead at the approaching Sacred Circle.

The Lord Guiron had broken that ancient law by looking into the eyes of Isar.

And now the Lord Khu-ren had looked at her.

She was flushed with pleasure and confusion.

After this she accepted the fact that she would see very little of her lord and that it was probable that they would have no means of meeting for a long time. He was very much among the more important of the priests and none of his duties took him anywhere where she was likely to be.

She managed to convince herself, because of the look she had received from him during the procession, that some day, some time, the moment would be right and they would be together.

Meanwhile she kept her feelings secret from her friends and apart from occasionally teasing her about the mysterious student who brought the necklace and then never called again, they allowed the subject to fade away.

The necklace became so much a part of her that they almost forgot there was a time when she did not have it.

The first time the Lord Guiron noticed that his jade sign had gone from her neck and she had faience beads in its place, he gave her a strange and penetrating look that made her heart beat anxiously. But he said nothing. And his thoughts she could not fathom.

Because she was anxious to make as much progress as possible, as fast as possible, towards the time when she would be ready for "spirit-travelling", she worked harder than any of the other students.

It seemed to her at times her teacher knew what she was trying to do and deliberately held her back.

"These things cannot be hurried, Kyra," he said to her one day, noticing the look of impatience on her face when she thought she was ready for a particular graduating test and was refused permission to take it. "Each stage of learning must be fully absorbed into the system of the student before he moves on to the next one.

"Think? What are your motives for taking this test now. Is it because you know you are ready, or is it because you are impatient to reach the next stage because of reasons quite unconnected with the growth of understanding?"

Kyra was silent.

She remembered a dream she had had the night before.

She was a small child and saw in the distance amazingly tall and beautiful Shining Beings. A feast was being prepared for them, and as a great honour she was allowed to help prepare the feast although all the other children of her age had been sent to sleep.

Excitedly she rushed about doing everything her elders told her to do, but as she laid each delicious bowl of food upon the place of the feast she sampled a little of it. It was legendary food. Nothing like it had ever come her way before. She ate from every bowl a morsel, no more, thinking all the time how lucky she was to be allowed to stay awake and serve at the feast. She would see the Shining Beings and hear their talk while all the rest of the children were asleep.

But before the Shining Beings arrived to eat, she was in pain and ill with all the bits and pieces she had swallowed, and she was sent home.

She missed the feast. She missed the Shining Beings.

"You see?" her teacher said, looking at her closely.

She flushed.

"I see," she said.

And she tried to be patient.

When her teacher thought she was ready, she took the test, and passed.

The next few years passed very fast and very busily.

There was much to learn and as long as Kyra knew the Lord Khu-ren was still at the Temple College and she had his beads about her neck she was content.

Of course she listened with great attention whenever he or anything concerned with him was mentioned and it was in this way she learned that in his own language "Khu-ren" was a reminder of the Being's radiance in eternal life and its secret and spiritual name.

She sat one night watching the stars and thinking about this for a long time. Names were important. His parents and the priest who named him at his birth must have known that he would be a special person, with spiritual powers well above his fellow men. To be a Lord of the Sun so young he must have travelled a long way on the journey of enlightenment before his present birth.

She thought about her own name, Kyra. It was not easy to put into common words but it meant in the ancient language of their people which was now almost forgotten, "balanced for flight on the point of beauty".

Maal had told her this and Karne had laughed.

"What does Karne mean?" she demanded.

"Axe-head," Maal had said, and she remembered how Karne had not been sure whether to be pleased or insulted.

Her studies in the Mysteries grew deeper and deeper and ever more difficult, but the College policy was sensible and their concentrated sessions of deep meditative work and spiritual discipline were interspersed with periods where different but related faculties were called into use.

Kyra's favourite of all these periods was the one when she was taught the whole process of making pottery, from finding the most suitable clay, cleaning it of impurities, kneading and thumping it to remove the air bubbles trapped within it which would make the pot explode when it was heated, to working it with her hands into beautiful and pleasing shapes.

She learned to build the little stone and earth oven and how to keep it burning at the right temperature.

She learned to scratch designs upon the surface of her pots before they were fired, and even how to use salt and ash and certain powdered rocks to change the colours of the clay.

The teacher encouraged them to become totally immersed in what they were doing and to forget everything else.

"Become the pot you make", he said. "You are not making a pot. You are making yourself."

One Spring Kyra moved to the College of Star Studies further South and learned to calculate the movements of the Sun and the moon and the Stars.

She was privileged to be present at the ceremony at dawn on Midsummer's Day when the great, dazzling orb of the Sun rose directly above the Sun Stone and shafted light like a knife straight into the eyes of the High Priest who stood in the dead centre of the Great Circle.

It was at this moment that he lifted his arms and spoke in a loud and awe-inspiring voice.

And it was at this moment that he saw Visions.

It was from these visions that the whole wisdom and teaching of the Temple of the Sun took its form.

Around him the highest priests of the community stood and listened to his words. Beyond them were the ring of Standing Stones brought in the ancient days from a Temple of great Sanctity in the far West, the giant Trilithions and the Circle of the Immense Stones from the

131

Field of the Grey Gods, each linked to each with a lintel of finely worked stone.

The students and lesser priests stood outside the Stone Circle but were no less moved by the impressiveness of the occasion . . . The darkness bursting into light, the inspired voice from the Spirit Realms speaking through their High Priest, the huge, oppressive rocks . . .

Kyra's heart beat until it hurt against her ribs.

She knew she was present at the meeting of great forces and the men within the Circle at that moment might well be possessed and in great danger.

She knew one of them was the Lord Khu-ren and as it grew lighter she could see him, his eyes shut and his face lifted to the sun, an expression that was not his own transforming him.

As the words finished issuing from the mouth of the High Priest, all the spectators found themselves singing, starting with a hum, the sound rising and rising until it seemed to reach the highest point of the sky where the last star flicked out as their eyes followed the sound upwards towards it.

And then the sound burst and from hundreds of throats the hymn to dawn on Midsummer's Day rose and spread outwards until the whole landscape was in light and sound, even the sombre burial mounds that ringed the Temple at a discreet distance transformed to something beautiful and joyful.

The air was suddenly full of birds, flying and swooping and arcing in time with the hymn.

Kyra was moved to tears. She wished the moment could last forever. She felt great thoughts within her, great feelings of wanting to help the world, to lift all human spirits up to join in light and love and absolute understanding.

The love she felt even for the Lord Khu-ren seemed almost a little thing compared with the love she suddenly felt surging in her for all of Creation. It seemed to her there were no divisions. No one to love and not to love.

All was One and all was taking wing at this moment into timeless ecstasy.

132

She too shut her eyes.

And with Khu-ren she stood as though enclosed in a crystal of light, the walls of which were fading even as she became aware of them, the light from outside breaking through to them.

As its unbelievable brightness touched them they both faded from sight.

She knew they were still there. She felt herself aware of herself and yet she could not see any part of herself. Only light. She felt herself aware of him, and yet she could not see him. Only light.

She remembered thinking with great joy, "We exist . . . although all our visible and physical parts are gone! . . ."

And then . . . and then . . .

Someone pressed her arm.

It was Lea.

She opened her eyes and stood dazed upon the grass outside of the Great Circle. Her body visible again.

"Come on," said Lea, "it is over. We have to go now."

But there was something more.

She could feel the pull.

She looked into the Circle and the Lord Khu-ren's eyes were looking deeply into hers, gravely and with concern.

She was shaking uncontrollably from her experience and was very pale.

Lea put her arm around her.

"What is the matter? It is not cold."

"No . . . not cold . . ." muttered Kyra with her teeth chattering.

"What is it then?"

"Did you not feel anything?" Kyra asked, her eyes lost and bewildered in this ordinary world of moving people and pale sunlight on grass.

"It was very moving," Lea said. "The High Priest spoke with Spirits."

"And you?" asked Kyra.

"I?" Lea said surprised. "Nothing happened to me."

And then . . .

"You mean the singing? It was wonderful."

"It was beautiful," Kyra said, her voice quite faint with awe.

"Yes, it was very beautiful," Lea agreed, thinking of the singing.

Kyra said no more but allowed herself to be led away.

About noon, the morning ceremonies over, the students were spread out upon the grass well beyond the outer circumference of earth ridge and ditch, resting and talking amongst themselves about the experiences of the day.

Kyra was apart from the others and was lying flat on her back with her eyes shut, trying to recapture that marvellous moment of somehow being united with Khu-ren as though they were the two halves of the same Being enclosed in Light, when she felt a shadow fall across her. She opened her eyes and looked straight up the tall body of the Lord, to his face leaning over her, his dark eyes, made darker by the lines painted around his lids, looking into hers.

She jumped up instantly, colour flooding to her face, and then stood awkwardly in front of him.

Three midsummers had passed since he first came to The Temple of the Sun and in that time they had seen each other occasionally but had never spoken.

Now they stood together and did not know what to say.

She had grown taller in those three summers. She wore her hair coiled on the top of her head now instead of in a long and untidy plait as she had the first time he had seen her.

The cord she wore around her slender waist was black with a thread of gold to indicate that she had reached the level of studying the dark of the night sky and the gold of the stars.

"I wish to apologize," he said at last, very gently.

She looked surprised.

"I should not have taken you with me into the Light. But . . . I could not stop myself."

She lowered her eyes and stood very still, afraid that he would see her thoughts.

So it had really happened, and she had not imagined it!

134

But it was the fact that it was his longing for her that had brought them together that was the most wonderful thing of all!

They stood awkwardly and silently for a while and then he touched the beads he had given her which she still wore. She felt his hand lightly on her throat and currents of feeling passed through the whole of her body.

She looked up at him and her eyes must have shown it all.

He withdrew his hand and stepped back a pace from her.

There was a tense silence between them.

But when he spoke again his voice was well under control.

"The Lord Guiron tells me you are making good progress," he said.

"So he has asked about me!" she thought joyously.

The Lord Khu-ren smiled.

"Yes, I have asked about you," he said.

She blushed.

"And there has not been a time when I have not been aware of you," he said gravely, and she sensed a touch of bitterness and self-reproach in the gravity.

She thought he would hear her heart beating. Was this really happening?

"Kyra," he said, and her heart lurched with anxiety, "you know this cannot be."

"Why not!" the words burst out from her pent up heart with such violence she startled herself.

His eyes looked even darker now, and there was pain in them.

It was his turn to drop his gaze and turn away from her.

"It is not possible," he said firmly and harshly. "We must both accept it!"

And he turned and strode away.

She was devastated.

"No!" she shouted, but it was unlikely he could hear her. "I will *not* accept it. I will *not*!"

She found herself stamping her foot and shouting like a

small child and then she ran into the woods and sat weeping with her arms about a tree.

Priest? How could she be a priest with such longings in her, with so little self control.

She *would* not be a priest!

Why should she be a priest?

If she said today she was giving it up, would anyone stop her?

It was too much to bear.

She was not fit.

She wanted only one thing and that was to be with the Lord Khu-ren.

But—Khu-ren was a Priest. One of the highest. Would he give it up? Would he *have* to give it up?

Oh, how she needed comfort and advice.

But who could she turn to?

She had told no one of this love of hers. She had not wanted anyone, not even Karne and Fern to know about it. Somehow the very secrecy of it kept it safe. As soon as someone else knew, it was vulnerable, *she* was vulnerable in some way. She could not explain.

Even that it had become verbal and definite between Khu-ren and herself had brought about this danger now.

Before, when it was still secret, everything was still possible.

But now his words made her choke with sobs.

"It is not possible," he had said with such finality. "We must both accept it."

Sometimes she thought the Lord Guiron suspected. Ever since he had noticed the faience beads!

And then Khu-ren had said he had asked after her.

Should she go to the Lord High Priest now and ask his advice? But something held her back from him always.

She admired him. He was a great, great man. But . . . the story of the spirit lady of the lake and Panora always haunted her somehow. It did not fit with his honoured position as High Priest.

And there was always the shadow of the mystery of his relationship to Isar between them.

But . . . on the other hand . . . if the story of the lady

were true . . . he must know better than anyone what it was to love someone more strongly than one's duty to the Priesthood.

She would speak to him.

She would tell him she was giving up the Priesthood. Of that at least she was certain.

And she would ask him if it were possible for a priest of Khu-ren's standing to take a wife.

She felt better when she had made this decision.

She washed her face in a stream and returned to the others.

The Labyrinth and the Test of the Star

On her way back to the Temple College her friends noticed that she was very tense and silent.

"Tell me!" Lea said gently, and Vann took her hand and showed that he too would like to help.

"There is nothing!" Kyra said defiantly.

Vann and Lea looked at each other.

But they loved her enough to leave her until she was ready to tell them.

She could not at first find the Lord Guiron and, as she was weary from the travelling and the emotions she had been through, she fell down on her sleeping rugs and shut her eyes before she had even eaten the evening meal.

Her dreams that night were restless and disturbing. She tossed and turned so much that Lea who slept next to her woke her once and tried to quieten her with soothing words. After this she did not move about so much, but in her dream world she wandered hopelessly through a labyrinth.

It seemed to her that beyond every turn she would find the Lord Khu-ren. On and on she searched through the dark and hostile passages, but he was always just out of sight, just out of reach.

As she reached the same point at the Centre time after time, she sat down on the cold stone ground and wept. Around her the labyrinth crouched, in silence and in mocking emptiness.

She would never find the Lord Khu-ren. She would never find the way out. There was no way!

But as there is a way in, there is always a way out of a labyrinth.

Despair had closed her eyes to it.

She thought of conjuring up his image as she had done in the great cavern.

But he had spoken of "the illusions of love" in the same breath as "the illusions of fear".

And she was weary of illusions now. She had felt his touch upon her neck and it was this kind of reality she wanted now.

"I cannot help it!" she said defiantly to the invisible Spirit realms that she knew were always present, occupying the same "space" she occupied but in different form, in a different "reality".

"I am not like you! I have a body and my body has needs as well as my spirit. Why do we incarnate on earth if it is not to experience earth reality, earth love!"

She lifted her tear stained face and stared around her in the dark, defying the bodiless, formless Beings to answer her this riddle.

"The answer is . . . ," a gentle voice spoke behind her, and she spun round to see the girl she had twice seen before in vision form, the girl from the Island of the Bulls, the lithe, naked acrobat who danced with bulls and somersaulted over their fearsome horns and yet, at the same time, was one of the noble Lords of the Sun. "The answer is, my friend, as you would know if you stopped weeping and stilled your mind as you have been taught to do, that we incarnate on earth indeed to experience earth

reality, earth love. Spirit and body must both have fulfil-
ment on this plane and the love that can satisfy both is
worth a great deal and must be cherished."

"Then *why* did he say the love between us was impossible?"

"He too is body remember, great Lord of the Sun
though he may be. He does not know everything!"

"Then . . . ?"

"You must both learn to accept the *pace* of destiny.
Because you cannot have what you desire *now*, this moment, does not mean that you may never have it. There
are other lives than yours woven into the fabric of your
fate. Each may have to take its course before the time is
right for you."

"If only I could be *sure* I would have him in the end!"

"If it was sure that I would not get gored by those
horns I leap over in the palace games, I would not leap.

"You ask for certainty! You ask for the end of a challenge and excitement, of development and the joy of
achievement."

Kyra was silent.

Then said in a very small, sad voice,

"I really do not think I am strong enough to be what
everyone expects me to be."

The beautiful girl smiled and there was an element of
mocking mischief in her eyes.

"If you are not, then what makes you think you will be
worthy to be the wife of the great Lord Khu-ren?"

Kyra was trapped.

She sat, thinking very deeply, for a long, long time.

When she became aware of her surroundings again she
was no longer in the dark and oppressive labyrinth.

She was in the palace enclosure on the Island of the
Bulls, amongst the crowds she had encountered once before while "travelling in the spirit".

The crowds were shouting for the young acrobat to risk
her life against the monstrous stamping beast that tossed
its horns and raised red dust with its hard hooves.

The beautiful queen with the bare breasts and gold

snake ornaments and her court retinue were seated, as before, on the dais raised above the dust and sweat of the enclosure.

She raised her arm and, from a wall of translucent alabaster, the young girl Kyra had been speaking with in the labyrinth leapt gracefully into the arena of the bull, and as before danced to him while the crowd chanted and stamped and clapped, the rhythm quickening as the girl's movements flickered faster and faster.

Kyra stood paralysed with fear for her as the beast suddenly lunged forward. Quick as light the girl leapt, seized the horns and was over the fierce head and back almost before the creature was aware of it. Perfect agility. Perfect timing. Perfect sense of inner communication with the bull to judge its every twist and turn. In the split moment she was arcing across its back Kyra saw the two disparate beings as one. Harmony and beauty were there in that moment where danger and suffering should have been.

Once on the other side of the bull, separate from him again, the girl leapt up on the wall and stood arms raised, her face transformed with triumph and excitement as the crowd cheered and cheered.

Kyra felt tears of pride and emotion for her beautiful friend pricking behind her eyes.

And then she was awake and had the day to face, but she had made a decision. The way through a labyrinth, Maal had said, could as easily be the way of unfolding enlightenment as the way to confusion and despair.

She would not go to the Lord Guiron for his advice, nor to tell him that she was giving up her studies.

She would keep her love secret as before and she would demand nothing of the Lord Khu-ren or of Life.

She would concentrate on making herself worthy to be a priest.

And then . . . maybe . . .

But of this she was no longer prepared to think.

By the end of the Summer she was ready to take the Star test. Although her studies had been at the College to the South, her test was taken in the main Temple of the Sun.

On a clear, moonless and cloudless night, she entered the great Stone Circle of the Temple and lay upon her back on the grass, her feet towards the East where the Sun would rise.

She was alone and the whole night was hers.

This night she must not let her attention wander for an instant.

The Star the High Priest had chosen for her was rising at the moment she lay down and she must watch its progress across the sky, unwaveringly the whole night long. No matter how tired her eyes became she must not let it out of her sight for an instant.

The effect of the high earthen ridge around the Circumference was to cut out all sight of the landscape and the villages around. She was isolated in a Circle of Power in complete darkness, alone with the Stars.

As the night progressed she totally forgot herself lying on the grass. All that existed was the one star she followed, brilliantly in focus, while an incredible pattern of subtly changing points of gold moved round in the background of her vision.

The star she watched not only moved with slow but inexorable majesty across the dark forever hole of the night sky, but grew in brightness and in power until she felt it like a sharp needle point actually penetrating the centre of her forehead.

It seemed to her the earth bank and the Tall Stones surrounding her not only kept the rest of the world out, but concentrated the power of the stars and whatever realms of Reality that lay beyond her normal consciousness, until they grew in strength and became the only Reality of which she was aware.

It seemed to her the needle of the Star she watched pinned her through the centre of her forehead to the earth and she could not move her body. In her stillness she could feel the earth moving. She was no longer loose upon its surface but was joined to it by this thin, sharp

143

beam of force that passed from the Star to her, through her into the earth, and through the earth until it came out the other side to continue its journey . . .

Her mind ached with the strain of thoughts that were coming to her.

Her forehead ached with the pain of the sharp beam passing through it.

She felt very strange as she turned with the earth, feeling the earth move, and the Star stand still.

But the thought she was trying to grasp kept returning until at last her mind *could* encompass it.

It was the realization that the beam of force from the star that was passing through her and through the earth, and through the universe beyond, was returning to the Star of its origin from the other side!

As though the Whole Universe was a sphere, yet of such a kind that there was no material solidity to it whatever, and therefore no bounds of inside and outside.

She was like a bead on a necklace, threaded through the line of force that was curving with the Universe.

As she grasped this there seemed to be a kind of brilliant explosion in her mind, or was it in the sky?

But suddenly, from every star in the sky, there seemed to be the same fine beam of light, and each one was threaded through the pain in her forehead, through the earth, and through the Universe beyond and back again to its original Source.

The sky now instead of being black with separate points of light, was criss-crossed with fine arcs of light, each starting in a star, or . . .

Did they start in her head?

She could no longer tell if she was the centre from which all the beams were coming, or whether she was the passive recipient of the beams from the stars.

Was she the beginning of all things?

She?

Who was she?

She could not remember her name.

She thought and thought in a sudden kind of panic . . .

"What is my name?"

144

But she had no name.

The more she tried to remember the more the beams passing through her head hurt her.

At last exhausted and in agony, she accepted that she had no name.

And with that acceptance the pain ceased, and she lay in wonder, watching the cycles of light weaving their magnificent pattern all around her and through her.

The beauty of it! The blissful peace and happiness she felt that anything could be so perfect occupied her for the rest of the night.

And when the sun slowly rose and the vision faded, she remembered her name.

And with the remembrance she moved and felt pain in every limb.

Slowly she dragged herself to her feet and looked round her with weary and bewildered eyes.

The dawn light revealed the Circle as she had known it before, the grassy bank, the giant Stones. Above her the first flights of birds called cheerfully to their fellows.

Around her stood a circle of the highest priests in the Temple.

She looked from one to the other with aching, bloodshot eyes.

The Lord Khu-ren was amongst them, but she was too tired even to react to him.

The Lord Guiron spoke at last.

"My child," he said gently, "you must tell us all that happened to you in the night."

She began to shake her head, thinking how impossible it would be to put all that into words.

"You must try," the High Priest said. "It is important." He spoke quietly, but with great authority.

Stumbling for words the young girl started the story.

The priests around her stood silently, impassively, listening.

No one helped her when she could not find the words, but gradually, clumsily, the story emerged exactly as it had happened.

145

As she finished speaking, she could feel herself slipping into darkness, her body cold and infinitely weary.

Then for the first time one of the priests moved.

The Lord Khu-ren stepped forward and caught her in his arms as she fell fainting.

The Haunted Mound

The Winter passed in training for Healing.

They learned a great deal about the body and the natural ways it had of healing itself. They learned how the mind, clouded by fear and doubt, could hinder these natural ways, and how they as priest-healers could bring back confidence to the patient so that the ways of nature could work again freely.

It seemed the mental image a person held of himself had great power to influence his body. They were taught to change with great tact and skill the self image of illness the patient held tenaciously within his mind, to one of well being and health. The image changed, the patient visualizing himself well, the healer's work was done. Nature did the rest.

They learned that when the illness had gone too far for the patient's own body to heal itself, they could transfer the strength of their own life-force, to aid the natural healing processes within the patient.

They learned to do this by laying their hands upon the sufferer and directly "willing" the strength which they knew flowed through them from the Great Source of Life, to enter his body and make him whole again, to by-pass, to push aside, the impediment within the patient that was preventing his natural supply of life-force from entering.

They also learned to use the power of thought to do the same thing when they were too distant from the sufferer to touch him physically.

They studied how to prevent illness, what to eat and how to exercise. The movements they practised were always simple, slow and effective, control of body built up gradually stage by stage until it became a perfect instrument for the use of its owner on earth.

Kyra enjoyed the classes and worked hard.

But one day in early Spring when she was in the middle of a set of rhythmic movements, her concentration was broken by the sudden stinging of the thought that Fern needed her.

She had seen very little of Karne's little family lately as they had been busy having another child and she herself had been occupied with her own determination to make good and fast progress in her studies.

As the thought from Fern reached her, she stopped in mid-movement, and a look of puzzled concentration came to her face.

"What is it, Kyra?" her teacher asked.

"I am sorry," Kyra said hastily, "but I must go. I am needed."

The teacher did not question further but let her go.

She ran faster now than she had ever run. Her body was at its most proficient because of the training she had undergone, and the distance between the College and Fern's little house seemed much shorter than usual.

She found Fern alone with the new baby, weeping, Karne away from home with Olan, and Isar lost.

"Oh, Kyra!" she cried when she saw her. "You have no idea how I longed for you!"

"I felt it," Kyra said gently. "Now tell me."

She put her arms around her.

"Tell me."

"Isar has wandered off somewhere and has been gone

for ages. I have looked everywhere and all my friends have been helping, but no one has seen him."

"Was Panora with him?"

Kyra knew the girl spent a great deal of time with Isar.

"I have not seen Panora for a long time. I was cross with her once . . . Oh Kyra . . . I did not mean to speak so harshly . . . I think I was jealous because Isar seemed to prefer her to me . . . and I told her to go away. She did, and I have not seen her since. I thought perhaps Isar had wandered off to look for her. I know he missed her. I feel so ashamed! If only I could unsay those words!"

"Calm yourself. No words can ever be unsaid, but new ones can be spoken. Come, I will help you find him. But first you must be quiet. I must try to 'feel' where he has gone."

"Oh Kyra!"

"S-s-sh," Kyra said softly, stroking Fern's head. "Gently . . . you will make your baby upset."

Fern buried her face in her second child's soft body and rocked backwards and forwards, her cheeks wet, but her sobs stilled.

Kyra moved outside the house and sat in the garden, first letting the beauty and the peace of the Spring leaves and flowers distance her from the disturbing anxiety and fear of Fern.

Then she began to empty her mind as she had been taught to do.

Dark and disturbing impressions began to come to her and at first she thought she was witnessing a burial, and her heart jerked to think it might mean Isar was dead.

She struggled to regain her concentration and this time received impressions of a lake, a mist, a shadowy figure of a woman.

"Guiron's lover!" she thought with shock.

Again her own thoughts having intruded she had to force her way back to meditative calm again.

But no more impressions would come to her.

She would have sat longer, trying yet again to see Isar, if Fern's anxious face had not appeared.

"Did you learn anything?" she asked, her eyes so full of pain, and yet so trustful that Kyra could work miracles.

"Something," Kyra said guardedly, "but I cannot work it out yet. I need more information."

"Try!" Fern said, tears beginning again. "Oh Kyra, I *love* him so!"

"I know," Kyra said soothingly. "I know. We will find him. Is it possible for a neighbour to look after your baby while we go and search?"

"Of course. They have been wonderful to me. Someone has even gone to fetch Karne and he is a long, long way away with Olan."

"Good. Find someone to take the baby, then find me an old and reliable villager who has a good memory for the old days."

Fern did not question the commands, but obeyed immediately.

The baby was happily settled. The oldest woman in the village was brought to Kyra.

"I believe," Kyra said to her, "there used to be a lake somewhere not far from the Temple, which was drained many years ago. Do you remember it?"

"Oh aye!" the old woman said, "I remember the lake."

"Where was it?"

"It were on the other side of the haunted mound," she said darkly.

Kyra looked enquiringly at Fern.

"I think she means that enormous mound we saw first from the ridge way when we arrived. It is supposed to be haunted. No one will go near it."

"Oh yes," Kyra remembered. "And the lake was there?"

"I suppose," Fern said, shrugging.

"Thank you," Kyra said to the old lady. "Come," she said to Fern.

They went as swiftly as they could but it was a long way and the sun had passed its zenith when they came within close sight of the weird man-made mountain.

"What makes you think he will be there?" Fern asked, still worried.

"I am not sure . . . but I kept getting a picture of that lake . . . so it is possible . . ."

"I am glad it is no longer a lake," Fern said, out of breath from trying to keep up with Kyra.

Kyra did not mention the other impression she had had, of a burial.

"Are you sure it was not another lake?" Fern suddenly felt anxious again. "A lake still filled with water?"

"No, it was the one that is now dry land. Of that I am sure. Do not be afraid."

As they approached the strange mound they noticed the signs of village life had ceased. It stood very much alone in a great bare space and they could see the flat plain to the West, now overgrown with reeds and marsh grasses, that had once been a lake.

They were just about to bypass the haunted hill and make for the area where the lake had been when Kyra's eyes were drawn to the top and she saw standing there a tall and impressive warrior figure. The sun was behind him, his silhouette black but surrounded by fire. His arms were raised and in one a battle axe caught the sunlight and flashed malevolently.

Her heart missed a beat.

She knew who it was with a strange and terrible certainty.

"Fern!" she cried.

Fern looked at her.

"I want you to promise me something."

"What?"

"You will stay here and not move until I return. If you do this I will bring Isar unharmed to you."

Fern looked as though she were about to promise, though puzzled, when a movement or a flash of light drew *her* eyes upwards to the summit of the mound.

"Isar!" she cried in delight and she was off towards him before Kyra could stop her.

To her the figure on the top of the mound was that of a small boy with red hair, no more than about five summers old, waving a bullrush from the marsh over his head.

Her mother's love propelled her up the side of that

151

steep and forbidden mound faster than Kyra could manage, and when Kyra arrived at the top mother and son were happily sitting side by side, arms around each other, kissing and laughing.

Kyra stared at them.

She knew she had not been mistaken in what she had seen, and she just as certainly knew that this was the child Isar with his mother and a bullrush in his hand.

The harsh, mocking sound of a rook as it flew off from the long grass on the side of the mound brought back the chill to Kyra's heart.

There were things she *must* find out before it was too late! Isar offered no explanations for his actions and his mother asked for none. The three of them made their way back to Fern's home as quickly as possible, there to find Karne returned, just about to set off with torches to look for them.

Kyra did not disturb their happy reunion with any of her own forebodings and when they had eaten and put the children to bed she kissed them both and returned to her College.

The next day she started enquiring about "the haunted mound" and tried to find out as much as she could about its history. The first people she asked knew nothing more than that it was haunted.

"What kind of ghost haunts there?" she asked. But no one seemed to know. She could find no one who had ever seen the ghost, nor even spoken to someone who had. The legend of its haunting must be very far back in the past.

From one of the oldest priests she managed to establish that the mound had been raised before the building of The Temple of the Sun.

"There is a legend that a great and powerful king from over the seas came to this land in the ancient days, conquered its people and lived in great splendour for many years. Some say it is his burial mound."

"He must have been very powerful indeed to command such a burial," Kyra said, looking round and comparing

152

the not inconsiderable mounds around the Temple which housed the dead of many noble families from many countries in the world.

"Aye," the old priest said. But that was all he knew.

And with this she had to be content for some time.

The lake that used to be beside the mound some old people remembered.

It had been drained during the lifetime of the present High Priest and she longed to ask him about the lake and the mound, feeling strongly that the two were connected, but she was still too much in awe of him to attempt a confrontation.

The Field of the Grey Gods
and the Return of Wardyke

At last the time arrived for her to study the choosing of the Stones.

The day their teacher chose to visit the Field of the Grey Gods was a bright and sparkling one. A day on which it was hard to believe in the dark side of life.

The students chattered happily as they wandered up the long path to the ridge way from the Temple. Vann picked some daisies and made little crowns for Lea and Kyra.

Kyra laughed and let down her hair which was now almost to her knees. She looked like a nature spirit as she began dancing along ahead of the others, her eyes shining, her crown of daisies slightly lop-sided, her gold and shining hair flowing out around her in the breeze.

She felt something good was going to happen today, and if it did not she would *make* it happen!

"Kyra!" called Lea laughing, but Kyra did not hear.

She knew the way to the Field and she had waited a long time to be allowed to visit it. There was no holding her back now.

At the point where the path from the Temple joined the ridge way some young trees had grown up since she, Karne and Fern had first stood hesitating there, and she did not see the figure resting in their shade until pirouetting happily, she arrived among them.

And then she stopped. Before her stood the Lord Khuren.

He had not seen her since the time she took her Star test and had fallen so wanly into his arms. It was difficult to believe it was the same girl, she was now so full of light and life.

Even the sudden shock of his appearance where she did not expect him could not discomfit her this day.

She met his dark eyes with a sparkling blue, and bowed to him with a slightly exaggerated and mocking movement, glancing up immediately to see how he was reacting.

He was smiling.

"My lord," she said, "I think this is one of the good days in the world!"

"I would agree," he said, his eyes following the light that glanced off her long hair.

"I think, my lord," she said, her face alight with mischief, "this day I am going to dare the gods to do their worst!"

And before he could grasp what she meant, she darted forward, flung her arms around him, stood on tip-toe and kissed him passionately on the mouth.

She had meant to dart away again and disappear along the ridge way before she could pay the penalty for her audacity, but she reckoned without his own feelings in the matter, and when the other students arrived several moments later they found the golden Kyra locked helplessly in the close embrace of the tall dark Lord from over the sea, both of them oblivious to the amazed crowd of onlookers.

The students of course were delighted, but their teacher was old and sour and might not have the same reaction.

When Lea heard him puffing up the hill almost within

sight of this astounding scene, she hastily touched Kyra's arm and called out to attract their attention.

And then it was for the first time the two dazed people saw that they were not alone.

Scarlet, Kyra drew back from Khu-ren, and he in his turn went a deeper shade of sunburn.

They would have stood there confused and shaken forever if Lea had not take the situation in hand and led Kyra away.

When the teacher-priest finally came to the trees he found only the lord Khu-ren standing there, the others running like children and laughing as they ran along the ridge path to the Field of the Grey Gods.

The hot and puffing priest bowed to the tall young man, mentioned the heat of the day and passed on.

"Peculiar look he had on his face," the old man thought, but then thought no more about it.

Khu-ren stayed there a long time, watching the landscape as it stretched below him in every direction, carefully winding several strands of very long and very golden hair about his finger until it became a ring.

The knowledge concerned in the choosing of the rocks followed naturally from all the other classes they had attended over the years.

The students had grown sensitive to the inner forces of themselves and of the world around them. Those who had not had left the College and returned to their homes.

Of those who remained some would study to be village priests, leaving the College when they had a certain standard of general knowledge in the different disciplines. Others would stay on and specialize, rising higher in the priesthood. Vann wished to stay on and specialize in Healing, Lea in Dream Interpretation, while Kyra looked to be a "spirit-traveller" and perhaps, eventually, a Lord of the Sun.

The choosing of the rocks suitable for the Tall Stones of a Sacred Circle was a specialization in itself, but they were all to attempt at least to understand a little of what was involved.

Kyra had seen the strange Field of grey rocks before on her original journey to the Temple, but many of the other students had not. They were amazed and somewhat apprehensive when they heard the legends that were associated with the Stones.

Not one of them dared approach the Stones until the priest, their teacher, had finally arrived, very red in the face and out of breath.

He allowed himself to cool down in the shade of the trees that edged the field while he discussed with them the method he proposed to use in training.

Today they would wander in the Field and each try to find a rock that gave them a particularly strong "feeling".

"You may find a rock that has vibrations for one of you, has none for another. This we will discuss later. The first stage is for you to get the 'feel' of the rocks.

"Now go!" he said, and waved his plump hand at the field.

The students scattered like feathers before a wind across the Field.

At first they darted from rock to rock, putting their foreheads against the cold stones, sensing nothing, and moving off immediately to another. But after a while they began to realize they were being too hasty. None of them was getting *anything* from the rocks, and it was apparent the teacher expected at least some of them to get *something*.

So they slowed down and gave each rock a longer time to respond to their overtures.

Kyra remembered her old village and the Sacred Circle there, and the training she had already received from Maal to feel the power in the Tall Stones. She had an advantage here over the other students and it was she who first found a stone that she was sensitive to in the Field.

It was a strange shape, almost like a throne.

She felt tempted to sit on it and pretend to be a Queen, with Khu-ren at her side as King. But she restrained herself and knelt beside it instead, her head resting on the hollow time and the weather had excavated.

There was something about it.

Several times she left it, not sure that she could feel anything from it, but several times she returned.

There was something.

She closed her eyes and concentrated, tried to feel deep into the Stone, to *become* the Stone in a sense, to feel it feeling *her*.

There was certainly something between them, but she could not explain it.

After a time she stood up and moved away.

"I do not feel vibrations," she said to herself, "I just feel a sort of sympathy. That cannot be what the teacher meant!"

And she firmly walked away from the Stone.

But whatever other one she tried, she could not get the one like a throne out of her mind, and so eventually she returned to it and sat upon it, waiting patiently for the elderly priest to work his way right round the field from student to student until he reached her.

She would tell him what she felt, though she was not at all sure that it was what she was meant to feel.

After a while she began to feel strangely drowsy . . . or was it dizzy?

The others seemed to be getting further and further away, the sounds of the birds and the talking of the teacher and the students fainter and fainter. She looked around her, slightly puzzled, but not alarmed. Even the colours around her seemed to be changing subtly and those that had been dark now seemed to be light, and those that had been light seemed now to be dark.

"How strange," she remembered thinking, and then she was conscious of nothing more.

When she awoke she was lying on the grass of the ridge path, away from the Field, the anxious faces of her teacher and her fellow students gathered closely around her and staring at her.

Vann who had great natural powers of Healing in his hands was holding her head. She felt life and consciousness mercifully flowing back into her body.

"What happened?" she murmured, her lips very dry.

159

"You must have found a powerful stone," the teacher said, and then to the others, "Stand back and give her some air."

Looking considerably relieved at her recovery the others moved back, only her special friends, Lea and Vann, staying close to her.

"Stone?" she muttered stupidly, not remembering anything clearly.

"One of the special Stones we were looking for," Lea said softly. "Remember?"

"You see you should not have spent so much time on it," the teacher scolded. "I meant you to locate one and then call me. I found you lying all over it!" he accused, "No wonder you fainted!"

She was amazed.

She began remembering now.

"But . . ." she began.

"You see," the teacher went on scolding, "the forces in the earth are very strong. In certain places stronger than in others. In certain rocks stronger than in others. In certain people stronger than in others! You must be very sensitive to energies and forces hardly felt by others, and you must have found a rock particularly charged with Special Power. You should have been more careful!"

"Oh," said Kyra.

While she was recovering the students went to the special stone Kyra had found and tested themselves against it. Some of them could feel strangeness in it. Others could sense nothing.

The teacher pointed out that this was why certain priests who had the aptitude for sensing power in rock, travelled sometimes days and months to places where a new Circle was to be built.

"Not everyone can feel the natural currents in the earth. Those who can, pick out the Stones and places of natural energy where they are to be erected. Once they are raised in their correct places by the correct ceremonial procedures and are used in a community as a Sacred Circle, the natural energies in the Stones and in the earth combine with the forces generated by the ritual worship of the people to become very powerful indeed. The Inner Circle of our Temple had power to transport the spirits of Initiates across the world."

Kyra remembered the meeting of the Lords of the Sun in that very Circle many summers ago when she was a desperate, half-tutored girl, asking for their help.

When she was strong enough to stand and walk, one arm linked through Vann's and one through Lea's, the teacher led the whole group back to the College.

As they walked they talked in little groups about the unseen threads of force that were woven through the fabric of the earth.

"Sort of keeping it together," one said.

"Alive," another said.

"I have heard," a third joined in, "that over great periods of time the pattern of flow sometimes changes and Sacred Circles have either to be abandoned or moved to find the new route of the energy flow."

"Almost like a river that changes its course?"

"Almost like that."

As they reached the crossing of the ridge way and the path leading down to the Temple, Kyra's attention wandered from what the others were saying and relived the moment of great happiness she had spent in the arms of the Lord Khu-ren such a short while before.

There was no sign of the young Lord now, but she noticed the daisy crown Vann had made for her lying on the grass where it must have fallen from her hair.

She smiled, relieved.

So strange had been the happenings since, she would not have been surprised if that incident had proved to be a dream or a vision.

It was not always easy to be sure which one of the different types of Reality one was experiencing.

She longed to see the Lord Khu-ren again, but it was not to be for some while.

Soon after the incident of the rock in the Field of the Grey Gods she visited Karne and Fern.

She found children in the garden playing happily, but Fern and Karne in some distress.

Isar ran up to her at once and took her hand and led her off to see the dam he was building in the stream. Seeing him today so full of childish fun she could not believe he was the same tall and vengeful warrior she had seen on top of the haunted mound.

After she had spent some time with him and helped him move a boulder or two, she managed to withdraw and visit his parents.

"What is the matter?" she asked at once, seeing their faces.

"Wardyke!" Karne said immediately, and her heart sank.

"He arrived here yesterday and wanted to see Isar," Fern said miserably.

" 'His son' he called him," Karne said bitterly.

"Oh no!" Kyra looked distressed. She had hoped they had heard the last of Wardyke when they banished him from their community and stripped him of all his powers as magician-priest.

"What did you do?"

"I told him to go, there was no son of his here!"

"And . . .?"

"He just smiled . . . and went."

Kyra looked surprised.

"But oh, Kyra," said Fern, "if you had seen his smile! I know we have not seen the last of him!"

"How was he? Do you think he has regained his powers in some way?"

"No, I do not think so," Fern said thoughtfully. "When I first saw him I felt almost sorry for him . . ."

Karne snorted and it was clear he had not felt the same.

"He has aged a great deal. His hair is quite grey and he is very thin and ragged looking. He must have been wounded in some way because his left arm and his left leg are sort of . . . well, he sort of drags them . . . he does not use them properly."

"Has he seen Isar at all?"

"No. Nor will he!" said Karne fiercely.

Fern looked less certain.

"Do you think he has?" Kyra asked her.

"It is possible . . . I cannot keep him with me in the house all the time. He runs about the village with the other children and plays a great deal down by the stream. It would be easy for Wardyke to come upon him one day."

"Of course his unusual red hair would give him away as your son," Kyra said musingly.

Karne looked at the long dagger Olan had given him that was hanging on the wall behind them.

"No, Karne. That is not the answer and you know it."

Karne knew she was right, but down here in the South ways were different, and many quarrels were settled with violence where in their small quiet Northern community it would have been unthinkable.

"Settled?" Kyra asked, seeing into his mind suddenly with great clarity. "Nothing is 'settled' that way. You just move the problem to another time, maybe another life, and have to undo what you have done in ways that may well be more unpleasant for you than the original problem."

"I know!" Karne said impatiently. "I know."

And he left the house muttering that there was much work to be done.

"He is very worried," Fern said gently in his defence.

"I know, and it is easy for me to talk about keeping feelings under control . . .!" she said wryly.

Fern could not catch the implications of the remark as she did not know about Kyra's love for the Lord Khu-ren.

"What will I do, Kyra," she pleaded, "if he were to take him away from me?"

"He has no right!"

"Of course not. But he might still do it."

Kyra was silent, thinking.

Fern went on talking.

"The garden and the trees watch over him and I can 'feel' when he is in trouble. But I fear one day it may be too late before I reach him. The feelings I get are not

163

specific. I feel danger and pain and love, but exactly *where* the danger is is not so easy.

"I have made friends with Panora again. I called her back and apologized. She is with Isar a great deal and I will warn her to watch our for Wardyke."

This did not comfort Kyra much. She had never been able to shake off the feeling that Panora´ was somehow malevolent.

She had told Fern of Panora's connection with the Lord Guiron, but for some reason Fern refused to accept it as a warning. She pointed out Isar was Wardyke's son and yet had nothing of Wardyke in him.

The two young women spent a great deal of that day discussing what to do for the best, and it was decided that Fern should try to talk to Wardyke about Isar and to Isar about Wardyke, and to let them meet, but at first only in her presence.

"If you forbid him to see Isar he will do everything in his power to take the boy from you. You must be subtle. You must be cunning. You must be watchful. Isar is held to you and Karne by bonds of love and trust that nothing can break. Wardyke will accept this when he has tried and failed, but never if he is prevented from trying."

Fern admitted to still being very much afraid of Wardyke.

"But he had no powers as magician now," Kyra said.

"I know, but I still fear him and I cannot bear to speak with him. When he came yesterday, I hid, and Karne did all the talking."

"I think that is unwise. Karne is anxious and impatient, and does not always consider the full implications of what he says or does. You must discuss the matter with him before Wardyke comes again and make Karne understand it is the only way to keep Isar. You cannot hide him forever."

Fern nodded sadly.

The work at the College was becoming more and more

demanding and Kyra had little time to visit Karne and Fern again.

Her experience with the rock in the Field of the Grey Gods, combined with the remarkable advances she had made in all her studies, earned her a special meeting with the Lord Guiron.

"I have been watching you, my child," he said, "and have decided that if you wish it you may enter now the first stage of priesthood."

This meant she would be qualified to be a village priest and would have a ceremony of inauguration.

She gasped.

"But my advice to you is not to leave the College at this stage, but to study for the higher grades. I think," he said, looking deeply into her eyes, "you have the capacity to enter the highest grade of all."

One of the legendary Lords of the Sun!

She was overwhelmed.

She had dreamed and longed for this, but it had seemed so impossible.

"I remember you had experience of 'spirit-travelling' long before you came to us as student. You still have much to learn as I am sure you realise, but the Lord Khu-ren tells me, and I have noticed, that you learn fast."

Kyra blushed with pleasure and her hand went involuntarily to the faience beads about her neck.

She saw Guiron's eyes follow the movement of her hand and smile with amusement. How much did he know?

There was an awkward silence between them for a moment, Kyra's heart beating fast with joy at the implications of what she had just been told.

"Your inauguration as a priest will be at noon six days from now. Prepare yourself."

She bowed, but did not turn to go as was expected of her.

He raised an eyebrow inquiringly.

"My Lord," she stammered, and stopped.

He waited patiently, a very impressive figure.

She trembled with the audacity of what she was about to ask.

"My Lord . . ." she brought out with difficulty again . . . "is it possible . . . I mean . . . is there a law against the marriage of priests of the highest grades?"

She had said it, and she was scarlet!

He turned away from her and walked two or three times across the room, his face lowered and in shadow.

She was alarmed.

"I . . . am sorry . . ." she muttered.

He came to stand at last before her and his face was hard and composed as she had never seen it before.

"There is no law," he said, "but it is not the custom, nor is it advisable."

She bowed hastily and retreated backwards from his presence.

Outside, she stood in confusion. She felt she could not face her fellow students and went for a long walk by herself.

She followed the path from the Temple to the ridge way, not noticing the quiet fields on either side, the silent burial mounds, the woods and houses that stretched beyond.

Her journey was in the past, marking the moments in her life that had led her to this point, and wondering about the moments in her life that would lead her on beyond it.

So absorbed was she that his arms were about her and his lips on hers before she even knew he was there.

"My lord!" she gasped, and then gave up everything of past and future to the beauty of the present moment.

When they at last had drawn apart and were sitting close together on the grass, she said,

"The Lord Guiron said it is not the custom, nor is it advisable, for priests of the highest grades to marry."

He untied the coil of her hair and shook the golden shower of it about her shoulders, twining his fingers in it to pull her head back to kiss her lips again.

"It is not advisable, nor is it the custom, but it is not against the law," he said.

"You mean . . .?"

"I mean . . . take one step at a time, my love . . . You are entering my class as a student . . . not as my wife . . ."

She flushed and turned away, ashamed that she had presumed so much.

"On the day you have learned all that I have to teach and we stand equally within the Inner Circle of the Priesthood, I will ask you *then* if you wish to defy custom and ignore advisability. I will not take you as master to student, lord to awestruck girl!"

She buried her face in her knees, not wanting him to read in her eyes how much she wanted to be taken now. "Dignity" and "Equality" were cold, hard words in the turmoil of her present feelings.

He must have felt it too because he suddenly stood up and said sharply, "Come. The sun is setting."

They did not touch again, nor speak, as they walked down the gradually darkening path towards the Temple.

Kyra's Inauguration

In the next few days Kyra had many formalities to attend to, and most of them in the pouring rain.

Her student friends were delighted with her success but sorry to see her move out of their immediate circle. She would now live on the other side of the Temple among the other priests who were continuing their studies, and would be cut off from her old companions in many ways.

The last but one night before the ceremony, they made an enormous bonfire in a field some distance from the College and had a wild party, all their years of serious study forgotten, and they danced and sang as they used to dance and sing in their home communities when they were still carefree children.

Someone smuggled in strong ale and at the end when the rain that had been threatening all evening started to fall really heavily, the party became a disorderly but cheerful scramble in the mud.

The dawn found many a bedraggled student fumbling his way home to the College sleeping quarters, and the classes that day were very subdued.

If the teachers knew of the event, they gave no sign. It is possible such parties were not unknown in the College.

They had chosen the last night but one for the party, because the actual night before had to be spent by Kyra alone in the Sanctuary, meditating.

Her head ached from the previous night's revelries, but she had learned to ignore natural pain in herself and soon had it under control.

Much more difficult it was to control her thoughts.

But she had not come this far without learning anything and, difficult though it was, it was not long before she was in deep meditation.

This night she must speak with Spirits and listen to their guidance and advice.

With the dawn the priests of higher rank arrived to prepare her with prayers and incantations for the day. She had special oil from an exquisite gold jar rubbed gently into her forehead, and she was dressed in a plain white robe with no decoration or ornaments. It seemed to have been woven in one piece and was beautiful in its elegance and simplicity.

They made a move to take the necklace of faience beads from her throat, but she put up her hand to protect it from them with such fierce determination that the priest in question drew back his hand in some alarm and looked for guidance from his fellow priests.

No words were said, but the Lord Khu-ren stepped forward and took her hand away from the necklace, lifted it slightly and dropped it down underneath the white robe so that no sign of it showed. But she knew it was still there.

He avoided looking into her eyes when he did this or giving any sign to the others that there was anything special between them, but she felt his hand as he moved the beads, and her heart quickened.

They both knew that wearing the beads on the day of inauguration was breaking with an ancient custom and they both took it as a kind of secret sign that this would not be the only custom they would break.

When it was time to leave the Sanctuary she was stunned to see how many people had gathered to watch the procession . . . *her* procession! She wondered if Karne and Fern were there. She had sent a message by Panora, but had been too busy to visit them herself with the news. How proud and pleased they would be to see her walking in such a noble throng!

How she wished Maal could be there and all the people of her home community.

And then she felt ashamed.

The messages she had received in the night had made it clear to her that she was an instrument of the Spirit Realms and the God from which All things come.

Her only power came from them, her only skill was to open herself and allow their energies to work through her. She was nothing but a willing channel through which the innate life Force of the Universe could be concentrated where it was needed most.

The force and meaning of this suddenly struck her as she walked the long, long avenue to the Sacred Circle.

The crowds that pressed in on every side became a blur. The tall and magnificently robed figures of the men and women of the priesthood ahead of her became strange and alien.

What were they doing with such finery?

They were not gods to be worshipped and obeyed.

They were servants of the Great Spirit and were there to obey.

And then another thought struck her with the suddenness of rain.

The Lord who walked ahead of her, a cape of blue and gold sweeping over his bare shoulders to drag upon the ground behind him . . . what of him?

If she had given up her selfhood, would he be taken from her too?

She had felt so sure that day upon the ridge way when he had talked of the time when she would stand equally

171

with him and he would ask her to be his wife that there would be no question but that she would say yes.

What if at that point she was told by her Spirit Lords that she must not join with him.

What then?

Would she obey?

The procession she had thought would be a triumph and a joy, now oppressed her heart.

She kept her eyes lowered, watching her bare feet walking the cold, damp earth.

The sun shone but it had not yet dried up the moisture of the past few days.

Her old misgivings began to trouble her.

Was she fit?

Could she possibly carry the burden of being a priest?

She had enjoyed the dancing at her party.

She had enjoyed the touch of the Lord Khu-ren's hands and lips.

She knew he suffered too. She had seen the shadows in his dark eyes. But he was stronger than her and accustomed to being a priest.

Perhaps . . . and here she looked up quickly to see how far they were away from the entrance to the Circle . . .

Perhaps it was not too late . . .

She had not spoken the words of vow yet.

She had not received the Mark of Power.

And then . . .

And then . . .

She remembered the girl acrobat's words in the labyrinth when she had said she was not worthy to be a priest . . .

"If you are not, then what makes you think you will be worthy to be the wife of the great Lord Khu-ren?"

And he had said: "I will not take you as master to student, or lord to awestruck girl."

And the more she thought, the more she knew that their meeting and everything in her life so far had led step by step with ordered certainty to this place, this ceremony.

172

She *must* trust the overwhelming feeling that she had that there was reason in it.

The Spirit Lords had let her keep her faience beads in spite of ancient custom decreeing otherwise. She would take this as a sign he and she were meant to be together.

She would go on.

She felt the power of the Great Circle as she had never felt it before, closing in around her as she entered it. She was exhilarated, but afraid.

There was now no going back.

The ceremony was long and impressive.

The low drumming of the musicians, the chanting of the ancient words of initiation, the careful circling of the priests in their ceremonial robes, the occasional sips of a special and potent drink from a golden cup held by the High Priest himself, all served to make her feel less and less like Kyra and more and more like some strange and supernatural being.

She hardly felt the new robes being put upon her, the heavy pendant about her neck, the cloak of blue and gold, similar to Khu-ren's but not as grand, and finally the circlet of jet beads that fitted around the high gold coil of hair that sat upon her head already like a crown.

When this point was reached she thought all must surely be finished, but there was one thing more.

The others retreated from her, bowing, leaving her alone with the Lord Guiron, the Lord High Priest.

"My lady," he said quietly, "I once took something from you and promised to return it to you when you were ready for it.

"The time has come."

And he stepped forward and held out his hand palm upwards to her.

On it lay the stone sea urchin she had found in the great cavern.

It was hers.

She bowed her head and took it, feeling strength and confidence coursing through her as she did so.

173

"Use it well," he said gravely, "you have now the mark of the priest upon you."

He too bowed and retreated from her.

She stood alone as the sun sank and the crowds faded away.

Ancient Relationships Made Clear

Some while later when Kyra was greatly absorbed in her new studies she felt another call from Fern that could not be ignored.

She asked permission to be absent and went at once to the home of her brother and his family.

As before Isar was missing.

She questioned Fern about Wardyke and whether they had followed her advice. It seemed they had and all had been going fairly well.

Wardyke was allowed to meet the boy. He had settled in the neighbouring village under Olan's old enemy, Hawk-Eagle, and came only occasionally to visit. The visits were not pleasurable for any of them, but they passed uneventfully enough and Wardyke seemed content with the way things were.

"And Panora?"

"Oh, she has been a great help to me," Fern said warmly. "She always stays with Isar when Wardyke is with him. He never sees him alone even if Karne and I are not present."

Kyra was thoughtful. This news did not comfort her.

"How long has he been missing this time?"

"He was not in his bed this morning. I do not know if he left in the night or in the early morning before I woke. He often goes out into the garden or down to the stream as soon as the first light comes, so I did not begin seriously to worry until he missed his midday meal. He never misses that!"

Kyra could see she was very worried.

"I was feeling ill at ease all morning. My garden seemed to be trying to tell me something, but somehow I did not associate it with Isar."

Kyra knew the difficulty of interpreting "feelings" where there were no words to act as guide lines.

She noted this second disappearance had also occurred while Karne was far from home.

"I have already looked at the haunted mound and the lake," Fern said despairingly.

"You must not worry any more now," Kyra said firmly. "I found him the last time and I will find him this time."

She wished she felt as confident as she sounded.

She left Fern to attend to her other child and as before sat in the garden and tried to "feel" the presence of Isar. Her mastery of this technique had developed since the early days and she slipped into meditative silence almost immediately, her inner senses scanning the surrounding landscape for any traces of Isar's thought flow.

The impressions she was receiving were from the other side of the temple, from the Field of the Grey Gods.

They were not very definite, she could see nothing of Isar, but she kept remembering the Field of the Grey Gods and could not put it out of her mind. There was always the danger that her mind had wandered into a memory of her own or was even picking up the thought flow of someone else, but this impression was persistent and the only one she had, so she decided to act upon it as she had before.

She told Fern that she thought she had located Isar, that he was quite safe and she was not to worry.

"I will come with you," Fern at once insisted.

"No," Kyra was firm. "It is a long way and you have another child who needs you. I will bring him safely to you, but you must not worry if it is not before the sun sets. He had wandered further this time and it will take longer to bring him back."

Fern's eyes were full of tears as she watched Kyra leave, but she had great confidence in her and knew that if anyone could find Isar and bring him safely home, it would be Kyra.

As Kyra hurried back to the Temple she wished she had Fern's confidence in herself. She fingered the stone sea urchin in her carrying pouch and it seemed the strength it gave her lent her speed and she covered the ground much more swiftly than she normally would have done.

She bypassed the Temple and came along the ridge way from near the Sanctuary, passing the junction of the Temple path and the ridge way that meant so much to her in terms of personal happy memories, without even a glance.

The evening light and long shadows were upon the Field of the Grey Gods when she arrived, and the scene that she saw before her struck a real chill into her heart.

Seated on the throne of rock that she had found was a great King clad in strange and foreign robes. He was dark as the Lord Khu-ren was dark, but there the resemblance ceased. Where Khu-ren was tall and slender, his features fine and chiselled, the King was huge and broad, his features handsome but coarse.

Kneeling in front of him was a slighter man, dressed all in black, apparently from the splendour of his garb a man of importance in the court, but from the way he knelt, something in the way he moved his hands and head, even from this distance, Kyra could sense there was something obsequious and sinister about him.

It seemed to her (strange that she had not noticed this before!) they were not in the field of scattered rocks at all, but were in a great hall built of giant slabs of uneven rock fitted skillfully together. The King's throne, which at first had seemed to her the rock she had sat upon and fainted, was larger than she remembered it, and carved with unusual devices.

Upon a stone pillar beside the two men was the carved statue of a huge bird, watching the scene unblinkingly.

The same feeling she had had when she had sat that first time upon the rock came over her now. A sort of drowsiness, a sort of dizziness, as though she were not seeing what she was seeing.

She gripped her stone sea urchin and prayed for help not to lose her senses as she had done before, and feeling strength returning to her limbs she took a bold step forward.

With that movement, in that instant, the scene before her shattered like a dream on waking and she was staring amazed at the Field as she had known it before, full of scattered random rocks, and on the one she thought of as a throne sat the small boy Isar, with Wardyke kneeling in front of him and Panora perched on a rock beside them in the very place where the stone bird had been.

Kyra gasped and rubbed her eyes.

The scene did not change again.

The three had turned towards her and Isar called out delighted to see her. He jumped off the stone and ran to her.

"See what a great place this is, Kyra," he chattered happily as she put her arms about him. "We have been playing games."

She looked into his guileless eyes and looked beyond him at the half crippled Wardyke now standing stiffly waiting for her approach, Panora smiling her unpleasant, secret smile.

"Games?" she asked, looking directly at Wardyke and Panora.

"Yes, games!" Isar answered, but the other two said nothing.

"Your mother is worried about you," she scolded the boy. "You must not run off like that without telling her where you are going."

"Panora told her," Isar said confidently.

Kyra looked at Panora.

178

The girl shrugged shamelessly.

Kyra knew now that she could never trust her again.

She sighed.

"Come," she said, and took the boy's hand.

The other two remained behind watching as Kyra and child became smaller and smaller in the distance.

The moon was out before Isar was safely home.

"Do not trust Panora or Wardyke again," Kyra said to Fern. "Keep Isar close to you. I cannot tell you yet what is going on because I am not sure, but I am going to seek help now and we will soon know what is best to do."

She left Fern worried, but Isar promising never, never to leave his mother's side again until he had permission.

In the morning she went to the Lord Khu-ren and told him gravely that she must have his help.

They had treated each other with great formality since she had entered his class and nothing had passed between them that would have made any of the other priests present suspect they had anything more than a teacher-student relationship.

They had avoided each other away from the classes as well, not trusting themselves.

This was the first time she had approached him privately. He looked into her eyes and knew it was a matter for a priest and friend, not for a lover.

"Come to me after the lesson is over today," he said.

She nodded, but hesitated before she turned to leave.

"I would like to meet you beside the Field of the Grey Gods," she said tentatively but earnestly.

He looked surprised, but he agreed.

And so it was that they met that afternoon beside the field of scattered rocks and Kyra talked and talked, telling him everything she could think of that would be relevant to the situation.

He knew already of Wardyke's role in her former life but he had not known he was Isar's father.

She told him of the strange destiny that seemed to link Guiron and Isar. She told him of the haunted mound incident, and what she felt about Panora. She described the strange scene she had witnessed in this field the day before and of her own experience with the "throne" rock.

He listened very attentively to it all.

"I did not know who to turn to," she said apologetically at last. "The only other possibility would have been the Lord Guiron, but he is somehow involved . . ."

"You were right to come to me. I understand."

"I hope you do not think . . ." she stammered a little, embarrassed that he might think it was an elaborate way of attracting his attention to her again.

"No, I do not think . . ." he said gently, amused.

He raised his finger to his lips to indicate that now he wanted to be in silence to think it through.

They sat beside each other, silently, not touching, for a long time.

At last he stood up.

"I want you to stay here," he said. "Do not interfere in any way whatever happens—unless I specifically call for your help. Understand?"

"What are you going to do?" she cried, alarmed.

"There is nothing much I can do until I know how everything fits together. I am going to sit upon that throne myself and see what happens."

"Oh no!" she cried. "I fainted. It was horrible!"

He smiled and touched her on the nose.

She felt very foolish suddenly.

He was a Great Lord of the Sun, and she had been a green student on her first lesson about rocks.

She sat down on the bank and watched him walk into the field.

He sat upon the stone shaped like a throne and became very still.

He sat for a very long time.

Nothing changed. The field remained a field of scattered rocks. He was still the Lord Khu-ren whom she loved.

But he was as unmoving as stone.

The sun set and she began to shiver with the evening chill. She wondered what she would do if he sat there into the night. He had made her promise not to do anything unless he called to her for help.

She went into meditative silence herself, but could hear no call for help.

Nothing at all.

At last he moved, stood up and stretched himself.

She was so happy the anxious vigil was over she ran across the field to him and flung herself into his arms. She was bitterly cold now and he held her close to warm her. She was so thankful to have him back that she kissed him again and again on every bit of his face that she could reach.

He laughed and tried to hold her off.

"Wait," he said, shaking her and laughing, "you will make me forget all the important things I have learned while sitting here."

She jumped back immediately.

"Oh . . . I am sorry . . . please forgive . . ."

"All right! All right!" he laughed, "you do not need to go so far away." And he put his arm round her shoulders to give her warmth and comfort as they walked back to the Temple and he told her all that had come to him while he was seated on the "throne."

It was a story almost complete in every detail that seemed to make sense of all the bits and pieces Kyra had been worrying about.

It seemed that in the ancient days, before their Temple had been built, a great warrior King had come from over the seas, indeed from Khu-ren's own country, and had conquered much of the land around them, which at that time was full of wandering tribes, each under the leadership of a chieftain.

The King set up court in that very place. Many of the rocks that they could see scattered about the field were in fact part of the walls of his great palace. Kyra had not been wrong in her vision.

The stone that looked like a throne had indeed been a throne, but the weather, time and conflict had reduced it to its present ambiguity.

His god had been in the form of a large black bird, and it was he whom Kyra had seen upon the column.

Both his close friend and adviser and his beautiful queen he had brought from his own far country, the three sustaining each other against the alien nature of the land to which they had come.

All went well for many years.

They lived in a luxury that no one in the land had ever seen before, and the queen and he were idyllically happy in their love for each other.

But a shadow was not far from their lives.

One of the most powerful of the local chieftains, who had been befriended by the king and invited to his court as an equal, fell in love with the beautiful dark queen.

For a long while he watched her, in the movement of dance, in the stillness as she sat beside her lord.

But one day he could bear it no longer and he approached her.

She turned her head towards him slowly as he spoke the words that had for so long been burning in his heart.

Her almond eyes were dark with scorn.

Bitterly he retreated and did not rest until he had devised a way of killing the king and his friend-adviser. So cunningly did he do his work and dispose of the bodies that no one but the queen suspected it was he, and she was helpless and unable to convince others.

It was not long before the murderer, mourning apparently so sincerely the disappearance of his friend, had managed to take his place as king.

On the day he was crowned he asked the former queen to be his wife.

She refused.

He raped her.

And later when he was asleep she left his side and flung herself into the lake where she and her lord had been happy to sail on many a peaceful summer afternoon.

From that time on nothing went right for the new king.

He was broken with remorse for what he had done to the woman he loved and gradually his enemies destroyed him and the palace he had taken as his own.

He died in battle and through many other lives on this earth and on others he paid for his lust, treachery and violence, until at last the guilt was worked off.

He was born again on this earth, at this time, and led a good life.

"He became," and here Khu-ren paused and looked hard at Kyra, "the High Priest of this Temple, the Lord Guiron."

She gasped.

"Everything in his life went well until the night he spent in the mist on that lake. He had no surface-memory of the story I have just told you. The whole debt had been paid and he was clear to live now an enlightened life.

"But there were other threads of destiny woven into this tale that had not yet been worked through. The friend of the King still harboured malice and feelings of revenge. The Queen had never been reborn but had haunted the lake waiting for the return of her lord.

"Guiron was confronted by the image of the woman he had loved and he made the same mistake again! She refused him and he forced himself upon her."

They had stopped walking and were standing in the dark, Kyra almost not breathing with the interest she had in the story.

"And so the whole cycle of purgation has to start again."

"How do you mean?" Kyra asked breathlessly.

"Guiron, horrified at what he had done, drained the lake and destroyed the image of the woman, thinking once again to escape the consequences of his action.

"Whether he remembered now the whole story from the past I do not know. But it is possible."

"Isar?" asked Kyra anxiously.

"The murdered King."

"Wardyke?"

"The murdered King's friend."

Kyra remembered that the demon figures associated

183

with Wardyke had reminded her of the gods and demons of Khu-ren's land.

"Panora?"

"A kind of half-human creature, half-spirit."

It seemed to her now that Wardyke and Panora were there to play their part in arranging the vengeance of Isar against Guiron, whether the two protagonists wished it or not.

Kyra was silent in the dark, clinging to Khu-ren's arm.

When would it end? If Isar carried out this act of vengeance the cycle of purgation would have to turn for *him* through aeons of pain.

How long the threads of cause and effect that wove about their lives!

How strangely they played their parts in other people's dramas.

That Wardyke should father Isar and that *she* should be instrumental in bringing him face to face with Guiron after all that time!

Khu-ren put his arms around her.

"You are shivering, my love."

She clung to him and without either of them intending it they found themselves together in Khu-ren's warm sleeping rugs for the night.

A Wounded Friend and a Lake
That Is Not a Lake

As soon as she could Kyra told everything she knew about Isar to Karne and Fern. They sat for a long time discussing it and their suggestions ranged from leaving the Temple environs and moving back to their old home, to facing it out here and now.

In the end they were all agreed that moving their location on the face of the earth would do no good whatever, nor would trying to destroy Wardyke and Panora physically. It was decided that the only reasonable course they could take would be to watch the relationships between Wardyke, Panora and Isar closely and try and counteract their influence on him in every way possible. They all knew that not much purpose was served by forbidding someone to do something. Their only hope in saving Isar from the consequences of a course of vengeance was to influence him with their love and convince him of the beauty and necessity of forgiveness, so that when the final confrontation came he would not choose to go the way Wardyke and Panora wanted him to and he would be strong enough in himself to withstand their pressures.

Kyra left them soberly and sadly considering the future,

with promises of help from her at any time they needed her.

She told them also of her love for the Lord Khu-ren and of his assistance in the matter.

Fern looked at her with tears in her eyes, knowing what it was to love.

Whatever the plans of Wardyke and Panora were at that time they seemed to leave Isar alone for a while. Perhaps they feared Kyra's interference. Perhaps they knew the powerful Lord Khu-ren was now involved. They may have even thought to lull Isar's family and friends into a feeling that all danger was past. At any rate Isar was still very young and they could afford to wait.

Isar grew daily closer to his mother and her gentle teaching.

Karne too spent much more time with him and when he went on journeys for Olan, riding on a horse, he took Isar with him sitting in front of him.

The boy had an amazing knowledge of the countryside and many times set Karne on the right path when he was about to stray. Apart from this, which could have been explained by the fact that Isar had lived in this area before, there was not much sign that there was anything unusual about him. He loved to ride, to run, to jump, to play fighting with cudgels as other boys did. But his greatest joy of all was to carve wood into beautiful and fantastic shapes. With this skill he gave both Karne and Fern great pleasure, especially as he chose the wood with care and never harmed a living branch.

Meanwhile the Lord Khu-ren and the Lady Kyra struggled to keep their love for each other under control.

Apart from that one night when Isar's story was revealed, they did not see each other except as master and student in the class among the other priests.

Kyra could see, when she was thinking sensibly, that a priest of Khu-ren's stature could not live a normal family life without jeopardising his work as Lord of the Sun.

The control of the subtle and complex inner forces of

his Being necessary for the great work he had to do across the world in "spirit-travelling" would be endangered by family distractions and worries.

The only way they could be together would be if they had equal powers and worked in unison. Their bond of love would then aid and strengthen them. But as long as she was still a feeble and unformed girl, demanding his attention away from his work, instead of aiding him in it, there would be difficulties.

She knew also that if she chose this way, graduated to stand beside him as an equal in his work, she would have to give up any idea of having children of her own.

A mother with children could surely not be a Lord of the Sun.

A mother with children must be a mother.

These were not easy days for her.

One night in sleep she had a dream that she knew at once was not a dream, but a cry for help.

She could feel great pain but at first could not locate the source or cause of it. Then impressions of noise, of shouting, heat and dust, and blood. Pain seemed everywhere in her, but visually she could see nothing but a sort of whirling reddish fog. Then she felt hands pulling at her and the pain grew worse, until she could hear herself screaming . . . then through the sound of screaming and people's harsh voices shouting in a language unknown to her, she struggled to interpret another sound which she knew was of great importance but which she just could not grasp with her mind.

The pain passed through her like a wave and her whole dream went black.

She was awake, sitting upright, feeling no pain but an overwhelming sense that she was needed somewhere.

But where?

If only she could isolate the other sound and recognize it she would know where she was needed.

She tried to calm her mind.

"Slowly," she chided herself, "you must go into the Silence if you want clarity of thought."

Her mind was at first quite blank as she removed the disturbances of her own life from it and then she deliberately put herself through the dream again, but this time she kept consciousness.

She knew she was succeeding when the terrible pain began to return to her body. She almost wavered then and backed away but her training stood by her and she forced herself to go on and feel all that she had felt before, hear all that she had heard before. This time she recognized the other sound, the sound of thundering hooves.

The Island of the Bulls!

Her friend, the beautiful acrobat.

For a few moments her mind was in complete disorder as she tried to cope with the emotions of worry and fear for her friend, and the decision as to what to do.

The Lord Khu-ren this night was on work of great importance in another country. He had entered the powerful Northern Inner Circle of the Temple at sunset and must not be disturbed until dawn. It would be dangerous both for him and for the situation he was at this moment helping in his "spirit" form.

She alone must help her friend.

She pulled her long woollen cape around her and left the room of sleeping people. She entered the Great Circle of the Temple.

She held her sea urchin talisman tightly in one hand, asking for power to "travel" and her faience beads she touched for comfort with her other hand. Her forehead she laid against one of the Stones in the Outer Circumference of the Circle she had on several occasions found had special significance for her.

The night was very dark and she felt very much alone.

"I must not be afraid," she told herself. "Fear will prevent my 'travelling'."

And indeed while she thought about herself and her fear she stayed where she was, but when she started to think about the girl, the force of her affection for her made her forget herself, and suddenly she was no longer in The Temple of the Sun.

She was in a high walled room in the Palace on the Island of the Bulls, wall paintings flickering in the firelight of torches, her beautiful friend lying very still and covered in blood upon a cold slab of stone.

Around the walls people were gathered weeping, but near her two priests of her own culture were working upon her, one washing the blood away from the wounds, the other sprinkling herbs into the cleaned gashes and uttering incantations.

Kyra moved forward to stare down upon the pale face of the girl. The people in the background showed no sign that they had noticed her arrival or were aware of her presence. Only the two priests reacted in amazement at the sight of her.

In appearance she was very different from the people of their land. Her long cloak of fine gold hair flowing loose made her appear to them like a shining being from another realm.

Bowing slightly, they retreated, and it was clear to her they now expected her to save the girl.

As soon as she had established that the life force had not yet left the bodily sheath entirely, she indicated to the priests that the mourning, miserable people were to leave. This they did at once, though under protest.

When the room was clear except for the two priests who stood well out of the way and projected only confidence, Kyra leant over her friend again.

Remembering how Maal's little stone sphere of power placed upon his chest had revived the pumping of his heart when it had almost stopped, Kyra now placed her sea urchin talisman between the girl's breasts, folded her limp hands over it and then placed her own hands upon the girl's forehead. All that she had learned in Healing came to her now and her love for the girl, her longing for her recovery, gave impetus to the forceful flow of life that she willed through herself to the girl from the great Source beyond.

When she could see the pumping of her heart was gradually becoming stronger she began to massage her limbs, forming a strong visualisation of the acrobat refreshed and renewed, energetic and healthy again. At the same time she never ceased to will the force of life to flow through her.

When she was sure the immediate danger of death was over, she looked to see what the wounding of the bull's harsh horns had done to her. She found deep gashes and broken bones.

She called the priests back to her side and asked for clean cloth, more water and more healing herbs.

Together they stanched the bleeding, set the bones, bound the wounds with clean linen and healing herbs.

And only when this was done did Kyra dare to remove the talisman of power and call the girl to wakefulness.

As she opened her eyes and saw Kyra's loving face above her, she smiled a very small but very happy smile.

"I called you," she said, and shut her eyes again.

Kyra dismissed the priests and sat beside her friend, holding her hands, loving her.

Kyra was moved and touched that she had been called. It would have been more likely that she would have called one of the great Lords of the Sun, of which, after all, she was one.

"No," the girl whispered, as though Kyra had spoken this aloud. "I wanted you. I wanted to show the Lord Khu-ren that *you* could do it."

Kyra looked her surprise.

"Ah yes," the girl smiled wanly, "I have loved him too. But that was long ago. I did not wish to give up the excitement of my life here and so I let him go. It was meant to be. You and he are for each other. I have seen it and I accept it."

Kyra did not know what to say.

The girl shook her head very slightly. It still pained her greatly to move in spite of the numbing herbs.

"Nothing," she breathed. "Say nothing."

Kyra sat still holding her hands, feeling all that was between them and between them both and the Lord Khu-ren.

Yet another strange thread she had not been aware of in the fabric of her life.

"I will sleep now," the girl whispered at last. "You must go. I will be all right now."

"What about . . . ?" Kyra did not like to say anything about her future as an acrobat, but the thought came unbidden and the girl caught it.

Again she moved slightly. This time it was almost a shrug of the shoulders.

"My name is Quilla, which means in my language, 'flight'," she said.

Kyra leant forward and kissed her on her forehead.

"You will fly again", she said gently, "and I will visit you again."

"Who knows," and here Quilla's lips formed a smile with a touch of mischief in it. "I may come to your wedding!"

Kyra smiled too, also with a hint of mischief in her eyes.

"You are welcome!"

On that warm note they parted, Quilla to sleep and Kyra to find herself in the anxious arms of Khu-ren who had returned at early dawn from his exhausting night of "spirit-travelling", to find Kyra lying in a dead faint on the cold dewy grass beside one of the Stones of the Great Circle.

When he had taken her home and warmed her and scolded her roundly for being there at all, he listened to her story with great interest.

When she had finished he sat so gravely thinking that Kyra began to grow alarmed.

"Is it her you really love?" she burst out at last.

He looked at her as though she had said something stupid and childish.

She *felt* stupid and childish.

But when he took her in his arms and covered her with the warm fur of his sleeping rugs she felt very different.

When Kyra had first entered the class of "spirit-travelling" she had made amazing progress, partly because she had had some experience before, and partly because she was determined to master it as fast as she could.

But after this time with Quilla both Khu-ren and herself began to notice a disturbing thing. She tended to faint a great deal during and after "travelling" and many times failed to achieve separation from her body in spite of every sign that she was doing it right.

She managed two visits to the Island of the Bulls before it became too obvious for them to ignore that something was wrong.

Quilla was healing slowly but surely. Her quicksilver personality was impatient to be at her old trade, but there was no way she could be allowed to, or even be capable of it, for a long time.

"I have always been short on patience", she said gloomily, "and now I suppose I will *have* to learn it!"

It was after this visit that Kyra took so long to come out of a faint and felt so ill when she did that Khu-ren decided to think seriously about allowing her to go on at all with her training.

She was in despair.

It mattered so much to her to marry Khu-ren, and she was as determined now as he had originally been, that they would not marry unless they could work together as well.

"Perhaps your real role in life is to be a Healer," suggested Fern when Kyra poured out all her troubles to her, "and not one of the Lords of the Sun at all."

But Kyra would not accept this.

"I know I can 'travel'. I know it is in 'travelling' I can be of most use to Khu-ren and my fellow beings."

"But you cured your friend Quilla . . ."

"But I 'travelled' to do it!"

Fern sighed. She was very fond of Kyra and knew how she felt.

And then her baby stirred inside her own body and she looked at Kyra with a look of revelation.

"You are with child!" she almost shouted.

Kyra looked astounded, and then she remembered the night when Khu-ren had told her the full story of Guiron and Isar and she had not returned to her own sleeping place.

The two girls stared at each other.

The realization of what this meant slowly dawned on Kyra.

The joy that she first felt to be carrying his child turned to despair as she realized she would now have to give up all thoughts of "travelling" and being his equal and his wife.

"I will not chain him to me with this child! Oh Fern! What am I to do!"

It was a cry from a very deep source of pain.

Fern held her silently in her arms, as once Kyra had held her.

"There must be a meaning in it, my love, there must be a way!" she said gently.

"What meaning? What way?" sobbed Kyra.

Fern stroked her hair.

"How many times did Maal tell us there is no way in the confines of our bodily existence that we can see enough of the picture to know what the meaning is?"

"I know . . . I know . . . but . . ."

"But this has happened now. It is a child of love at least."

And Kyra felt a twinge of shame to be so complaining to Fern when Fern's child had been forced on her in fear and hate, and she had carried it bravely and cherished it with love.

Yes, her child was certainly a child of love.

It would change the course of her life, but who was to say this change was not meant to be.

"You will speak to the Lord Khu-ren about it?" Fern asked after a while, when Kyra was calmer.

Kyra hesitated.

"Yes!" Fern said firmly.

"Yes," agreed Kyra.

When Kyra left Fern she knew that she must walk and think alone for a while before she faced her Lord.

Without realizing it she found herself following the tracks that led to the Haunted Mound and the one-time Lake. So deeply was she engrossed in thought that she had climbed the mound before she realized it and was sitting on the top gazing at nothing, her thoughts all of the child within her and what role it would play in the world when it was released from her body.

She felt at peace now as though Fern were right.

It was meant to be and its influence would be for good.

She began to feel very drowsy and very happy.

She noticed a flight of water fowl across the sky and heard the splash as they landed on the lake.

Smiling, she looked down at the shining waters and the birds swimming elegantly beside the reeds. She picked up a pebble and threw it hard so that it reached the water and she watched the circles as they grew out from the central impact.

And then the warm peacefulness of the scene began to change and she felt a little cold. She noticed mist was beginning to gather on the far side of the lake and drift across towards her.

"I must go," she thought, but she was so happy and comfortable where she was she did not move.

She lay back and watched the drifting clouds pass by for a long while and then told herself again that she must go.

She sat up and noticed with some alarm that the mist had completely covered the lake now and was creeping up the mound on which she was seated.

Startled, she stared into the uncertain moving cloud, and saw the faint figure of a woman emerging towards her.

For what might have been an instant or a million sun cycles the two women stared at each other, Kyra and the beautiful wife of the long dead King, and then with a sharp intake of breath Kyra realized where she was and what was happening.

She jumped to her feet, a sharp pang of fear stabbing through her heart.

"There is no lake!" she cried aloud, "No water birds swimming on water, no mist, no beautiful living Queen!"

And with that cry the whole scene changed and she was alone and frightened on the mound, with a dry plain beside her, and a cloudless sky above her.

She scrambled down the slope as fast as she could.

What further role these ancient actors were to demand of her she did not wish to think about.

Khu-ren was almost knocked down by the force by which she flung herself upon him as he emerged from the Temple.

He tried to hold her off and steady her at least until they could reach a place of greater privacy, but she was in such a state of perturbation, he could do nothing but put his arm about her and lead her boldly off in front of everyone.

So disturbed was she that the story came out backwards and the news about the lady of the lake came before the news that Kyra was with child.

Khu-ren was bewildered at first, but eventually made sense of it all.

"So," he said calmly, "we are to have a child."

"Yes!" shouted Kyra as though he should have grasped this point a long time ago.

"This probably explains why you have not been too successful with your 'travelling' ", he said with maddening self-control.

"Forget the 'travelling'!" cried Kyra in exasperation, her own feelings in the matter having changed since she had spoken to Fern. "That is not important! What is important is that our love has given us a child!"

"Hmm," he said, but he could not keep the act up much longer and when she threw something at him his face broke into the expression of delight he was really feeling.

"I have decided everything," Kyra said later. "I refuse to let this interfere in any way with your life."

He looked at her and laughed.

"And how do you propose to manage that, my love?"

"Well, I will leave the Temple and become an ordinary mother living in Fern's village. You will continue with your work here as though nothing has happened . . . but perhaps . . . you will visit us from time to time?" Her voice had started very briskly on this proposal but by the end

195

it had trailed off somewhat into a kind of pleading query.

"Oh," he said, his dark eyes sparkling with mockery. "That is very kind of you."

"Seriously . . ." she said.

"Seriously?" and he laughed again.

"Well . . ." she began to wriggle a bit with embarrassment. "What do you suggest then?" She demanded at last, quite flushed.

"I suggest we marry. No!" he said and put his finger to her lips to stop her interrupting. "Listen for once. You will leave your studies for a while and when you are ready to take them up again we will continue with them until you join me as Lord of the Sun."

"But . . ."

"Our child will live within the Temple community and have great advantages. If he shows signs of power he will be trained as priest. If not he will choose whatever else he wishes to do . . ."

"But . . . how will I look after him properly if I am working as a priest?"

"You will find a way."

"You make it sound easy."

"It will not be easy. I do not promise you that. We will have strains upon us that at times will be hard to bear, and he will have pressures that perhaps a child in an ordinary family would not have . . . but . . . I am sure for all that he would not wish that he had not been born, nor us that we had not brought him into Life."

"And what of the others?"

"What others?"

"Other children if we marry?"

Khu-ren was silent for a while.

"We have started on a course we both knew we should avoid. We did not avoid it. Now we must follow it through and make of it what we can.

"If it means giving up everything we expected of life, then that is how it must be. There are many ways to live a life and there is no going back now."

She was silent at last.

He was wise, and she loved and trusted him.

Wardyke's War

Kyra slipped into the new way of living quickly and more easily than she had thought she would.

She left the classes of "spirit-travelling", but there were a great many other things she still needed to learn and for some of them she joined her old friends Lea and Vann again. Both had been inaugurated as village priests and both had chosen to remain at the Temple for further training. Most of their original class had left and the three grew closer together than ever before.

Her husband had a great deal to do but they had many times of tenderness and peace together.

The Lord Guiron had blessed their marriage in a formal but simple ceremony, but Kyra could not shake off the feeling that he had some kind of premonition or foreboding about it. His words almost took the form of a spell to avoid harm rather than of the usual marriage blessing, and she noticed him many times looking at her in a strange, gloomy and penetrating way.

She tried not to worry but knowing the extent of his

powers as a prophet and priest, she was very ill at ease and found herself trying to avoid his presence.

As the child came nearer to birth she had to face another problem.

Day after day she had an overwhelming longing to visit the Haunted Mound and the site of the old lake. She was determined not to go there again after her last experience, but she had to fight something in herself to stay away.

Fern and Karne were having their troubles too.

Isar was no longer young enough to keep under surveillance all the time. He had grown very tall for his eight summers. He was handsome and proud and did not care to be told what he should do or not do. Both Karne and Fern respected him for this, but given the circumstances of his past it made it more difficult for them to keep him from harm. They fortified him as best they could with the beliefs and understandings that they had of life, but they had the impression that he did not always agree with them. Other influences were at work upon him at the same time and he was young and impressionable, not always capable of seeing things as clearly as an experienced person might.

Wardyke became the right hand of his Spear-lord, Hawk-Eagle, and encouraged trouble between his master and Olan. The two land owners were constantly quarrelling, the ownership of the lands bordering each other always in question.

Fern was concerned to hear the men talk of fighting for the land, the one determined to oust the other.

"But this is foolishness!" Fern cried to Karne. "There is enough for both."

"Try telling that to old Hawk-Eagle! It is he who is always taking more. Olan has given in many times to keep the peace, but he is gradually being squeezed into a position where there is not enough land to feed his own people. We cannot let Hawk-Eagle take any more. *That* would be foolishness!"

"Surely you can talk to him?"

Karne laughed.

"Of course we have *talked*, my love! But Hawk-Eagle does not understand our language, and of course now he has Wardyke at his elbow all the time there is even less chance of a reasonable settlement."

"What about the priests at the Temple? Can you not ask them to settle it?"

"I am afraid, my sweet innocent, the priests at the Temple are so busy reaching for the other kinds of reality, they do not pay much attention to this one!"

"I am sure that is not true!" Fern said indignantly.

"True or not, it is none of their affair. We must settle this between ourselves."

Karne had become Olan's most respected friend and tenant, and Wardyke Hawk-Eagle's. It was strange how another confrontation between these old enemies seemed now inevitable.

Fern thought of calling on Kyra for assistance, but knowing that her time for delivery was near and having heard that she had not been at all well of late, she thought she had better not worry her.

Isar spent more and more time away from home, and when questioned where he had been boldly refused to answer.

One day Karne came storming home, his face a study in the conflicting emotions of anger and anxiety.

"Do you know where that boy is this very moment?" he demanded of his wife.

She looked startled.

"With Wardyke! And that is where he has been every time we have asked him for his whereabouts and he has not replied."

Fern felt sick with worry, more for the fact that the boy was keeping his meetings with Wardyke secret from them than that he was with the man. After all, they had not forbidden him to see him.

Such a little while ago they had been so close and happy together, but recently she had noticed a sullen streak, a secretive look. She might have guessed Wardyke was behind it.

When he returned that evening she contrived to speak with him without Karne being present. She did not want the confrontation to be an angry one.

"I hear," she said gently, "you have been spending a great deal of time with Wardyke and Hawk-Eagle lately?"

The boy looked at her with expressionless eyes. He neither denied it, nor agreed with it.

"You know, of course, that Hawk-Eagle and Olan are enemies?"

"I know."

"Do you know the reasons?"

"Olan tries to keep land that is rightfully Hawk-Eagle's away from him."

"That is not so, but we will not discuss that now."

"What then?" the boy said coldly.

She hated the way he spoke and how he had changed. She thought back to the time when he used to sit peacefully creating beauty with his wood carving. He had not touched his tools for a long while now. Wardyke had always had the power to destroy what was good and creative in people and bring out what was destructive and restless.

"You know Karne and I do not like Wardyke, nor trust him."

"I know."

"And yet you still see more of him than of us?"

"He is my father," the boy said, lifting his head defiantly.

"Yes," she said and her voice had lost its gentleness and had an edge of great bitterness to it. "Yes, you can call him that, if that is what you mean by 'father'!"

The boy was silent.

"You know he forced himself on me and I hated and feared him?"

Again Isar did not reply, but she thought she detected a slight uncertainty in his eyes. This was not quite how Wardyke told the story.

"Karne has brought you up, fed you, protected you and loved you. To me *that* is fathering!"

"What if Wardyke is sorry for what he did and wants to make amends?" Isar's voice was less cold now, less sure that he was right.

"Then we will welcome him as friend," Fern said, "but do you think this is how it is? Think."

Isar thought.

"He does not visit as a friend, but entices you away and makes you lie to us and keep secrets from us. He encourages a man to rise in violence against another man, knowing that in the process Karne who has cherished you, and even your mother, may very well be killed. Does this seem like 'trying to make amends' to you? Or does it seem like vengeance?"

Isar was still silent, his face dark and confused.

"I will say no more about it, nor will I forbid you to see Wardyke. See him, but *think* about what you see. You are old enough now to judge for yourself."

She left him alone and went for a walk in her garden, trying to regain her peace of mind, trying to calm the anger and the hate that still burned for Wardyke in her heart.

She did not know how to break the link between Wardyke and Isar. It was of double strength if Kyra's amazing story had any truth in it. Not only was Isar Wardyke's natural son, but they had been friends for long ages before she or Karne had ever come between them.

In a moment of despair she thought she would abandon all efforts to interfere in what must be a very strong and significant liaison and then her love for Isar, the boy, her child, and the thought that whether she liked it or not she *had* become involved in this ancient drama and must have some role to play, decided her to keep trying, keep loving, keep interfering.

The day before Kyra's child was born the longing to visit the Haunted Mound grew so overwhelmingly strong that she slipped away from the Temple College without Khu-ren's knowledge and walked the distance as though in a dream, all rational control gone.

She was not well, and had not been for some time, but she *had* to reach the mound!

Busy about their own affairs, no one paid particular attention to the young priestess, heavy with child, and clad in a long, flowing blue cloak, passing their way and climbing the steep sides of the forbidding man-made mountain.

Out of breath and dizzy with the strain of it she flung herself down on the top and sobbed with relief. She did not know why she felt so relieved, she knew only that those long days of fighting and struggling within herself to stay away from this place were over and she was where she was meant to be.

After a while she fell asleep with exhaustion and the dream (or vision?) that came to her was not a comforting one.

She was lying on a couch somewhere in a strange and foreign place and her body was racked with the most terrible pains she had ever felt. This time she knew it was her own pain she was suffering and not that of anyone else. There was no cry for help except from herself and, although she could feel the pain, she could not move her limbs, nor open her mouth to utter the cry for Khu-ren that she longed to give.

In the dark recesses of the hall around her she saw her old enemies, the demons, half-animal, half-man, that had haunted her before. They were crouching and leering, occasionally taking a darting step forward and then retreating to the shadows again, as though they were waiting for the pain to increase and she to become weaker before they dared approach too near.

Fear and pain occupied her entirely and she felt desperately alone.

She called in her mind for Khu-ren, for Maal, for all her Spirit Lords and at each call the demons cringed as though they had felt a lash. But she began to feel weaker and weaker with pain and even her mind-calling began to fade, and her tormentors, noticing this, drew nearer.

Suddenly, through an archway that she had not noticed before two figures came and stood one on each side of her.

Through her agony she recognized the tall and bulky figure of the ancient King she had seen in the Field of the Grey Gods and the tall and elegant figure of the sad Queen of the lake mist.

They had walked into the room together, but as though they were not aware of each other's presence. Now, standing on either side of her, their eyes met and it seemed as though they noticed each other for the first time.

Great joy came over their faces and they took each other's hands and held them over her and then, as silently as they had come, they walked away, but this time hand in hand and very much aware of each other.

While they were present the demons held back, but as soon as they had disappeared through the archway, they surged forward and, screaming with agony, Kyra was torn apart.

As darkness and pain overwhelmed her, she was shaken awake by a hand and she found a startled Isar looking into her eyes.

"Kyra!" he was calling. "What is the matter? Why are you screaming?"

She sat up at once trembling with the horror of the experience and flung her arms around her young nephew.

"Why are you crying? What is the matter? Are you in pain?"

She heard his anxious questions, but could not answer them.

"I am going to die," she kept thinking. "That dream means that I am going to die!"

And now she knew why she had come to the Haunted Mound.

The child she was bearing would be Isar's Queen, but in bearing her she was going to die.

"No," she sobbed, "no! I will not! I will not!"

"Kyra, let me take you home to mother," the anxious boy pleaded, pulling at her arm.

"No!" screamed Kyra and with astounding force she pushed him aside and stood as tall as she was capable of upon the very top of the burial mound.

She shook her fist at the sky.

"I will not die!" she shouted fiercely. "I will play my part if I must, but I *will not* die!

"I am *Me*! Kyra. I have my own destiny . . . not yours alone!"

"What are you talking about?" the bewildered boy thought she had gone mad.

She looked at him suddenly and there was hate in her eyes.

"I do not see why I have to die for *you*!" she spat out.

"Kyra!" he gasped.

And then she fainted.

He stared at her in horror for a few moments, convinced that she was dead, and then turned and ran to fetch help.

When Kyra became conscious again she was in Fern's house and in extreme pain. She remembered the dream and it was as though the pain she was feeling was the same. The terror on her face startled Fern.

"Do not be afraid, my love, it is only the baby coming. Nothing to be afraid of."

"Khu-ren," sobbed Kyra, sweat pouring from her.

"He is coming," soothed Fern. "Isar has gone to fetch him."

"Fern, I am going to die," Kyra burst out.

"Nonsense," said Fern calmly. "There is a new life coming here, not an old going!"

"I had a dream . . ." gasped Kyra.

Fern wiped the sweat and tears gently from her face.

"I do not know anything about a dream, but I do know a great deal about having babies. You are having a bad time, but you are not going to die."

"But I dreamt . . ."

"I do not want to hear about any old dream!" Fern said sharply. "You priests know a great deal, but not everything. Dreams can be misinterpreted just like everything else, and you know as well as I do that if you believe you are going to die, you lessen your chances of living.

"Now stop being a priest for a moment and be a *woman*. Push!" she commanded.

Kyra pushed.

Meanwhile Isar had found Khu-ren and the two were hurrying back to Isar's home. As they went the boy told Khu-ren the circumstances of how he had found Kyra and the strange things that she had said.

Khu-ren's face grew darker and darker.

"Boy, I am going to run and my legs are longer than yours. I would be grateful if you would return to the Temple and find the Lord High Priest, and bring him to your home."

Isar turned instantly and was gone.

He was really troubled by Kyra's insistence that she would have to die for *him*.

By some strange quirk of fate Hawk-Eagle and Wardyke chose this night of all nights to attack the village of Olan. Of course they had no way of knowing about the drama that was being acted out in Fern's little house. Karne himself was unaware of it as he had been all day with Olan preparing defenses, knowing that the time was near when the talking and the insulting would stop and the violence begin.

Fern had been too occupied with the crisis of the moment to send word to him and could think only of fetching Khu-ren and seeing Kyra safely through the delivery of her child.

It was obvious to her the birth was not going as well as her own had done and that Kyra and her child were in very great danger, but she managed to keep her fear from showing and continued to help her friend in every way she could, with calmness and fortitude, praying all the while for the arrival of Kyra's husband.

The dream Kyra kept muttering about seemed to be their worst enemy. There were times when Fern felt Kyra was so sure she was going to die, she just seemed to give

205

up trying to live. At those times Fern used all her energy of love to sustain her, but if Khu-ren did not arrive soon she did not know how much longer she could keep her going.

The attack Hawk-Eagle and Wardyke had planned to launch that night was delayed a while because Wardyke had intended Isar to be at his side and Isar had disappeared. He had been in the village all day seeing the preparations for the attack. Wardyke had thought the boy had seemed a bit restless and unsettled and if he had not been so busy himself he would have worried about it. As it happened it was only when the moment for attack arrived that Wardyke realized Isar was missing and something was wrong.

He tried to stall Hawk-Eagle for as long as he could without telling him his reasons, torn between the two fears, one that the boy was in the victim village and would be destroyed with the other villagers, and two that he had betrayed them and the other village was prepared for the attack.

Isar had been very uncertain of his loyalties since his talk with his mother. He had grown very close to Wardyke with the help of Panora and had thought his loyalties lay with him, but since his mother had commanded him to think for himself, he had been noticing things about Wardyke that he had not noticed before. Things he did not like.

Wardyke himself had been so busy plotting with Hawk-Eagle he had not noticed the change in the boy.

Confused and distressed by the violence that was threatening to break upon the people he now realized he truly loved, the boy left Hawk-Eagle's village determined to warn Karne, but en route for his home he had seen Kyra upon the Haunted Mound and had become enmeshed in that particular crisis, totally forgetting the other.

In some ways he had always felt the talk of attack was just talk. He never really believed Hawk-Eagle and Wardyke would do it, though within the last few days he

206

had realized Hawk-Eagle's greed for more land and power was very strong indeed, well matched by Wardyke's greed for vengeance against Karne who had been the instrument of his downfall as magician-priest.

It was when he finally grasped that real violence was to occur that Isar knew that he had to choose, and he chose to return to Karne and Fern.

But it was perhaps his former affection for Wardyke that made it easier for him to forget the urgency of the message he should have delivered to Karne and Olan when another crisis arose.

Wardyke thought he had some control over the situation but he reckoned without Hawk-Eagle's own personality. Having decided to attack, and this had been largely on Wardyke's recommendation, he would not be held back.

If the boy had gone back to his old friends, too bad for the boy. All the more reason to start advancing before they had too much time to prepare a defence.

Wardyke was torn between his love for Isar and his hatred of Karne and Fern.

But his wishes no longer carried any weight. As before, he had unleashed forces of hate and violence in people he no longer could control.

The attack was launched.

Fern struggling with Kyra was horrified to hear the sound of shouting, fighting, screaming, the roar of flames, distant at first but coming nearer all the time.

She feared for Karne, for her children sleeping snugly in the other room, for Kyra struggling to give birth. She feared for Isar somewhere on the road to or from the Temple and prayed now that he would not return, but that someone would see their plight and come to their aid. But she knew these villages were small and the wooden houses easily burnt. Before help could reach them there would be nothing left but cinders and charred bones.

She had a terrible choice to make, to seize her children and run, leaving Kyra who could not be moved to face death alone.

She screamed to all the Spirit Lords that ruled the world to help her in this, the worst moment of her life. She could not leave and yet she could not stay!

As though in answer to her prayer the hanging rug that covered the doorway to her house was swept aside and the Lord Khu-ren strode into the room.

"Go!" he shouted at her. "Take your children and go!"

She gathered them up and ran, as she saw him bending over Kyra.

Outside was chaos and confusion.

The men were fighting as best they could, but fire arrows were being shot by skilled bowmen at the straw roofs of the houses and the men were hindered by the smoke and flames, and the fleeing, screaming women and children.

Briefly, in the light of flame, she saw Karne and Wardyke locked in battle, both using the long daggers the Spear-lords had introduced into the country.

Olan was on the ground with Hawk-Eagle's spear through his stomach.

She looked no more, but ran, her heart breaking.

In Fern's abandoned house, the roof on fire, Kyra gave the last push that brought her baby into life.

Guiron and Isar entered and it was Guiron who seized the child and ran with her to safety.

Khu-ren lifted his unconscious wife.

Isar seized a cudgel that he used for practice fighting and ran wildly towards the battle, his eyes ablaze.

"Wardyke!" he screamed seeing Wardyke about to drive his dagger through Karne's fallen body.

Wardyke looked up and saw his son, his ancient friend, with cudgel raised in hate and anger against him.

"My King!" he cried.

"No!" Isar shouted. "That was another time. Another place. *Now* Wardyke . . . *now* is the time to live!"

And he stood so fiercely strange, this boy who was at once a boy and yet a King, that Wardyke fumbled with his dagger and dropped it, and stood staring, not knowing what to do.

And in that moment one of the fire arrows loosed from the bow of one of Hawk-Eagle's men, passed through his heart and he fell in death.

"No!" cried Isar, and a boy again in tears, he flung himself upon Wardyke's body, but there was no way he could bring him back to life.

Karne staggered to his feet in time to see Hawk-Eagle raise his dagger against the boy and with a cry of rage he stepped between them, his love for Isar giving sudden strength to his already wounded body.

Hawk-Eagle fell and rose no more.

The New Spear-lord and the New "Traveller"

Many days and nights passed before Kyra regained consciousness, but when she did she was amazed to find herself still alive.

Ashen and pale and thin she was, but still very much alive.

She looked around her room savouring each familiar thing.

"I did not die!" she whispered to herself with joy. "I did not die!"

And then she remembered her baby, and her head turned with anxiety to look for her.

"Yes," Fern said gently, sitting beside her. "Your baby is safe too."

Kyra smiled with great joy.

"A girl,"

"A girl," Fern confirmed.

"I will call her Deva. It means 'shining one' in a language I once heard in a dream."

"You and your dreams!" teased Fern. "I thought you said you dreamed you were going to die?"

Kyra was too weak to say any more, but she smiled a very little ashamed smile.

Fern kissed her.

"Yes," she said, "I know your next question. He has been with you day and night all the time. He will be back in a few moments."

Kyra shut her eyes, this time to sleep in peace.

When she awoke the Lord Khu-ren was beside her.

When Kyra was a little stronger they had a simple ceremony to bless and name the baby in the room where she lay, as she was still too weak to move.

Karne was there, bound with bandages but in reasonable health, and Fern with their children, Isar standing separately like a man in his own right looking with very shining and loving eyes on the new baby who was dark of complexion like the Lord Khu-ren and the original Queen who had lived so long ago and had been his wife.

The Lord Guiron performed the ceremony and the blessing with humility and warmth.

There seemed to be no shadows present except perhaps for Panora who watched from the background with a peculiar brooding look in her eyes, unnoticed by the others.

Deva smiled when she was named.

Indeed a shining one!

"Is she not beautiful?" Kyra whispered to Khu-ren.

"You are both beautiful," he said with a smile and put his arms around the two of them.

"Come," Fern said firmly to the others, "we must leave Kyra to rest now. She is very weak and if Deva is anythink like my children she will need a great deal of looking after."

Kyra was too weak for a long time to take care of Deva properly. Fern stayed with her, glad of the temporary home for her small family since their own had been burned to the ground.

When Karne and Isar returned to the village the day after the birth of Deva they found a desolation worse than they had expected. There were very few houses still standing but fortunately there were fewer dead in either village than Karne would have thought possible in such a fierce battle. The survivors who had fled in the night had returned to wander aimlessly among the ruins of their homes, uncertain of what to do next.

Isar slipped away from Karne and sought out the body of Wardyke. It was lying where it had fallen, so burnt and charred it was almost unrecognizable.

The boy squatted beside it and wept, his heart almost breaking. There had been so much of Time and Mystery, love and treachery and pain in their relationship and now Isar knew in a way he could not have explained that his path and Wardyke's would not cross again.

In the moment he had denied the past, he had broken free of Wardyke's spell, a spell that had been upon him since before he left their home in the land of the Long River and the desert that flowered after every flood. It was his friendship for Wardyke who was in trouble and sentenced to death that had made them flee across the sea and come to this strange and barbarous land.

It was Wardyke's idea that he should set himself up as King and Wardyke who organized the ignorant wandering tribes to pay tribute to him and build his palace and supply him with his wealth. Wardyke who sniffed out gold like a dog sniffed excrement. Wardyke who destroyed his enemies, manoeuvred his friends, while he and his beautiful Queen lived in love and joy, thoughtless of anything that could harm them or change their earthly paradise.

When a certain chieftain had come to their court, joined the feasting and the hunting, it was Wardyke who had warned that he was not to be trusted. But thinking that it was jealousy because this man was the first he had loved beside Wardyke himself, Isar had taken no notice.

For the first time he had not taken Wardyke's counsel and it was his undoing.

Many times since then the three of them had been reborn in other lands, in other worlds. The old score had at last been settled and he had been at peace upon a world in another galaxy, a world of many suns where light was danger and they had lived in darkness underground, seeing with their minds, peaceful amongst themselves.

213

The ache of longing for his Queen who had never been reborn, but had clung tenaciously to the place where she had died, had at last healed. He lived with no memory of this ancient wound.

And then, in the darkness that was not darkness to him, he had suddenly felt a shaft of pain through his heart and his friends mourned his death.

In that instant he was conceived in the womb of Fern, called thither by Wardyke's relentless spirit.

The stirrings of these memories had been with him since his birth, like dark shadows at the corner of his eye which, when he turned his head, he could not see.

In dreams images haunted him from the past, but he only partially recognized them, and the soft arms of his mother had dispelled many of the dark traces from his mind.

Standing on top of that ancient hill, surveying the lake, he had remembered, fleetingly, and again on his one-time throne . . . but in each case the memory had slipped like a dream slips, like an adder slips under rocks, to lie in darkness biding its time, but out of reach of the conscious mind.

It was only at the moment when he faced Wardyke in battle and saw his weapon raised to kill Karne whom he loved, the moment that Wardyke called him King, that the whole memory had come flooding back and he knew he had to make a choice.

The choice was made in an instant from deep inside himself and there was no going back.

But now beside the body of his friend his heart ached and he wished life's justice was not so long and so inexorable.

He felt a hand upon his shoulder and looked up to find Karne beside him, looking on him with great tenderness and understanding.

He stood up.

"We have to attend to the burials and the rebuilding," Karne said quietly. "No one else seems to know what to do."

He looked at Isar deeply.

"I need your help," he said with humility.

Isar looked from Wardyke's body, to the living warmth of love in Karne's eyes.

"You have it," he said with dignity.

Karne bowed his head slightly and the two began the task of making order out of chaos.

As soon as someone took the initiative the helpless villagers were willing enough to work. They had been used to a Spear-lord and an ordered routine and they seemed to need someone to tell them what to do. Without meaning to take over Olan's place, Karne found himself issuing orders.

In the bustle of work Isar's painful memories faded and he found comfort as a boy again, running messages for Karne, organizing the clearing of the old burnt wood away and advising where new timber suitable for building could be found.

Karne noticing that many of Hawk-Eagle's villagers were wandering among his own with as much despair upon their faces and with expressions that showed they were equally at a loss to know what now to do with their lives, and, suspecting that the villagers themselves had not had much to say in the attack but had just been doing what they had been told to do by their Spear-lord, he gathered them together and made a great and moving speech suggesting they all forget the past and join together to rebuild the future. There were not many dissenters to this idea. Quite a few of the villagers had sons or daughters who had married into the other village, and relatives and friends had been involved in the fighting, caught up by Hawk-Eagle and Wardyke in a war that was not really their war.

Isar stood beside Karne on this, and Hawk-Eagle's people, recognizing him as Wardyke's son and hearing him join with Karne to plead for peace, agreed.

Sadly not only Olan had been killed in the fighting, but his beautiful daughter as well, and Olan's widow was now alone.

The bodies of the dead of both sides were gathered and a great funeral pyre was built.

But those of Olan and his daughter and of Hawk-Eagle were kept separate for they were of the tribe that had separate burial mounds.

That night there was great sorrow and mourning.

Priests from the Temple arrived and the High Priest, Lord Guiron, said words of comfort and prayer to the bereaved from his own heart, as well as the ritual words that were expected of him.

Karne watched him very closely, wondering what he was thinking and if he remembered anything of his old connection with Wardyke and the young boy who stood beside him, mourning.

But if he did, he gave no sign.

The words were simple, moving and sincere.

When the ashes the following dawn were gathered and placed in pottery urns for burial, Panora slipped forward and placed a garland of flowers around Wardyke's urn. Karne could see that she was weeping and as she turned to leave he caught a look in her eye towards the Lord Guiron and the boy Isar that chilled his blood.

The old score was not settled as far as she was concerned and she would not let it rest.

But Isar did not see it. He carried Wardyke's ashes to the burial place and laid them down with the others killed in battle, Panora's flowers still upon the urn.

That day passed in raising the burial mounds.

The next in clearing the ground for rebuilding.

And the third day they started serious work on reconstruction.

While Khu-ren was with Kyra, and Fern was temporarily released from her duties as nurse, she returned to see what she could salvage of her old home.

Olan's wife found her there sad among the trampled ruins of her garden, thinking of Wardyke and how years ago he had destroyed with fire her beautiful living wood. She sat on the ground and lifted broken fronds and branches gently, seeing how much she would have to cut away to let the new growth through, speaking words of comfort and tenderness to them.

Olan's wife watched her for a while and then moved closer to her.

"Have you words of comfort for me too?" she said with pain. "Olan and my daughter have no roots hidden in the earth to send up leaves again in Spring."

Fern looked up at her and opened her arms. The proud, tall woman, the warrior Spear-lord's wife, sat upon the earth and buried her face in the peasant girl's breast.

Fern kissed her and stroked her hair.

"*I* have no words," she said softly. "The words are in your own heart. Listen to them."

The older woman's tears fell upon the young woman's arm.

"Sssh," Fern whispered. "Listen to them."

Gradually Olan's wife quietened and she lay listening to the beat of Fern's heart, puzzling a little about what Fern meant, wondering what she was supposed to hear.

She began to feel drowsy and at peace. Sleep had not come her way since that terrible night. Fern rocked her gently and whether she was asleep or not she did not know, but she felt a calmness come over her, a calmness which seemed to shade into a feeling first as though there were a glimmering of hope and then growing into the strength of a conviction.

Wherever she looked in Nature there were correspondences that ran through the lives of everything, a cyclical pattern, a constant ending and beginning, destroying and renewing, and wherever she looked she saw *no waste*. Everything that existed continued, even if in another form. She thought about the caterpillar and the butterfly. She thought about the fallen dead leaves in a forest, nourishing the new and living tree. If such things were without exception in Nature, Man, the most complicated and subtle creature of all, the most difficult to bring to maturity, would hardly be the only one to be denied renewal, the only one to be *wasted*. The slow and painful struggle he had to reach complex consciousness *must* be for some continuing purpose.

217

Olan's wife opened her eyes and there were now no tears in them.

She looked at Fern and Fern knew she had heard the words in her own heart.

"You see!" she said gently, releasing her from her embrace.

"I see," the woman said.

With Karne's supervision and energetic work the stricken homes began to rise again, but almost without anyone realizing it the two villages that had been so separate and so different began to merge into one large straggling village with a great deal more open space between the houses than there had been before. Not everyone rebuilt their homes in exactly the same place, relatives in one village moved nearer to relatives in the other, some chose new land but some stayed with the old.

Also, without anyone realizing it, Karne was increasingly consulted on every decision that had to be made. At first he turned always to Olan's widow for the final permission for any move, but she knew as well as he did that the decision was always his, and she agreed almost without thinking to whatever he proposed.

At last she said he need not consult her any more but do as he thought fit.

Hawk-Eagle had no wife, nor heir, and so his people tended to turn to Karne too.

On the day the last house was rebuilt the villages decided to hold a celebration.

Kyra was still too weak to attend, but Fern and her whole family were there and all the people from both villages gathered round one central fire and drank strong ale and feasted well into the night.

At the height of the festivities Olan's widow called for silence and was placed high upon a rough platform of wooden beams.

The tall woman stood beautiful and elegant in the firelight and the villagers gradually became silent, all faces turned to her.

"It is not easy for me to speak without my husband at

my side," Olan's widow said, "but what I have to say I say with his authority behind me.

"Before he died," and here her voice broke slightly, but she resumed in clear and ringing tones within moments, "his most trusted friend and confidant was Karne whom I think you all know." She turned and pointed to Karne who was standing near the platform with his arm around Fern and his latest baby on his shoulder.

A cheer went up that rang so loud the very sky seemed to receive it!

Fern flushed with pride and turned her face into her husband's shoulder.

He looked embarrassed.

"With your permission," and Olan's wife looked around smiling at the happy, friendly faces around her, "I would like to ask Karne to be Spear-lord of this fine new village in the place of both Hawk-Eagle and Olan."

Another cheer went up.

She held up her hand for silence as the cheering seemed to be getting out of hand.

"You will know it is not the custom for one of the local people to be the Spear-lord of a village. In asking this I am breaking with long years of history and there are many people who might object most strongly to this move."

Cries of "No! No!" came from the crowd.

"Other Spear-lords in other communities," she reminded them, and the crowd grew silent to think about this. This could be dangerous.

It was indeed a break with custom and with history.

Karne thought about it too and knew that it was honour beyond his dreams, but responsibility and challenge as well.

He looked at Fern.

She shook her head slightly.

"It must be your decision," she said softly but firmly.

He looked around at the faces of the villagers. He knew they wanted him. He knew he was capable of the task. But . . . Hawk-Eagle was not the only member of the Spear-lord race who wished to keep their ancient privileges to himself.

"What do you say, Karne?" Olan's widow looked at him straight and steadily. "My husband believed your people were ready for responsibility and this made him many enemies. What do you say?"

Karne took a deep breath and stepped up to join her on the platform.

"I say Olan was right and I will stake my life to prove him so!"

The roar of approval that went up this time could be heard far and wide and could not be stopped by any one until it had spent itself naturally.

The dancing and the singing that followed this was truly wild and joyful.

Dark destruction past, the moment of regeneration is always one of joy.

Within the next few days calmer discussions were held both with the villagers and the Inner Council of the Priests at the Temple.

It was agreed after some small dissension, that though unorthodox, the move was a good one.

Karne was installed as Spear-lord in a ceremony presided over by the Lord High Priest, and given official authority by the highest powers in the Temple. They hoped by this means to avert angry reaction from other Spear-lords who feared their positions would be usurped by commoners and local peasants.

Messengers were sent across the land where the rule of the Spear-lords had most hold, to explain that it was now possible in certain very specific circumstances, for a local man held in great respect by the community, to succeed a Spear-lord, but only at the discretion of the Priests of the Inner Council of the Temple, and after rigorous investigation.

He would hold his authority in trust for the Temple and it would be removed from him if he abused it.

Olan's wife bade farewell to the village she had lived in for so long and returned to the house of her parents.

Fern and Karne moved into the Great House and

within days Isar began carving every wooden post and beam he could find in it with beautiful designs.

Karne took charge of the running of the village and Fern set about creating another garden that would bring delight and peace to all who walked in it.

Meanwhile Kyra gradually grew stronger, but Vann who attended her as Healer had to tell her that in bearing Deva she had suffered such damage that she would never again be able to bear a child.

When she heard this she dropped her face into her hands and sobbed, but the Lord Khu-ren who came to her soon after this took her hands and lifted up her face.

"My lady," he said tenderly, "we have Deva and we have each other. Why do you weep?"

She felt ashamed and dried her eyes.

Deva fed upon her mother's milk and grew delightfully round and rosy.

When Kyra could walk again she carried her on her hip everywhere she went and talked to her as though she could understand all the things her mother said. Deva chuckled and looked around with large, dark eyes as though she were surprised and joyful to be alive.

"Do you think she will have powers to be a priest?" Kyra asked Khu-ren eagerly. "She should, with both of us so deeply involved."

He smiled and shrugged,

"She is herself," he said.

A shadow crossed Kyra's face.

"Is she?" she asked sadly. "Remember the dream I had upon the Haunted Mound the night she was born? I sometimes wonder," and her face was pensive, "what claim we have upon her if she is that ancient Queen . . ."

Khu-ren kissed her into silence.

"She is Deva now . . . our child . . . enjoy her . . . love her. When she is grown to be a woman it will be her decision what place she takes. You know as well as I do that no one is born exactly as they were in a previous life. The differences in Deva and in Isar now may change the destiny that seems to us so closely and inevitably linked."

"But the dream?"

He smiled.

"You thought it meant that you would die in bearing her!"

Kyra laughed.

"Oh well," she said, "I see I am not to be allowed to worry!"

"That is right," he said, and left her.

Gradually Kyra resumed her studies and her work. Deva was looked after by Fern while her mother was busy, and the great house of the Spear-lord Karne became a second home to her.

Isar was always at her side and it was he who taught her how to walk and how to say her name.

Kyra had made it clear that Panora was not to be allowed anywhere near her daughter and if Panora was at Fern's house Deva was to be brought instantly back to her mother.

Fern's first trust in Panora had disappeared, but the girl still came to the house as though she were welcome, and Fern could not bring herself to be unkind to her. She was always ill at ease when the girl was around and kept a close watch on the children, but Panora showed no signs of harming them. She was in fact most helpful and kind, singing to them and playing with them as often as they wished.

Fern kept her word to Kyra and kept Deva out of her way, but Isar was often off with her, apparently visiting other villages far afield.

It was after such a visit when Deva was three summers old that Isar brought news to Karne that Hawk-Eagle's brother, who had been living all his life on the other side of the Western mountains, had at last received word of Karne's position in Hawk-Eagle's old village and was intending to do something about it.

"What is he intending to do?" Karne asked Isar curiously.

"That I do not know. I heard it as a rumour from people who had not even met him."

At the time of Karne's installation as Spear-lord there had been a certain amount of restlessness amongst the warrior race, but as no one had a personal stake in the village concerned and the Priests of the Inner Council of the Temple of the Sun had great authority, nothing had been done about it, but Karne knew it would not take much to rouse them if they had a specific leader who had a claim on the village.

He was loath to give up his position now, not only because he enjoyed the responsibility it gave him, but because he felt he had really made a positive contribution to the wellbeing of his people. The village economy was healthy, the people happy and well fed. Other villagers came to admire his work, and the carvings of Isar upon the houses were becoming famous.

He had introduced the system of the Seven Elders from his home community and the villagers really felt it was their village and took great pride in it.

His greatest triumph was that several Spear-lords in the district, on seeing how well the community was run, had allowed their villages the privilege of the Seven Elder system. They still retained ultimate control, but many matters were turned over to the Elders, and the Council of Elders could bring to the attention of the Spear-lord any problem the villagers had that the Spear-lord might have overlooked.

On the other hand, other lords, those who had been Olan's enemies in his lifetime, turned the other way and became more self-assertive, determined not to relinquish the smallest part of their power and privilege.

During the first processional Karne and Fern attended, walking with the traditional splendour of the warrior caste behind the priests along the Sacred Way, they could feel the antagonism building up around them, particularly as the crowd cheered incessantly whenever they appeared.

Fern was afraid and her heart was very low. She had no wish to be a great lady walking in grand robes and living in a house too big for her needs. She had no wish to stir up change and restlessness. To her each person's life should be spent in perfecting his private relationship with the Universe. From this all else followed. Pushing and jostling for power positions relative to each other to her was a waste of precious time and energy, and could lead nowhere but to sterility of Spirit and thence to the destruction of the material world around.

To know one's true Self and one's position in the scheme of the true Universe could be compared to a person, seeing clearly, walking forward and attending efficiently and steadily to the real needs of his fellow human beings and the natural world of which he was an integral part.

Not to know one's true Self and one's position in the scheme of the true Universe could be compared to a blind person blundering and stumbling about in a room full of unfamiliar things, knocking them over, breaking them, and achieving nothing.

Karne would have agreed with much of this but he was caught up in action now that was running too fast to be stopped. His strength was that he had been long enough with Maal, Kyra and Fern to know the value of deep thinking, and to have a reasonably clear idea of who he was and why he was, and yet enough joy in physical and challenging action, enough excitement in quick decisiveness, to ride the coming storm with some elation.

He held his head high in the procession and his eyes sparkled to meet those of his adversaries.

He believed what he was doing was right. The old warrior caste and the old ways had served their purpose. His people, or at least some of them, were ready now to think for themselves and be more than.chattels.

At the same time as these thoughts were occupying the minds of Karne and Fern, Kyra was facing the most difficult part of her training.

For years they had been trained to sense the inner levels of their own thoughts, to use them for greater understanding and awareness. They had been trained to go beyond even the innermost levels of their own consciousness and join with the great flow of spirit-consciousness all around them, again to use what they found there for

224

greater, deeper awareness and understanding of every-thing, great and small, that comprised the Whole, the All.

She worked hard, struggling many times and through many difficult trials to reach the state when she could feel that she was as ready as it was possible for a human being to be to take the final step to become Lord of the Sun.

At noon on one never-to-be-forgotten summer's day she passed from Tall Stone to Tall Stone in the Northern Inner Sanctum of the Temple, touching her forehead to the Sacred Rocks until she felt their power working through her. And then, standing in the centre of the Sacred Inner Three, she closed her eyes, feeling the throbbing of their energy through her body and the strength of the earth through the bare soles of her feet.

Around her she could hear the faint swish of sound as the priests, touching hand to hand to form a continuous circle, walked round and round the outside of the Stones, adding the strength of their spiritual experience to the forces in the Circle of Stones.

She began to feel stranger and stranger, as though all the blood, all the life force in her was draining out. She briefly remembered the first time she had felt this and had thought she was dying. This time she knew better but she could not quite dispel a tiny thrill of fear as finally her body went cold and numb and she could no longer move a limb or command a single bit of it to do her bidding.

She tried to concentrate on the feeling that was coming to her from the stone. Tried to concentrate on the words that were forming in her mind that she had been taught to use at the moment of separation.

"I am not Kyra. This body I lend back to the elements from which it came. It is nothing to me. I am Nameless, Formless. I am the point of consciousness on which ev-erything rests. I am conscious of Everything and am no longer limited by that discarded shell I see below me. I AM."

It worked!

She could see her body surrounded by the Three Stones that symbolized the God-Spirit, its manifestation in mat-

225

ter, and the human Spirit which formed a bridge between the two.

She could see the priests moving and murmuring, round and round the Circle. She could see the outer Rock Circle, the earth bank beyond, the Colleges, the priests' houses, the burial mounds, the forests, fields and villages . . .

She was high . . . high . . . high . . .

She knew this time she had a particular mission. It was not enough as she had done before to blunder accidentally into far-off lands. It had been decided where she would go and whom she would meet, and her journey must be controlled and her arrival must be accurate.

She deliberately blanked her mind of any distractions, and visualized in passionate detail the mountain area her teacher, the Lord Khu-ren, had described for her.

First she saw in her mind's eye a terrain of enormous dimensions, plains that seemed to lie in baking sun forever and ever, and beyond them the rising foothills and then the mountains themselves. The greatest mountains on earth.

She visualized herself as an eagle flying closer, and as she approached the range her vision became more restricted in scope, but in detail more and more explicit.

At last she stood upon the mountain side and saw around her a proliferation of beautiful plant life, from the enormous bushes richly decked with clusters of waxy purple flowers to the tiniest ferns and mosses.

She looked around and could see for a great distance in every direction and there was no sign or mark of man anywhere.

She lifted her gaze and beyond the mountain where she stood she saw, rising to the blue immensity of the sky itself, a giant peak of virginal crystal, the sunlight glancing off the sharp facets of its sides, the rock she knew to be below the ice and snow darkly silent and brooding.

She stood very still and watched the eagle whose body she had borrowed lift off and fly to a craggy place a long way to the East.

She felt the mountain silently about her and its power

was greater than the puny Stone Circles her people built to lend them strength for their little excursions into Reality.

This Rock seemed Conscious. She felt its Thought examining *her*. She was afraid of the force she felt, the unusual strength of the thoughts that came into her mind.

The air, the watching plants, the invisible rays from the mountain itself seemed to be working on her, purifying her, clarifying her mind until she could see everything, not only the things around, but everything in great and perfect detail from every angle simultaneously.

Vision upon vision of incredible intricacy arose for her and she saw the beauty of her earth contained like a leaf in amber, its own beauty far outdone by the beauty of that which contained it and was everywhere around it.

Even the crystal giant above her she could see now was just one peak in a series of peaks, each shimmering with a richer and more brilliant light.

She felt her heart would burst, unable to contain so much visionary splendour, so many feelings crowding into her of understanding and awareness. She wanted to cry to the Lord Khu-ren for help, to escape from this throbbing, powerful place. If what she had been taught about earth currents was correct this place must be the centre of them all.

Her people were right to send her to these mountains to test herself against them.

The vast energies that had formed them were still within them and she knew that now and for as long as they stood they would be a challenge worthy of any man's acceptance. Some would test themselves bodily against the rock faces and the ice and ultimately against the peak of peaks. Others would stay in meditation and in silence absorbing the spiritual energies to the limit of their endurance and capacity.

Feeling herself almost at that point she began to tremble and as though in answer to her unspoken plea for help she noticed that a man had joined her.

He came crawling out of a hole in the rock face of the

mountain and stood before her blinking owlishly in the light.

He was the thinnest man she had ever seen, a skeleton with a fine white pall of skin drawn over his bones, but his eyes were alive and dynamic.

She remembered now she had seen just such a ragged, ancient, bony man amongst the grand Lords of the Sun.

"Yes," he said smiling, and when he smiled his hideous skull face became beautiful. "Yes, we have met before."

She felt better now that she was no longer alone. She knew also she had succeeded in her task, because he was the man she had been sent to meet.

"My lord," she said reverently, bowing, "I am greatly honoured to be in your presence."

He moved his bony hand to indicate the beauty of the mountains around them.

"It is not I!" he said, and she understood he meant her to be reverent towards the mountains, not to him.

"I have been sent, my lord," she said softly, humbly, "to learn from you."

He smiled again, this time amused.

"And what is it that you have been sent to learn?"

"If I knew that, my lord, I would not still need to learn it!"

He nodded, pleased by her reply.

"But I can teach you nothing," he said gravely.

"Could I at least ask you a question?"

"You may ask, of course, but whether I can answer it is another matter."

"I must ask it. It is something that has worried me from time to time but I have never dared put it into words before."

"Ask it then."

"You are a man of great understanding . . . perhaps the greatest in the world . . ."

He stared at her expressionlessly, neither denying nor accepting the compliment.

"Would it not be better for the world if you were among people giving of your understanding to them . . . helping them with their lives . . . rather than staying locked up in this cave . . . in this mountain . . . benefitting only your own spiritual development?"

She poured out the words, horrified at herself, hardly realising what she was saying until she had said it.

He looked at her long and unblinkingly. It did not seem that he was offended. Nor did it seem that he intended to answer her question.

"I am sorry . . ." she stumbled out, trying to break the silence somehow.

He lifted his hand to make her silent, and then carefully chose a flat stone and sat upon it cross-legged, going almost immediately into a kind of trance.

She watched him for a while, puzzled and ill at ease, at a loss to know what to do next.

At last she felt the need to sit beside him, cross-legged too, and so she did.

She stared at the scenery around her, wondering at its beauty and its remoteness from any other living human being, and wondered about the question she had asked. She was not even sure why she had asked it because the training she had received at the College of Priests had stressed again and again the power of the flow of thought from one person to another, so that it was quite acceptable to her that a holy man or hermit, while taking no apparent part in the world's affairs, could indeed have a profound influence upon them by the strength of the beam of his trained and concentrated Thought directed into the minds of certain receptive people who were concerned in the world's affairs, and who were affecting men's lives every day, and yet had never themselves had the time or opportunity to develop their own minds to the point to which they should have been developed if they were to bear such responsibility and wield such power.

She knew also that immature and receptive people were also open to influences from unscrupulous and evil sources, and a man such as the hermit beside her had valuable work to do in intercepting and counteracting such influences.

Because he could not be *seen* to be doing anything in the Outside world most people accepted as the only world,

229

it did not mean he was doing nothing in the worlds that existed out of sight but were just as significant.

She realised she had asked the question because she had accepted the answer when it had been given to her at the College with only part of her mind. She needed the actual experience of sitting beside this man on the mountainside (and yet in "spirit" form only!) "feeling" his thoughts within her head, to know that what she had been told was indeed true.

They sat in silence for a long time and Kyra had never experienced before such profundity and clarity of understanding.

She would have liked to have stayed forever, but something was pulling her away.

As though he sensed it, he looked at her and the strange, silent spell that had been on her and in which she had understood so much was broken.

He stood up, bowed slightly to her, and returned to his cave.

She saw that the afternoon must have progressed a great deal since she arrived, and a long purple shadow from the immense peak was lying across the land almost to the horizon. Everything in its path had a strange softness as though it were dissolving.

She too stood up and forced herself to shut her eyes and remember who she was and where she had left her body.

She longed to open her eyes again, to stay in this powerful, beautiful place but she knew she was not ready to leave forever her husband and her daughter, no matter how much beauty and understanding were offered in their place.

With this thought she was home and she opened her eyes to the encircling stones of the Northern Inner Sanctum of The Temple of the Sun.

Before her stood the Lord Guiron and the Lord Khuren, and behind them many faces she knew of the Temple Priesthood.

She was shivering and very, very tired, but before the

minutest detail of it could fade she was forced to give a description of everything in absolute completeness.

At the end she was allowed to go and she knew by the faces around her that she had passed the test.

The day of her inauguration as one of the select group of Lords of the Sun was a very great day for her.

This time after the long procession down the Sacred Way a great many of the community around were allowed into the Sacred Circle in orderly groups.

To call all the Lords of the Sun together needed great power and the Outer Circle was filled with concentric Circles of people, male and female alternately, each turning rhythmically within the next, until the Northern Inner Sanctum itself was reached and that was surrounded only by the highest priests.

Deva and Isar hand in hand were among the outermost children's circle, and Fern and Karne were with the Spear-lords and their ladies.

The fact that Karne's sister was to be inaugurated as Lord of the Sun gave him extra status in the eyes of the ruling caste, and many who were wavering which way to go now joined his side against the dissidents.

The low and vibrant sound of drumming set the pace of the circling figures.

The Lady Kyra, the Lord Guiron and the Lord Khuren, being the only three Lords of the Sun present, were alone in the Inner Circle, each standing regally against one of the Standing Stones, facing the great Central Three, the focus of power, their backs to the moving rings.

As the drummers increased the speed of the beat, the speed of the circling figures increased, and so did the build-up of energy.

Gradually, as the humming, vibrating note that issued from the throats of the encircling people and the drums of the drummers grew louder and louder, and the energy generated by their bodies and thoughts grew stronger and stronger, Kyra noticed changes happening within the Inner Circle.

At first a kind of flimsy shadow appeared before each unoccupied Stone, hardening at last into what appeared to be the full bodily forms of the other Lords of the Sun.

She felt great joy to see Quilla from the Island of the Bulls, now quite healed, standing straight and tall in her traditional dress, supple and graceful as ever. Kyra was glad the bull's horns had left no scars to mar her beauty, but even as she thought this a little thought that should not have entered her head as one of the Great Lords of the Sun entered hers, and she looked quickly at the Lord Khu-ren to see if he was looking at the girl of flight with more than ordinary interest. If he was, nothing showed upon his face and Kyra was ashamed to have even entertained such a thought for an instant at a time like this.

She met the eyes of the old hermit from the great mountains and she knew he at least had seen her thought. She flushed. But his eyes were amused, not accusing.

Then there was no more time to think irrelevant thoughts. She "left" her body against the rock and in "spirit" form moved slowly around the Circle bowing to each Lord in turn, receiving each one's blessing, each one making a sign particular to his or her race or culture on the newcomer's forehead.

She received the sign of the Circle, the sign of the Star, the sign of the Crescent Moon, the sign of the Tree of Life ...

The ancient hermit of the mountains made no sign at all but looked deeply into her eyes and she saw a vision of her world, among a myriad other worlds, all reflected in the small black circle in the centre of his eyes.

When she had completed the round she knelt in the centre of the Stone Circle and bowed so low that her forehead rested on the earth.

From the earth, through her forehead, she heard the drumming and the throbbing of the vibrations set up by the people of her community and she was filled with great love and a feeling that all that she heard was the beating of her own heart. She loved all things as she loved herself because they *were* Herself.

She did not know how long she stayed thus.

At last she lifted her head slowly and looked around.

The Lord Guiron, the Lord Khu-ren and the Lady Kyra were alone in the Inner Circle.

No one else was in sight.

The great Outer Circle was completely empty.

She looked dazed.

"Come," the Lord Khu-ren said, and took her hand.

They followed the High Priest, Guiron, out and across the little wooden bridge.

The Circle of Power lay behind them, dormant.

Panora's War

Panora was not at the inauguration of Kyra as Lord of the Sun. She was in the far West visiting Hawk-Eagle's brother, Nya.

Nya had not seen his brother since they had been children and he knew nothing and cared nothing about him, his land or his people. Nya's people were mountain nomads and lived wild and scattered, coming down to the settled communities in the valleys only to raid and take what they needed for the winter months, sometimes trading their furs, sometimes not.

It was Vann, Kyra's friend, who had first brought Nya to the notice of Panora. His own family had suffered greatly at the hands of Nya and his rough people, and it was in telling the story of one of Nya's raids that Vann mentioned he was one of two sons of a man called White Hawk. Panora knew that Hawk-Eagle's father had such a name and knew also that he had died in the clutches of a bear when his sons were very young, one coming East with a relative, the other staying in the mountains.

No sooner had she skilfully extracted from Vann the

exact location of Nya, than she had sent a series of messages to him bringing to his notice that his brother had been murdered and his village taken over by his murderer.

When she could slip away unnoticed herself she traveled West to seek him out, stirring trouble against Karne all the way, and promising the anxious Spear-lords a leader who would restore their threatened privileges to them.

Nya's camp was in a forest by a waterfall and Panora was treated with great suspicion when she first appeared, but so unafraid was her carriage and so flattering her words of welcome to Nya and his untidy band of ruffians that she was soon accepted and was squatting with the lord himself, tearing at a boar steak and swilling ale as though it were her usual drink.

"What is your interest in this?" Nya asked at last, when he had listened at length to Panora's speech on how it was his duty to march East and seize back his brother's land.

Panora was careful how she answered.

If she were truthful she might have said that she had no interest in the particular case at all, but that she was tormented by an ancient spite which she saw a way of satisfying by using Nya.

She was tired of the kind of servant-to-master relationship she had with her father, tired of the settled orderly existence of the Temple and the communities around it. She had a kind of aching itch deep inside her that would not be cured until everything the Lord Guiron and the Temple stood for was overturned, and Isar was King again, her mother Queen, and she a princess treated royally.

Until Wardyke's coming she had not even known what it was that ailed her and made her so dissatisfied. He had filled her head with stories of ancient times, the splendours of her mother's palace and the wrong Guiron twice had done.

He had poisoned her mind against Karne and Fern whom at first she had felt to be her friends. And when

Wardyke was killed Panora had brooded long and bitterly on how she could avenge not only his death, but that of her ancient royal mother as well.

On hearing of Nya, and feeling the stirring of anxiety among the Spear-lords that their long established powers were being undermined by changes and decrees from the Inner Council of the Temple, she saw her chance.

A war would relieve her restlessness.

A war would ease her dissatisfaction. It would destroy the upstart Spear-lord and the treacherous priest.

The Temple would be razed to the ground and she would build a palace for her mother, the Queen, and her mother's chosen husband, that would out-rival the ancient palace that had stood upon the Field of the Grey Gods.

She would be powerful and grand instead of a servant-messenger, a half-grown child tolerated everywhere, but nowhere loved.

She would be the instrument of vengeance, the instrument that would change the balance of power in the whole country.

The more she thought about it the more grandiose her schemes became.

But to start them she needed to use the weapons of a band of violent men, and then she needed violence to breed violence, hate to breed hate, and in the final holocaust she needed power to destroy what she wanted to destroy, and build what she wanted to build.

She must not lose control as Wardyke had lost control.

But these thoughts she did not express to Nya.

"Justice is my interest," she said sweetly.

He snorted. It was not a word much used in his vocabulary.

"All right," Panora tried again. "Hawk-Eagle was my friend. I want vengeance."

That he understood.

"And you," she added, "will get his lands, his riches, great honour and power as Spear-lord. No longer will you have to live from day to day in the mountains, killing for every scrap of food. Food will be plentiful all the year

237

round. People will respect you and you will live in a great house with furs upon the floor. Your lady," and here she looked at the filthy ragged crone at Nya's side, "will wear jewels and soft clothes and drink sweet wine instead of goats' milk and bad ale."

Nya's woman showed her rotten teeth in a greedy smile.

Nya looked with disgust at her and this point did not seem to attract him.

"Perhaps," Panora said to him softly, "you would prefer another woman. One of the East, bred among the Spear-lord caste, fine of feature, tall and straight of limb."

This pleased him better and he smiled at last.

"You say there are many who will join us on the way?"

"Yes."

"I will serve under no other man!"

"No," Panora said, "you will be leader. They will follow you. It is your vengeance that will be done, your land that will be reclaimed. They will help you because your cause helps theirs."

Nya thought about it from every angle. It seemed a good enough proposition to him. He and his men enjoyed fighting and to gain so much this time would add to the attraction.

But being treacherous himself he was always on guard against the possibility of treachery in others.

"And what do you take when all the fighting is done?"

"Nothing of yours."

"What then?"

"I take what is rightfully mine."

"And what is that?"

Nya was not entirely a fool. He wanted to know exactly where he stood before he committed himself.

"A place of honour too."

"Aha!"

"But it will not conflict with yours. I promise. You will have your brother's land and much besides that you have conquered. I will have vengeance for my friend and a place of honour I have always been denied."

"Hm-m," Nya thought about it.

"Surely if I show you the route to take where the most will join your force, give you aid in every way from my knowledge of the Temple area, a small reward of land or honour from your bounty would not be too much to ask?"

Nya shrugged.

"We will see. I will think upon it this night. In the morning I will give you answer."

Much time that evening was spent in drinking and carousing.

When they finally retired to sleep Panora could not imagine any one of them being in a fit state to think anything through!

She settled under a hide tent in a ragged sleeping rug beside a bad-smelling woman and her four children, and thought about the future and the palace she would build, riches, power and glory.

In the morning Nya gave the answer "Yes", and voices and fists were raised with guttural shouts of affirmation.

At the turn of the next moon cycle the band moved off, pillaging as they went the villages that would not join with them, growing in strength with the ones that would.

Back at The Temple of the Sun little Deva, the Shining One, sleeping beside her mother, woke screaming in the night, and spoke of horrible hordes marching upon her loved ones with death in their eyes.

Kyra was troubled but rocked her to sleep pretending that there was nothing to worry about.

This was the first time that Deva had revealed a dream and Kyra was not sure if it was the result of far-sight or of the usual childhood fears when faced with a new and inexplicable world.

She and Lea and Khu-ren discussed it, but he could find out no more about it as in the morning Deva had completely forgotten she had suffered it at all.

"Let it rest at that," Kyra said. "I do not want to raise these fears again by probing. She is too young."

But Khu-ren spoke to Isar and asked him to keep his ears and eyes open for any more rumours like the one he had brought about Hawk-Eagle's brother.

239

Isar's fame as a wood carver was growing rapidly and he often spent time in distant villages carving for people who admired his work. He had great pleasure and satisfaction in this and Karne saw that he had training with the best craftsmen in the Temple area.

It was on a day that he was very far from home that he heard the first rumours of a vast army that was moving across from the West, devastating everything in its path. He even saw straggling groups of refugees, carrying what possessions they could upon their backs and telling horrifying stories of murder and rape, burning of homes and stealing of crops and cattle.

"Their leader is a giant with long black hair and beard, his eyes like the dead," someone told Isar.

"And at his side is a strange creature, half demon, half little girl. He seems to do everything she tells him, and yet great warriors tremble at a look from him!"

"Sometimes flocks of giant black birds follow them for great distances and eat any crops that have been left behind or hidden. The villagers are starving!"

Isar was horrified. He mounted Karne's horse and rode as hard as he could to the Temple. Arriving there he found others before him bearing the same kind of tale.

Some of the Spear-lords who had taken to the new ways and appreciated the help of the Elders, and were loyal to the priests, had come as soon as they heard of the trouble, and the whole Temple community was in an uproar.

The Lord Guiron called all the messengers together and he and his chief priests listened gravely and silently to all the differing accounts. Through the exaggerations and the distortions he managed to build up quite an accurate picture of what was happening.

So it was coming about as he had feared!

Kyra remembered her daughter Deva's dream.

She also remembered she had not seen Panora anywhere for a long time. She started to make enquiries and

240

it soon became clear that no one, not even the Lord Guiron had seen her. Nor had anyone missed her.

Kyra was convinced "the strange creature, half demon, half little girl" with the advancing hordes was Panora.

This was Panora's war.

The Lord Guiron and his priests called a meeting of all the friendly Spear-lords and the Elders of their villages and sent them back to their communities with words of strength and comfort, advising them to prepare defences but to do nothing until they heard from the Council of the Priests.

"You will have protection from us," the Lord Guiron told them. "It is only in the last resort you will have to fight."

He then called upon the Lord Khu-ren and the Lady Kyra to visit him in the privacy of his own house.

"There is much that has been unspoken between us in the last few years," the Lord Guiron began.

Khu-ren and Kyra were silent, not sure what was coming next.

"I speak of the story that began in the Palace they now speak of as the Field of the Grey Gods."

The Lord Khu-ren nodded. How long had he known that they knew? There had never been any sign.

Guiron's face seemed very tired and old, as though he were oppressed with memories too sad to carry further.

"I have paid for that ancient guilt many times and now it seems not only I, but those I love and cherish, will have to pay again."

Kyra put her hand upon his arm with warmth and sympathy.

He was such a great Lord and yet at this moment to her woman's heart he was like a lost and desolate child.

"This war," Khu-ren said, "has roots in other matters than your guilt. People used to privilege are fighting to keep it against the tide of change. This is an old story, nothing to do with you or what you have done."

Guiron sighed.

"There is no time for games. What you say is only partly true. The flame that sets this mess of straw on fire is Panora. She lives only as long as my guilt lives. She plots only as long as my guilt is not expurgated."

"I have often wondered why you have kept her by your side," Kyra said thoughtfully, "was there no way . . .?"

"No way," Guiron answered gloomily. "Nya thinks he comes to reclaim his brother's land. The other Spear-lords fight because they think they are being threatened by a change that is to their disadvantage, but none of these made a move until Panora drove them to it. They are her warriors, her minions, whether they know it or not."

"What does she hope to gain? Killing Karne and his family will not satisfy her vengeful nature."

"Karne must go because he was the enemy of Wardyke. I must go because of what I did to her mother. But with us must go all that we stand for, the good and gentle changes Karne has made in village life, the Temple and its mighty power.

"I have 'travelled' to her camp and looked into her eyes, and seen there the destruction of this whole Culture, the Temple laid to waste and in its place a palace of great magnificence in which the King Isar and his Queen Deva rule, their Warder and their Guardian, the Princess Panora.

"The Princess Panora grown in power beyond all belief.

"The Princess Panora ruling her King and Queen of Straw, and her kingdom of devastation!"

Khu-ren and Kyra were silent, the realisation that what he said was true bringing a chill to their hearts.

"What can we do?" Kyra spoke at last, her voice trembling.

Guiron's shoulders were hunched. He was tired and he had lost all will and hope.

"She is no ordinary girl and she has been learning from The Temple all these years," Khu-ren said. "She has been feeding on us, biding her time and now she is more deadly than a viper between the breasts of a girl."

Kyra shuddered.

It was no satisfaction to her now that she had never liked or trusted Panora.

"I think," the Lord Khu-ren said, "we should go into the Silence and seek the answer there."

The Lord Guiron suffered himself to be led to The Temple and thence to the Northern Inner Circle of Great Power.

There the three who were Lords of the Sun stood until dawn, deep in the Silence within themselves, seeking guidance from the Spirit realms around them and within them.

It took Panora more than a moon cycle to gather the army she thought sufficient for her purposes and move it within striking distance of The Temple.

Nya's men, unruly and greedy, were overloaded with the feasting and the pillaging on the way, but Nya still thought he was the leader of the expedition.

Panora moved among the gathering armies, her strange hypnotic power strengthening their purpose and confidence whenever it showed signs of wavering, feeding their fears, their hates, their greeds.

She was everywhere and nowhere. No one could find her, but she could find everyone. If a group of Spear-lords began to have their doubts when they noticed it was against The Temple itself they were making their advance, and not just against the upstart Karne, and held a secret meeting, Panora was suddenly and mysteriously in their midst making them see that it was the Temple and the Lord High Priest who were their enemy after all.

"Karne may be killed by one spear thrust, but if The Temple is determined to break the power of the Spear-lords and promote the common people to their ancient privileges, a hundred Karnes will spring to life whenever one is killed!

"You must destroy the Lord High Priest and The Temple at his back if you are to keep your way of life.

"You see that. You are not blind. You are men of action and of power. Use it! No priest living in his dream world can stand against you.

"Take the Temple! Make it yours! Instal it in *your* people who will look out for *your* rights!"

She stood amongst them strangely grown in height, a spear raised in hand, eyes like demon eyes enflaming them to action.

On the day when she thought the time was near to strike she vanished inexplicably from their midst and reappeared in the garden of Fern's house where Deva was playing happily unaware of all the threats of violence and of war.

The child looked up to see a strange girl standing beside her. Before she could utter a sound, Panora had seized her and whisked her away.

Isar, coming at that moment out of the house, saw it happen and ran like a deer in the direction they had vanished. They had moved so fast that by the time he could see clearly the trackway he thought they had taken, it was already empty.

Distraught with fear for Deva's safety he rushed to the field where Karne kept his horse and forgetting that his father would need it, he leapt upon its back and galloped off in the direction in which he was sure Panora had gone.

Panora meanwhile made sure that she kept just out of reach of him but left enough evidence of her passing for him to follow easily. It was part of her plan that he would be with Deva away from the battle and out of reach of any of their family or friends.

It was nightfall when Isar finally tracked Deva down. She was sitting in the doorway of a derelict house far from any other habitation and crying for her mother.

When she saw Isar she flung herself into his arms and clung to him sobbing with relief and joy. Gently he soothed and comforted her and then, when at last she was quiet and he looked around for the horse, it was nowhere in sight.

He asked Deva about Panora but the little girl just shook her head and looked so full of fear he left the matter alone. There was no sign of her. It was clear she meant Deva to stay there, far, far from possible help.

As darkness was fast closing in upon them he decided

the most sensible thing would be for them to stay in the half-ruined house overnight and try to find their way home in the morning.

He told Deva this and spoke with such calm authority that she who loved and trusted him was quite content and began to look on the whole thing as an adventurous game. But she was very careful never to leave his side and, weary as she was, she followed him everywhere as he gathered straw and built a soft bed for them in the most sheltered part of the almost roofless house.

When she complained that she was hungry he promised her he would find her food in the morning, but meanwhile she must sleep and he would tell her a story to lull her off to dream land. She settled down happily in his arms and he told her story after story until at last he felt her go limp and her breathing settle soft and rhythmically.

But he could not sleep himself. He lay cramped and troubled all the night with thinking upon the matters that had occurred, the war that was brewing and the part his one-time friend Panora was playing in it.

Many thoughts came to him in that long, long night and many decisions were made.

Meanwhile Panora had returned to her army and, finding her commander-in-chief, Nya, lying in a state of drunken stupor, gave the command to advance herself, in his voice. The moon rose full and brilliant above the plain and the hastily constructed defences of Karne and his Spear-lords showed up clearly.

The priests had sent word that this would be the night of the battle and Karne, lying in a ditch waiting with his men, could feel it in the air. If the sky had not been so clear he would have been sure there would be a storm, so hot and breathless and oppressive it was.

He was momentarily surprised and anxious that Isar had not brought his horse to him in answer to the message he had sent, but as everything was in such tension and confusion, he dismissed the worry by telling himself Isar could probably not find him. He had indeed moved his position several times.

The priests had sent word that no one was to attack, only hold themselves ready to defend. They had hinted before that there were other ways of defending enemies than by force of arms, and weapons were to be used only as a last resort.

Karne and his friends, remembering the legendary powers of the priests of the Temple of the Sun, were thankful that they at least were on their side.

There was something non-human and supernatural about Panora, but the rest of their enemies were ordinary men like themselves, and this was a relief.

The enemy had no such comfort.

Now that the moment of confrontation had come not a few of them had misgivings about raising arms against the mighty Temple priesthood.

Panora seemed to be everywhere at once and it was her energy that flowed through them like strong ale.

As the moon reached a height sufficient to flood the whole battle plain with eerie light Panora gave a shriek that made every one of her enemies' blood run cold.

It was the sound of Vengeance and with it the whole dark plain seemed to come alive, bushes and stones moved, the very earth itself heaved to spew out a dark horde of fighting men.

As they advanced they chanted a savage and relentless chant that added to the chill already in the hearts of the defenders.

They knew they were outnumbered beyond belief and as thy lay helplessly in the ditches and behind the hastily erected banks it seemed to them their case was hopeless.

But even as the first line of attackers came within spear throw a wondrous thing happened.

Upon three burial mounds, and clearly visible in the moonlight, three figures suddenly appeared, luminous and larger than life. The Lord Guiron in the centre, flanked by the Lord Khu-ren and the Lady Kyra.

The advancing army paused, its derisive and impressive chant cut off in mid breath. Ten thousand men stared at the three upon the burial mounds and as the centre one

246

raised his arm and pointed they raised their eyes to follow it.

Above them the moon that had signalled their attack and had been showering its light upon their enemy now seemed to have a weird shadow of blood creeping across its face.

They stared horrified, as gradually the shadow spread, the light dimmed, and the ghost of the moon, each detail of its pock-marked face clearer than it had ever been, looked down upon them in a sombre and ominous silence.

Even Panora was momentarily stunned and in that moment Guiron spoke with a voice of thunder that carried across the plain with more than human strength.

"You have dared to challenge the authority of The Temple of the Sun.

"You will advance no further.

"Between you and the innocent people you wish to destroy is a wall of power. If you touch it *you* will be destroyed. If you go back to your homes and live as you have always lived in peace and harmony with your neighbours, no harm will come to you."

"Do not listen to him!" screamed Panora. "He is no more than a priest frightened of losing power.

"We are the power now!

"We take!

"We break!

"We make a new world that will be ours!

"Advance!"

Her voice, like Guiron's, carried with an unnatural force across the echoing plain. Her power of personality, like Guiron's, was more than natural at this moment.

Half of her dark force moved forward under the strength of it, the other half hesitated and stayed where it was, confused and dismayed. But in the section that moved forward there were more men than the defenders had at their command.

As they advanced the two figures standing on the burial mounds to the North and South of Guiron raised their right hands and pointed dramatically. Between their pointing fingers a lightning bolt seemed to shoot across the plain.

Again the advancing army paused.

Again Panora drove them on.

"Beware of the wall of power!" Guiron roared. "No man may pass unscathed!"

"It is a trick!" Panora screamed. "You can see there *is* no wall!"

The moon had come clear of its ghastly shadow now and the light shone full upon the plain.

There was no wall visible.

The horde advanced again.

"Now!" shouted the three great Lords of the Sun with one voice and in that instant total confusion broke loose upon the plain.

Some screamed as though they had been burned as they touched an invisible wall of fire. Others shrieked with fear as the sky rained vipers and poisonous adders. Yet others leaped back from demon figures burning with unearthly light. Some saw long dead relatives raise spears against them. Others were engulfed in a black and suffocating fog. Leaping flames chased others back.

In the days to come each one who survived this terrible ordeal had a different tale to tell.

No one saw the same enemy.

No one penetrated the invisible wall.

"Advance! Advance!" shrieked Panora, mad with disappointment at the frustration of her plans.

"There *is* no wall. It is a trick!"

But her voice was lost in the shrieking of the damned and the stampeding of terrified men.

The battle that was no battle was a rout.

The defenders, still untouched behind the lines of their defence, gazed with horror and with awe at what they saw.

They saw nothing of wall, or fire, or fog or vipers . . . nothing but men screaming in fear and agony and falling about in the dark and running back from whence they had come.

They stared amazed.

And when they turned to look upon the three burial mounds there was no sign of the three Lords of the Sun.

And when they looked at the moon it was as bland and pale as ever.

Weeping with rage Panora watched the scene and knew that she had lost.

Never again while they remembered this night would any man rise against the power of The Temple.

But even as she despaired she remembered she had one last trick to play.

She had the children. Deva, the beloved of Kyra, Khuren *and* Guiron, and Isar, the beloved of Karne and Fern.

Swiftly she left the shameful scene of her defeat and travelled to the derelict house where she had left her captives.

She would triumph yet!

But even this victory she was to be denied.

Dawn light was breaking as she came upon the place and the children had left.

Above the house a wheeling flight of enormous black birds were screeching in the sky.

Panora shook her fist at them.

"Why did you let them go?" she screamed.

The birds wheeled once more and flew off across the horizon. Even her familiars had deserted her.

Bitterly, but still determined to salvage triumph from the wreckage, she set off in search of the children. She knew the horse had left them and they would not be able to go far on Deva's little legs.

But what she did not know was that Kyra's love had located them and even at that moment the Lord Guiron and herself, now in their bodily form, were hastening to the place where they knew the children would be.

Weary and bedraggled from journeying and hiding, Panora was in time to see their reunion in a little forest glade.

Kyra gathered both children to her breast, tears of relief falling upon them. She had played her part as great Lord of the Sun as it had been required of her, but now she was woman and mother, desperate with weariness and weak with relief after the long anxiety.

The High Priest stood aside and watched them, his face filled with remorse and love.

When Kyra had welcomed them enough and they turned to him, he stepped forward and knelt upon the grass, taking Deva's little hand in his and bending his large head to kiss her fingers.

Isar watched him warily.

"My lady," the Lord Guiron said with great humility, "I ask your forgiveness for all that I have done."

Deva, dark and beautiful, with the light that she was named for shining from her eyes, smiled not like a little girl but like a great Queen.

She raised him with a gesture and said softly and graciously,

"Go in peace, my lord, there is no longer anything to forgive."

And as she said this they heard a cry from behind them and looked round to see Panora crouching beside a tree, her eyes still dark with pain and hate.

Deva took a step towards her, in spite of Kyra's warning hand.

"You must go," she said with authority in her voice. "You have wandered too long between two worlds. I know myself how fruitless and lonely this can be.

"Choose spirit-world or earth-world, one or the other, and learn to live there without hate or bitterness. When you are ready, age and die as other people do. When you are ready, be born again as other people are."

Panora stared at her. It was as though the figures in the forest glade were frozen in time.

The old man, the young woman, the boy, the girl child and the girl demon were all poised on a moment of change, Panora's decision affecting all their lives.

At last Panora moved and it seemed to them that the hate and bitterness had gone out of her eyes.

She bowed her head to Deva, her one-time spirit mother, and Guiron, her earthly father, and before they realized she had it on her, she seized a dagger that was hidden at her waist and plunged it into her own heart.

They all gasped in horror as she fell.

Kyra held Deva and Isar back, and only Guiron moved forward swiftly and cradled the strange limp creature in his arms. He had to lean close to hear the words that she murmured as she died.

"If my mother forgives you, so do I," she whispered and the ancient feud died with her.

Guiron turned and looked at Isar with a question in his eyes.

"We have much living to do without bothering about old tales," Isar said, looking at him straight.

"So be it," Guiron said, bowing his head. "I thank you, and I will not cross your paths again."

At the time they did not know what he meant by this but when they returned to The Temple he told the Inner Council of Priests that he intended to reign as High Priest and recommended that they accepted in his place the Lord Khu-ren.

He would not explain his reasons, but neither would he be diverted from his decision.

Kyra and Khu-ren understood but said nothing.

He told them that it was his intention to leave his country and wander a stranger in strange lands for the rest of his natural life, teaching and healing where he could.

That way he hoped to atone for all the years he had worn the Crown of the greatest Priest in the land, knowing that he was not worthy of it.

Khu-ren's Inauguration

The inauguration of the Lord Khu-ren as the High Priest of the Temple of the Sun took place in two separate ceremonies, the first at the Southern College of Star Studies at the moment of the Spring Equinox, when day and night were equal in length and all nature was poised ready for the great surge of Summer growth.

At the moment of sunrise the Lord Khu-ren stood at the Standing Stone that marked the Spring Equinox and was transformed by the beams of the rising sun as it touched the gold that was everywhere upon him, from the band around his forehead to the sandals upon his feet. He seemed to be made of light and as the reflection of the sun from the gold upon his body reached the priests who were gathered around him they all bowed to him and then rose to full height to sing a song of praise and glory to the Sun and to its father, the Spirit of Light, and its servant, the Lord Khu-ren.

Deva, the Shining One, had the task of bringing the High Priest's crown solemnly along the processional way from the Midsummer Sun Stone to the Lord Guiron, whose last work as Lord High Priest was to place it upon the head of his successor.

Kyra, in long blue robes, threaded with white and gold, watched proudly from her place at the head of the Inner Council of Priests.

Deva, small as she was, carried herself like a queen, and her father, tall and handsome, bore himself with dignity and humility as the greatest power in the land.

From the ceremony at the Temple of the Star Studies the procession moved solemnly and sedately the long distance back to the main Temple of the Sun.

Night was passed at the Sanctuary, the other priests and Spear-lords camping on the hills around, while the new High Priest sat alone in the centre of the Sanctuary and communed with Spirits.

At dawn the procession moved off again to the Temple along the Sacred Way, the Lady Kyra walking beside the Lord Guiron, a few paces behind her the Lord, the High Priest.

Within the Great Circle concentric rings of people were moving to the sound of drums. The Lords of the Sun were to be called to take part in the final ceremony.

As Kyra took her place in the Inner Circle with the Three Great Stones at its centre and waited for the Lords from across the world to come and pay their respects to her husband, her mind went to the stone sea urchin she had found so deeply buried in the earth.

It lay in her chamber now and was not with her in the Circle, but so vividly did she think about it, so accurately did she visualize it in every detail that it was as though she held it in her hand and gazed upon it.

Its centre became the centre of the circle she was in.

Her husband was waiting, crowned and magnificent, in the very centre of both the Stone Circle and the Stone talisman she held in her mind. From him radiated out beaded lines of power reaching to every point of the universe, and from every point of the universe beaded lines of power reached back to him at the centre.

The simple sea creature, immortalized in stone, was a symbol of the Universe!

She looked up and wherever she looked and wherever she turned she saw each and every thing joyously as itself and yet, at the same time, in its role as symbol, pointing to everything else.

The bird that rose in flight was the developing Being who sees everything from a new angle as it rises.

The blade of grass was the living Being who draws its nourishment from earth *and* sun, from dark *and* light, from matter *and* spirit.

The Tall Stones that surrounded her reached for the sky, but were embedded in the earth, and formed a circle that was at once closed *and* open.

The sunlight sparking off the faces of the minute crystals in the Stone reminded her of the flashes of inspiration she had experienced throughout her life which had led her spirit to rise, her vision to lift and follow the tall and magical Stones until she was carried up and up to be absorbed in one of those moments of amazement at the blue depths of the sky and the immensities she knew were beyond it . . . One of those moments when, balanced on a point of beauty almost too great to bear, she could sense the presence of an Intelligence and a Love so overwhelming that she could only presume it was what men called "God."

The words "Magnificence" and "Purpose" burst in her mind like exploding Suns.

She lifted her arms . . .

and her heart sang . . .

ALL TIME BESTSELLERS FROM POPULAR LIBRARY

☐	BEFORE MY TIME—Maureen Howard	03185-9	1.50
☐	AFTERNOON MEN—Anthony Powell	04268-0	1.95
☐	SEVEN RUSSIAN SHORT NOVEL MASTERPIECES—L. Hamalian & V. Von Wiren-Garczynski	00165-8	95¢
☐	A TOUCH OF DANGER—James Jones	08255-0	1.75
☐	TO KILL A MOCKINGBIRD—Harper Lee	08376-X	1.95
☐	SEVEN SHORT NOVEL MASTERPIECES—L. Hamalian & E. Volpe	08504-5	1.95
☐	DEATH IN THE AIR—Agatha Christie	04041-6	1.50
☐	YOUR SINS AND MINE—Caldwell	00331-6	1.75
☐	THE HESS CROSS—Thayer	04286-9	2.25
☐	THE UNORIGINAL SINNER AND THE ICE-CREAM GOD—Powers	04287-7	1.95
☐	HOW TO MEET MEN NOW THAT YOU'RE LIBERATED—Gellis	04288-5	1.95
☐	MARINA TOWER—Beardsley	04198-6	1.95
☐	SKIN DEEP—Hufford	04258-3	1.95
☐	MY HEART TURNS BACK—Patton	04241-9	2.25
☐	THE BERLIN CONNECTION—Simmel	08607-6	1.95
☐	THE BEST PEOPLE—Van Slyke	08456-1	1.95
☐	A BRIDGE TOO FAR—Ryan	08373-5	2.50
☐	THE CAESAR CODE—Simmel	08413-8	1.95

Buy them at your local bookstore or use this handy coupon for ordering: